THE COMPLETE CASES OF THE
ACME INDEMNITY OP, VOLUME 1

John Lawrence

JOHN LAWRENCE

THE COMPLETE CASES OF THE

ACME
INDEMNITY OP™

VOLUME 1

BY JOHN LAWRENCE WRITING AS

JAN DANA

INTRODUCTION BY

JOHN WOOLEY

STEEGER BOOKS • 2020

TABLE OF CONTENTS

THE OTHER OP
BY JOHN WOOLEY

HE WAS a hardboiled lone-wolf investigator whose real name was never revealed. And he was a true company man, identified only by the name of the business he worked for, with an "Op" (or, occasionally, "Dick") tagged at the end. His stories were tough and violent, and while they sometimes revealed him to be indecorous or not particularly heroic, he laid them all out in a straightforward, first-person style.

He was, however, *not* the Continental Op.

By December 1937, when *Dime Detective* published the first Acme Indemnity Op tale ("Riddle of the Rats," which leads off this volume), *Continental* Op creator Dashiell Hammett had hit full-blown celebrityhood, hanging out with playwright Lillian Hellman and her smart set of writers, film and stage people, and assorted intellectuals and *bon vivants*. In 1934, Alfred A. Knopf had published Hammett's *The Thin Man*, a hit novel that quickly led to a well-received series of movies from M-G-M. Those pictures represented one of many revenue streams flooding Hammett with the kind of cash it took to live the hard high life with Hellman and their chums.

By that time, The Continental Op was barely a dot in Hammett's rearview mirror. His 36 stories about the nameless operative of the Continental Detective Agency—

beginning with "Arson Plus" in the October 1, 1923 issue of *Black Mask*—had ended in 1930, the year after Knopf brought out his first two novels, *Red Harvest* and *The Dain Curse*. Both were constructed with connected Continental Op stories that had first appeared in *Black Mask*.

While Hammett did manage to turn out five well-received books in the '30s, including those two Op narratives, the author of the "other" Op never made it out of the pulps. All 24 of the Acme Indemnity Op's adventures, ranging from short stories to novel-length adventures, appeared in *Dime Detective*. Only now, nearly 80 years after the publication of the final Acme Op story, is he starring in his own book.

Every one of the two dozen Acme Op stories carried the same byline: a man (or woman) named Jan Dana. Evidence suggests, however, that the writer behind these tales wasn't named Jan Dana at all. Instead, he was likely one of that second tier of accomplished hardboiled writers (just below Hammett and Raymond Chandler) who threw millions of words into the gaping maw of the pulps.

A few months ago, I began my own research into Jan Dana. Aided greatly by pulp-scholar friends, I ultimately came up with a name that has been seconded by Steeger Books publisher Matt Moring, who arrived at the same conclusion in pretty much the same way.

That name is John Lawrence, a Canadian native well-known to fans of the hardboiled pulps, especially *Dime Detective*, which carried the exploits of Lawrence's Sam Beckett, Cass Blue, and, most notably, Lt. Martin Marquis, the Marquis of Broadway, a dapper little policeman whose blood, underneath his natty exterior, runs as cold as any reptile's.

AUTHOR, EDITOR, and crackerjack researcher John Locke was the first one to start helping me dig into the true identity of the Acme Indemnity Op's author. After I'd floated the idea to him about Jan Dana being a pseudonym, John responded by notifying me that (a) he could find no stories by a Jan Dana in any other pulp magazines, and (b) although Dana had done all those Acme Op stories for *Dime Detective*, absolutely no biographical information about Dana had been published in the magazine during the Acme Op's five-year run—"adding further evidence," John wrote, "that 'Jan Dana' is a penname."

Not long afterwards, he sent me a list of 27 "productive" authors working for *Dime Detective* and *Black Mask* (which became *Dime's* sister publication with the June 1940 issue, having been acquired by Popular Publications) during the time the Acme Op stories appeared. Just about all of the great second-level detective-tale pulpsters, from Dwight V. Babcock and John K. Butler to Roger Torrey and Theodore Tinsley, were there—and so was Lawrence. Locke figured there was a "90 percent certainty" that one of the authors on the list was Dana.

He was right, but I didn't have any idea which of the names it might be. Then, I remembered my collection of checks from Popular Publications, written to authors and artists. A notation on the front of the check would usually name the story for which the person was getting paid. I figured there was at least a slight chance that one of my dozens of paychecks might have been written to someone for an alleged "Jan Dana" story.

The chance turned out to be better than slight. After only a half-hour or so of searching, I hit paydirt. There it was, a check for $135.00 as payment for the short story, "Murder for Not Much," dated March 11, 1938, made out to, and endorsed by… John Lawrence. (The third Acme Op story to run in *Dime*, "Murder for Not Much" appears in this collection, which features the first six Op tales in order of publication.)

A few days later, when I contacted Matt Moring about my discovery, I found that he'd come to the same conclusion, and in the same way. He'd found two Popular Publications checks in his own collection, made out to Lawrence for Acme Indemnity Op stories.

ACCORDING TO John Locke, John Lawrence never contributed to the writers' magazines that proliferated during the days of the pulps. Many other pulpsters did, and those articles have yielded important insights into the working lives and thought processes of their authors.

In Lawrence's case, however, all the info we have on him comes almost entirely from two sources: an excellent, in-depth essay in Francis M. Nevins's *Cornucopia of Crime* (Ramble House, 2010), and an autobiographical piece in the April 1932 *Dime Detective*, the same issue that carried "The Scarlet Comet," Lawrence's first story for that publication. The Nevins piece offers substantial insights along with insider material from an extensive interview with Charles Spain Verral, Lawrence's best friend and fellow Canadian who, like Lawrence, moved to New York City in the 1920s and ended up writing for the pulps.

In his biographical piece for the '32 *Dime*, Lawrence names P.G. Wodehouse as his favorite author; golf, hockey, and squash as sports he enjoys playing; baseball as a sport he likes to watch; and "Leo's on 52nd street" as a place where he "spends as much time as I can afford." (At the time, New York's 52nd Street was nicknamed "Swing Street" for its proliferation of jazz clubs; Leo's was likely one of them.)

"Born—well, less than thirty years ago," Lawrence wrote, in that offhand, staccato style so favored by pulp authors when their words were about themselves, "in Windsor, [Ontario,] Canada. Schooled in Canada and Detroit, then the Royal Military College at Kingston, Canada, which they tell me is similar to West Point here. Law school in Detroit awhile, then the newspaper business for a year. Finally the stock-brokerage racket. Ten years in that—Toronto, Montreal, Detroit, Chicago and New York. Got my first fiction-concocting experience writing stock-market prophecies and advice. When, in due course, my customers all followed it and went broke, I grabbed the opportunity and bought a typewriter; started pounding."

The Nevins piece helps flesh out those bare bones, giving Lawrence's birthdate at February 4, 1907 and pointing out that while he began at the Royal Military College at the early age of 15, he left the school "prior to the graduation of his class, when he was not quite eighteen"—expelled, according to Verral, "for some escapade connected with drinking."

After the 1929 stock-market crash Lawrence alluded to in his *Dime* bio, he met Verral through a mutual Canadian friend who also lived in Manhattan, and the two hit it off.

"We became good friends," Verral told Mike Nevins. "He kept quizzing me about all the aspects of writing—plotting, knowing your market, and so on. He was a fast learner and could absorb what you told him."

In addition, he happened to know the right people to help him get a start. At the time they met, Verral's wife, Jean, happened to be editing for a new outfit called Popular Publications. According to Verral, "Jack heard through Jean that they needed a story at Popular to fill out an issue.

Jack got busy and banged out a mystery, and through Jean he got it sold to Popular."

That was likely a tale called "Private Enemy Number One," which appeared in the October '31 issue of Popular's *Detective Action Stories*. It was the first pulp appearance for Lawrence, and it got his foot in the door with the new publishing house. It also didn't hurt that Verral and Lawrence, who played tennis together six mornings a week—"indoors, at the old Armory on 14th Street," Verral recalled—began regularly scheduling doubles matches with a couple of guys named Harry Steeger and Harold Goldsmith, the very men who'd begun Popular.

The pulp careers of both Verral and Lawrence took off in the early '30s, with Lawrence doing the bulk of his work for Popular's *Dime Detective* as well as making forays into *Black Mask*. Verral, beginning in 1934, kept busy for several years with steady work from another publisher. "Charles Verral," explained pulp authority Don Hutchison recently, "along with fellow Canadian author Harold P. Montayne, wrote most of the Bill Barnes adventures in Street & Smith's *Bill Barnes Air Adventurer* magazine under the house name of George L. Eaton."

Interestingly enough, while fictional air war became Verral's meal ticket, the real-life version appears to have shot down his pal Lawrence's pulp career. In August 1942, Lawrence returned to his home country to enlist in the Royal Canadian Air Force. In the "Behind the Black Mask" feature for Nov. '42, *Black Mask* announced, "John Lawrence is now a Pilot Officer in the R.C.A.F. Reported for duty August 7. Good luck, Jack! Hope you can squeeze out a yarn now and then between more important chores."

It was not to be. Except for two 1943 appearances—in Popular's *Detective Tales* and *Flynn's Detective Fiction*—

with stories probably written before his enlistment, the once-prolific author went missing from the pulpwood pages. He didn't return until 1946, the year after his discharge, and then only for a handful of stories for Popular titles that ended in '48. Both the Acme Indemnity Op and the Marquis of Broadway tales had halted in 1942, and while one short Marquis encore came along in the June '48 *Dime,* the Acme Op proved to be one of the many casualties of World War II.

Nevins wrote that the postwar Lawrence, unable to re-establish himself as a writer, "found a job with the Canadian Advertising Agency in Montreal and later became public relations man for a knitting company and a silk mill in Toronto." He died in a hospital in that city on January 28, 1970, of cancer and emphysema, at the age of 62.

OF COURSE, it's possible that some of the Acme Indemnity Op stories were written by authors other than Lawrence, but there's a consistency with the ones collected here that indicates they're all the work of one guy—a writer whose characters often carried around sentimentality and cruelty in equal portions, and, as in the case of Marty Marquis and his tough-guy Broadway Squad, were hardly more virtuous than the crooks they chased.

While Hammett's Continental Op—based on Hammett's own time working for the Pinkerton Detective Agency—is pretty much just a guy doing a job, Lawrence's Acme Indemnity Op is more easily sidetracked, especially when it comes to women. He's more emotional. And, just like the hard guy Marty Marquis, he'll sometimes go out on a limb to help someone when he knows he's being a sap for doing it.

The stories here read a lot like the Marquis stories, right down to the frequent bursts of often unsettling violence. Pulp researcher Rob Preston has noted that the first Acme Op story with a New York setting, "The Judas Touch" (found in this volume) takes place on Broadway, the Marquis's home turf. And while the exact tale has so far eluded both Rob and me, we feel sure that the Hotel Montfalcon in "The Judas Touch" was used in at least one of the Marquis of Broadway entries.

There's also the fact that the Marquis of Broadway stories almost never appeared in the same *Dime* issue as the Acme Indemnity Op. Often, they alternated on back-to-back months. And in the rare instances when two of them showed up in the same magazine, one would be a short story, the other a novel or novelette—indicating, I believe, that there were only so many words Lawrence could write in a month, and he was hitting that ceiling with regularity.

Sure, all of this is circumstantial evidence. But it seems to me to at least indicate that the only Jan Dana to appear in the pulps was actually John Frederick Brock Lawrence.

BECAUSE OF both his social and as business relationship with the head of Popular Publications, it's easy to conjure up a scene of Lawrence and Steeger in the Popular offices, tossing around ideas and hitting on the notion of doing a series in the style of Hammett's Continental Op. It's also easy to imagine that Lawrence wouldn't have wanted to have his name associated with such a blatant knockoff. Then again, maybe the unwritten pulp rule about not having a writer appear more than once in a table of contents had more to do with it. This is probably why the Jan Dana *nom de plume* had been used only once before the Acme Ops began, on a non-character story called "Panamint Oil," appearing in the January 15, 1934 *Dime*. That one also contained "The Scarlet Casket," a Lawrence tale featuring his recurring New York-based investigator Sam Beckett.

Certainly, *hommages,* shall we say, to popular authors showed up regularly in the pulps. Perhaps the best-known mainstream writer to be treated in that manner was Damon Runyon, whose slangy tales told in the present tense by colorful, and colorfully named, New York characters became hugely popular in the 1930s. In their wake, plenty of stuff that could charitably be called Runyonesque appeared in the pulps, including a Hugh B. Cave series for the *Spicy* group featuring a character called the Eel, written under Hugh's "Justin Case" pseudonym, and Robert Bloch's wild Lefty Feep stories in *Fantastic Adventures.*

But, as you'll see, while the Acme Indemnity Op may have owed his existence to one of the greatest of the early hardboiled characters, he—and his creator—have nothing to be ashamed of. These are compelling, exciting stories, written by someone who, under any name, was a stone-cold pro. Imitation may be the sincerest form of flattery, but good imitation can be very fine indeed.

—John Wooley
Foyil, Oklahoma
29 October 2020

(In addition to those mentioned in the above text, thanks go to Tony Davis, Doug Ellis, John Gunnison, Peter McGarvey, John McMahan, and David Walker for their help and encouragement.)

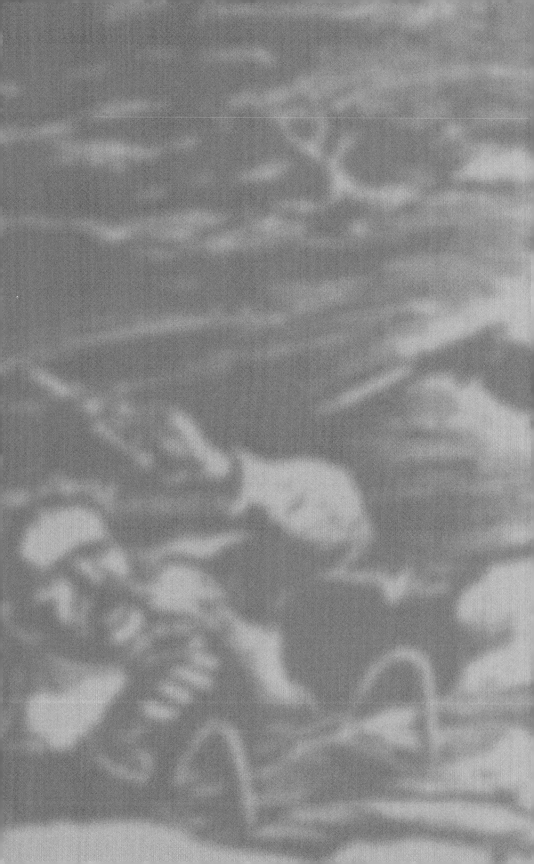

RIDDLE OF THE RATS

OUT OF THAT BLASTED WASTE
THAT WAS HELL'S HUNDRED HAD
SCURRIED AN ARMY OF RATS—
EACH WITH A BIT OF RED THREAD
NEATLY TIED AROUND ITS HUNGRY
THROAT. WHAT GRIM JOKE WAS
SOME UNKNOWN MADMAN WITH
A PERVERTED SENSE OF HUMOR
PERPETRATING ON THE CITY
OF HAVERSTON? WHY SHOULD
ANYONE DECORATE THOSE
SHARP-TOOTHED RODENTS WITH
CRIMSON CRAVATS OF DOOM?

CHAPTER ONE
THE FRIGHTENED CLIENT

I GOT track of the murderous Gino the first night I was in Haverston. That wasn't too difficult. Nowadays, crooks consider insurance detectives more as pals than as enemies, what with one thing and another, and we have to keep cozy with them a lot more than I, for one, would choose. The town had a sturdy little underworld—too damned sturdy, I thought, for a city of three hundred thousand—and I had no trouble circulating around. I ran into Ricci—his real name was Ricigliano—a natty little guinzo heister from back home, in a saloon known as Moore's.

He gave me a dazzling grin and a soft, moist little manicured hand and after we were at a table in the sawdust, "Well, riddle me. Here we have the Acme's favorite New York sleuth. Here we have a Michigan town half motors and half lumber. I doubt if there's a grand worth of ice in the burg. So what's the combination?"

"Looking for a no good wop," I told him. "Not you—though I'll make a note to check up on what you're doing here."

He chuckled. "It's my home town."

"Then you know every other Italian in town and can steer me to this stonemason, Gino. Right?"

A little wariness came into his wide grin. "Why should I? What do you want him for?"

I hesitated. "As nearly as I can figure out, to put a little folding money into his hand, take his sig and pat him on the head."

RICCI TWIRLED his glass and nibbled the end of his pointed little mustache, looked up at my eyes. "If that's a rib, you can save yourself trouble by finding him some other way. Your boss wouldn't thank you for pulling a fast one on me."

He gave a sudden frantic sob and whipped out a gun.

"It isn't important to pull a fast one," I growled. "At least, I don't think so. I'll be sure so, before I use anything you give me. If you don't like that, you can go to hell."

"Don't get huffy. You're asking me a favor, aren't you?"

"Not if it entails all this shadow-boxing. What's he done that calls for all this?"

Ricci shrugged. "I don't think the goof's done anything, but he's always thought he knocked somebody off in a drunken brawl about fifteen years ago. At least he used to go around muttering about it, though I don't think I even heard if anybody got killed."

I thought that over and was able to assure him: "That has nothing to do with my job, except that it may explain why he is such a hard gent to find. Where would he be now?"

"You might try a family named Carlucci."

I thanked him and paid for the drink, but having given me the steer, he wanted to supplement it. "You know, he's a little bit screwy," he warned me.

"In what way?"

"He's got a dementia praecox. There was that brawl, and then his family had a house on Hell's Hundred. You know what Hell's Hundred is?"

I said, "No," not entirely truthfully.

"It's a hunk of ground out at the east edge of town. It used to be a busy little community thirty years ago. There was a buggy-whip factory there and all the workmen lived around the place. The place went to hell when motor-cars came in and then there was a fire that gutted the whole piece of ground. It's about a hundred and twenty-odd acres, but they've called it Hell's Hundred ever since that. A lot of folks were killed in the fire and, after it was over, nobody wanted to rebuild on account of the swamps on the other side were moving in and—well, anyhow, the whole place just lies there, rotting. Up till about a year ago, there were a couple of squatters roosting out there—and Gino. He owned a little piece of ground, where his old man had lived.

"Like I say, the place was a real community up till fifteen years ago, with water mains and gas mains and all that and it seems when the fire gutted it, the water and gas companies just cut off the mains that went in there and sealed them up. Only, somehow, a lot of gas collected in the gas main and about a year ago got touched off. It like to blew the whole place out into the swamps.

"The squatters were killed, and some gent that was out there by accident, looking the place over to buy it. Gino happened to be in town or something and he escaped, but his place was demolished. What with one thing and another, you can see it's no wonder he's a little wacky."

I thanked him and hoped that Gino wouldn't be likely to pick on a total stranger like me as the cause of all his troubles, and Ricci agreed that was hardly likely. As I left, he reminded me: "I'm taking your word for it that you aren't you trying to jug him for anything."

I promised again that I would check up very carefully before I did anything with his tip. I meant it.

I went to check up.

HAVERSTON HAD plenty of night life and I rode through it, to my 'client's' house. It was nothing elaborate—a modest little six-room brick house in a middle-class residential neighborhood of the city.

I had to face a searchlight as I stood on the stoop and undergo a full two-minute inspection through the diamond-pane of glass in the front door before he unchained.

"I want to go over this again," I told him, as he switched on light in the brown-and-green living-room listlessly. "I think I may have found a way to locate this Gino."

For a minute, there was a sudden flaming of light in his red-rimmed, hunted gray eyes. He was a cavernous-faced, skinny, frightened old man—older than his fifty years, his hair almost white. He had some sort of shakes and he constantly balled a handkerchief in his sweaty left hand.

His voice was slaty, beaten, tortured. "Yes?" He said it wearily, as though unimpressed.

I slid hands in my coat pockets and set my jaw. "Don't give me that. When I left here this morning, you were on fire to have me find this Gino—so on fire that you shooed me out to get him before we went into it any deeper. Now you give me a bored 'Yes.'

"I was sent here to help you—or to recommend cancellation of your policy. You've got a hundred thousand on your life—had it just a year. Last week, they get the world's silliest communication from you, demanding to borrow thirty thousand on it, threatening, if the loan is refused, that they'll have to pay the face value to your estate within days. This turns out to mean you think you are on the point of being murdered by a man named Gino and that, by buying some property from him for thirty thousand, you think you can ward him off.

"Why they send me out here, instead of throwing your letter in the trash basket, I don't know, but here I am. I'm content that this Gino isn't going to knock you off in the next few minutes. There'll be plenty of time for you to tell me the whole story and particularly why—in view of the rush act you put on to have me locate him, this morning—you now give me only a 'Yes?' when I intimate I'm getting warm."

He mopped his face slowly, his hands shaking. His eyes were writhing on the rug. "I—I didn't expect you to—to find him quite so soon," he said fumblingly.

"God Almighty! Does that mean this whole thing is a hoax?"

"No! No!" he said hoarsely, quickly. "No—my God, no. I—but you see, there's nothing I can do—can do to him. There's no legal—no evidence—to have him arrested. He hasn't done anything—except threaten me by phone and—and things I can't prove."

"What things?" I snapped. "Tell me them, and I'll prove them."

He swallowed. "Even you can't do that. It—as I told you, he has a small tract in the property known as Hell's Hundred Acres. I—I wish to buy it from him."

"Why don't you?"

"Be—because I can't get in touch with the madman. For one thing he is suspicious of me—because he has some insane idea—God knows what it can possibly be—that I am attempting to trick him in the deal. Once, he was here in this house to sell and I—well, I stalled him off till next day. He—never returned. I think the man is mad. If I knew what was in his mind, maybe I could act intelligently."

"What's this deal about Hell's Hundred Acres anyway? Why do you want to buy and why does he want to sell—and anything else there is about it?"

HE LICKED his gray lips. "Yes. It must be that—must be something arising out of that." He was talking huskily, almost to himself. He looked suddenly up at me with eyes that had burning yellow lights in them.

"I told you it was a piece of ground—at the east end of the city—a piece of ground that must bear some curse. I have not told you the ghastly things that have happened there."

I let him tell me again all I'd got from Ricci with a few additions.

"It was once a prosperous section—the center of a small business colony—a buggy-whip factory.

"Up until two years ago, no one seemed to have the slightest interest in the place. The original families—foreign workmen mostly—either died or were lost track of somehow. The lots began to revert back for taxes. My brother and I are traders—mostly in timber tracts, but we sometimes handle urban property.

"Just over a year ago, he began to pick up pieces of this property. Why, I don't know. I was away on a trip through the northern part of the state. I got back here one night and opened the safe to stow some papers. I found options on practically every parcel in the whole tract of Hell's Hundred. I didn't know what to make of it. It was a gigantic undertaking, even though he bought the ground for practically nothing. I could not conceive what his plans were.

"I failed to locate him by telephone, but our one employee—a book-keeper—thought that I might find him out at Hell's Hundred.

"I started out—and this Gino appeared at the door. He wanted to sell me an option on his little piece of ground in Hell's Hundred. I—already in a panic at seeing nearly all our tiny capital involved in what seemed a disastrous deal—had small patience with him. My brother evidently had been negotiating with him and I am not sure he did not mistake me for Cyrus. We looked much alike. At any rate, he raved at me in Italian, as long as I was within earshot, obviously infuriated."

Beecher Lillian hesitated, mopped his jaws with a shaking hand. "I went out to the property. Before I reached it, then was a terrific explosion. I cannot describe it to you. It was as though hell, in truth, yawned open for a moment."

He shuddered, dropped his voice to a calmer level. "When we got there, we found that a spark must somehow have reached the gas main. There were a couple of tramps living on the property. We found only shreds of their flesh. Of my brother, we found only torn fragments of clothing."

He hesitated, trembling, and there was the horror of hell in his eyes.

I prompted gently: "And Gino?"

"Gino—when I recovered from the shock—Gino had disappeared. Weeks passed. I—you'll surely think I'm mad, but I must tell you this—I could not close my eyes in sleep, without my brother's face haunting me, urging me to take up the options—to buy the property. I became hag-ridden—and presently I did take up the options. Oh, it was not only these dreams, but my brother Cyrus was a shrewd man. Calm reflection told me he must have had some reason for his seemingly mad act. So I acquired the property. Which is to say—I acquired every last foot of it, save this lot owned by Gino.

"He—I cannot think but that he was irrational from the first. He was like a hunted thing the one night he came here. And, after the explosion, I never saw him again. Search as I would for him, I could get no trace. Nor have I ever gotten trace—till ten days ago.

"He called me on the phone. I know it was his voice, all right. He called me a thief, a blackguard who had tried to entrap him into the hands of the police, and he swore that he would kill me for it. He hung up without giving me a chance to discuss it with him. Twice more, he did the same thing. The man is, I am sure, mad. But I am equally sure that he definitely means to murder me."

"Because he threatens you?" I scoffed. "That usually means just the opposite."

HE LICKED his gray lips again. "You—you have not heard his voice. And there is not only his threatening. There is something else." He hesitated. "Six days ago, a young grocery clerk named Foxglove was cleaning the cellar of his home—on the north end of the city. Suddenly, he dashed up the stairs, phoned me that he was coming here with information of great importance regarding the property which, thanks to the newspapers, everyone knew to belong to me. He rushed from his house without enlightening his wife any further than that."

Again the scraggly old man mopped his livid face.

"He—young Foxglove—never reached here. After waiting hours, I called his house. His wife notified the police. We have found no trace of him yet. There was nothing in his cellar to show what information he might have come by. The police ransacked it thoroughly. Naturally, I cannot conceive of what he might have had to tell me. But—I can conceive, without too much imagination, why he did not reach here."

"You mean this Gino stopped him?"

"Yes. I am as sure of it as I am of your presence here. No, I cannot say why—I have no idea why. But in my heart, I know that Gino is responsible for his absence."

"Did you tell the police that?"

"Yes. They investigated. They assured me that Gino had left town a year ago and had not been back since. We—our police are a weak reed to depend on, unless there is money involved for them."

I growled: "It's a wonder you wouldn't tell me that this morning. However—what you want me to do is find Gino, buy his property and pacify him. Or do you want me to try and hang this disappearance of young Foxglove on him?"

The old man looked thickly at the floor, pushed hair out of his eyes. "I—I don't care what you do—if you can only make this mad Italian see that I had nothing to do—"

"How much will you pay for his ground?"

"Eh? He—he offered it for a thousand. It isn't worth half that. But I—I'll pay two thousand, gladly, if that will get rid of him."

"Make out a check."

I glanced over his shoulder while he sat at an old-fashioned secretary and scribbled a check—payable to me. I could not help seeing that he had exactly twenty-three hundred dollars against which to draw the two thousand.

I was disgusted, but I was vaguely uneasy, too. I knew that I should check with police headquarters. I could have brained the old fool for letting me tread on the edges of a police job without bothering to mention it. And I wanted to see the wife of this vanished Foxglove. On top of that, I had a morbid yen to see this Hell's Hundred Acres myself.

But—foolish or sane—I knew it was my business to contact this shadowy Italian with the bad conscience, Gino, at the earliest possible moment.

When Beecher Lillian let me out of his house there was no doubt that he was terrified to within an inch of his life. "For God's sake," he croaked, "don't do anything foolish. Don't mistake this Gino. He—he'll kill you, like *that!*"

"I doubt it," I said. "He doesn't even know I'm alive, yet."

CHAPTER TWO
RED THREAD

A THIN, needle-like rain was coming down as I turned back east. I had parked my rented car two blocks from the house, on the corner of Powell. I walked a block, passed under the strange green street lamps that guttered on the corners of this city. I walked half of the other block—and death reached for me.

There was an alley, midway the block. I was twenty yards short of it, when the huddled, crouched black thing leaped out of its yawning blackness, almost in my path. Surprise straightened me, brought me to what was supposed to be an instant stop—and the greasy, slick pavement betrayed me. My feet slithered, I almost did a split—and that flung me aside in the instant that stabbing, spitting orange flame lanced viciously at me.

The huddled thing was a black-cloaked man, but even in the spiteful flashes of the gun I could see no more. The jabbing reports were weird, flat and hollow in the falling rain. I slammed down on my back—and lead chipped pieces of wet cement from the sidewalk. The would-be killer simply stood there and slammed six crazy shots point-blank at me, while I flopped wildly like an eel on a line, finally spun into the gutter onto my face, yanking at the gun on my own hip.

One savage flame mushroomed at me and I ducked in fright, hitting my chin on the curb, as I got my own gun free. I snapped a wild shot at the dancing black thing—and he whirled and fled, back into the darkness of the alley.

I scrambled up, treadmilling in the wet, my eyes on fire. I stumbled over the curb and ran to the edge of the alley. I let three shots hammer flatly down its length, then peered in, prepared to issue a call to surrender—only to curse in my throat and race into the alley. It was merely a tributary of another alley that bisected the block. I could see vague light where it elbowed both ways thirty yards in.

I slid to a stop at the elbow, looked around. I saw nobody. I heard nothing—nothing but the soft patter of the rain. I ran to one end of the alley, saw nobody at all. I ran to the other and the three people I did see could not, for one reason or another, be the man who had shot at me.

I clenched my teeth and pocketed my gun.

I'm no coward but my heart was going ninety to the minute. I didn't understand yet why I was still alive. I had been caught flat-footed, utterly at the mercy of even a fair marksman, despite the floundering on the wet sidewalk. My would-be assassin must be execrable with firearms, but that did not cheer me up much. If he was stalking me— God knows why—there were plenty of ways he could get closer—close enough so that he could blast me out of existence with his eyes shut.

By then, I was awake to the true viciousness of this mad situation, and I began to understand my frightened client's terror a little more sympathetically.

I determined to do the only reasonable thing—to get Gino and get him fast, before he had a chance to play any more funny little tricks on me.

I DON'T know when I've blundered so much. I drove my car to the nearest drug store, found a city directory and found where this family of Carluccis lived. It was on the north side of the city. I loaded my gun again before I left my car parked near a railroad yards and set out for the address given.

I was in a section that was almost country. Gray, unpainted frame houses stood far apart, in rubbishy, over-grown fields that made no pretensions to being lawns. There were clumps of trees surrounding the clearing in which the Carluccis' house stood. From broken blinds on the windows, sick yellow chinks of lamplight streamed out.

Somewhere inside, a dog started yapping as I stumbled up the dirt walk to the sagging front door. I heard voices cease as I stood trying to catch a few words before knocking, so I knew there was no use trying to be cagy. They knew I was there, so I knocked.

A woman weighing two hundred and fifty pounds, with dirty gray hair, dirty black dress and a dirty, swarthy face, opened the sagging door to let out an odor of garlic and the piercing scrutiny of two coal-black eyes.

"Mrs. Carlucci?" I asked.

"Yes."

I gave a hasty moment's consideration to the question of whether these people would know about checks, decided they would and told her: "I'm an insurance agent. My company wants to buy a piece of property which I understand is owned by one of your countrymen." I brought out the check, waved it. "I have the check right here."

She suddenly loosed a flood of Italian at me, questioningly. I know Italian moderately well and what she asked me was could I say the same thing in Italian so that she could understand it better.

I looked blankly at her, and smiled apologetically. "I—I'm sorry. I don't understand Italian," I told her.

"Who you wish to see?" she said.

"A man named Gino—a stonemason."

She turned and spoke rapidly over her shoulder to someone in the room behind her, relaying my message and adding that I didn't understand their lingo. A grumbling man's voice answered. The man's voice, in Italian, said: "Hold him there, till I get Gino and Maria out. He is probably another of the cursed police."

The old woman turned back to me, looking dumb. "This Gino—where does he live?"

"I don't know," I lied. "I thought you might be able to direct me." A mangy yellow cur dog had its nose in the crack of the door, sniffing. I felt a small, round stone with the side of my foot, stooped, pretending to scratch my ankle while I picked it up and told her: "I understand this Gino is a distrustful man—very hard to make an appointment with and I—"

By then I figured there had been time for Gino—and Maria—to be on their way out from wherever they had been hidden so I let the cur dog have the stone with an underhand flip smack on his nose and he yelped shrilly, went racing back inside the door.

The old woman yammered wildly, automatically turned after him to see what had happened. I was around the frame shack in a matter of a second and at that I was almost too late.

A white blur that might have been a girl was running down the path away from the back of the house. A huge, shabby-looking Italian had just closed the back door and was jumping from the stoop after her when I centered him in my flash beam and let him see the snout of my gun.

"Stand still, Gino, or...."

The building fell on me.

I WOKE up, still on the wet ground, with a circle of dirty Italian faces around me. I did not have it clear in my mind just what had happened—whether the giant Italian had turned in mid-air and lunged at me first, or whether the stunning blow from behind had cracked my skull first. All I knew was that I had made a supreme fool of myself. I had had the Italian in my hands—I could almost smell garlic where he snatched at my throat—and I had not bothered to look in the darkness behind me. I thought grimly: sooner or later I'll wake up to the fact that I'm dealing with a guy a lot smarter than he looks, but by that time someone will probably be patting me in my foolish face with a spade.

I sat up, and saw what had socked me—a cold chisel wrapped in newspaper. It was lying at my right hand. I clenched my teeth and reached for it—and suddenly realized something else. In my right hand, tightly clenched, I had a piece of brown cloth and inside the brown cloth, something crackled.

I looked up at the hostile ring of faces. Somebody made a sneering remark in Italian and somebody snickered. My face was already purple with fury and mortification. I would like to have gone to work on the lot of them, but the concealed cloth in my hand—which I took good pains not to reveal—suddenly had my curiosity centered. I got up, looked for and found my pistol and flash in the mud, put them in my pockets and, after a minute standing there and looking foolish, being unable to think of anything else to do, I simply walked away. I was not simple enough to think that asking questions of this surly, inimical mob would get me anywhere. As a matter of fact, I was more than relieved to reach the road without them piling on my back.

I did not chance looking at my handful till I was in my car. I trudged grimly, still holding the rolled-up newspaper as though it were a club, till I could switch on my dashlight.

Strictly speaking, the thing passed into the nightmare stage then, but I did not realize it. I did realize, however, that the piece of brown cloth I held had once been a pocket, presumably on Gino's coat and that I must have torn it off in the momentary scramble. It contained a bewildering item: a small piece of paper, jaggedly torn along one edge and covered with faint brown writing. A closer look showed that it was part of a note, and that the other part had been torn away.

What I had was—

erground in

doned water

ballacite. I don't know

k Tony Gino,

as trying to

inced that I

ice for some-

y getting me

ff dynamite

p my exit. I

nest of hun-

ept alive on

am helpless

er finds this,

uch with my

ll him to use

ast open this

hat was the

n elbow joint

s hurt in the

to this terrible

ill not be long

And, running through the top of the note, was about six inches of crinkly, very thin, scarlet thread. It was as though the note had been attached to something.

It took me about four minutes, before I let out breath. I did not understand what I had—but somehow, I knew it was of importance and I was straining, trying to make sense of it. No dice—but certainly it brought up swarming questions to be answered, brought me back to cold earth. I decided to suspend my masterminding, to get down to brass tacks and chase down the things I had to chase down.

I looked at my watch. It was after two o'clock. I debated whether to call my client and could see no point in it. I decided to get back to my hotel and get some clean clothes.

All the way, I tortured my brain with the note, and I spent time on it after I got in, but I could not crack it.

I started running down the angles, as soon as I could.

I THINK I would undoubtedly have mentioned the note—and shown it—to the police lieutenant whom I interviewed, if he had been anything like a decent copper. But he had no sooner examined my credentials than a greedy look came into his little green eyes and he hurried me into his private office, closing all the doors. When he had eased his two hundred and fifty pounds into a swivel chair and offered me a cigar, he said: "Acme, eh? Well, we can do business, pally. Tell me what you're after and who you think's got it. We'll pick him up and shake him till he gives. I know without asking that you're not the kind of guy who expects something for nothing." The question mark on the end of his voice did all the asking necessary.

This to a total stranger, at seven o'clock in the morning gave me a funny feeling in my stomach. I recalled my 'client's' opinion of the police and for the life of me, I could not figure anything I could trust this fat slob with.

I told him that I was here only to look into the threats on Beecher Lillian's life and was trying to locate this Gino to ask him a few questions.

The incredible copper ignored most of it, and leaned across his desk to ask confidentially: "Just how much is this Beecher Lillian worth? Anything?"

I said that was none of my business, but that he had fair insurance.

It took a minute for the fat man to think it over, scowling at his blotter in a disappointed way. Finally he asked, "Well, what do you want to see me for?" plaintively.

"I thought you might help me pick up this Gino and set Lillian's mind at rest."

"Hell with his mind," the copper growled. "I heard he was going into bankruptcy and he's probably gone wacky. Besides, this Gino left town a year ago. I know, because we did look around for him."

That seemed to be that. I got out as fast as I could and he was growling at me before I was through the door, at that.

I WENT to the local office of the Acme and was in the door just a minute after the manager, a bright young lad who was very much perturbed about Beecher Lillian and very glad to see me.

After we had chatted a minute or two, I asked him: "What is ballacite?"

He wasn't sure, but thought it was some kind of a metal and went out to look it up in some books.

When he came back he told me: "Why, that's a very valuable metal. It's the lightest known, but in alloy it has the strength of structural steel. What's our interest in it?"

"I don't know yet," I told him. "What's it used for?"

"They haven't got it in commercial quantities yet but it could be used in aviation to double the safety factor. Also in long bridges."

"How much would it be worth in cold cash. Say, per ounce."

He had to go and look that up and make a phone call before he reported, a little awed: "Forty dollars an ounce—more than gold. Of course an ounce would be quite a bit more than an ounce of gold account it's so light. But what's this all about?"

"Maybe I'll let you know later," I said.

I quizzed him for quite a while about the affairs of Beecher Lillian and got no more information than I had had. The two brothers had come to town from Detroit some eleven years before and set up as traders in lumber land and ordinary realty. Both were bachelors and had practically no acquaintances. They were supposed to be doing just fairly well, hadn't made any very spectacular profits.

I SAT in my car, wrinkling my forehead over the note a while longer, then set out to find the wife of young Foxglove, the grocery clerk who had vanished while en route to Beecher Lillian's, after phoning that he had information regarding Hell's Hundred.

She was a rather brittle little blonde, without children, who still had kind of a sneaking hunch that her husband had merely used a neat means of walking out on her, and her surly answers to my questions were no help at all.

I examined the basement, in which something was supposed to have dawned on young Foxglove before he made the call and rushed out. For a million dollars I couldn't find anything in that basement different from a thousand I had seen.

The lines in my forehead were beginning to get permanent this time when I sat in my car again. I cursed the fate that had given me only routine brains. If I were, now, a movie detective, I was sure that I would have divined the answer to this weird puzzle long ago.

Then the newspaper caught my eye.

It was the rolled-up newspaper that had been used to wrap the cold-chisel when it landed on my head the night before. I had left it in the car, forgotten. It lay on the floor and it had, naturally, unrolled itself.

What was vaguely interesting was that a small piece had been clipped from the page that was outermost—not the first page, but the outside one as the paper lay.

I picked it up and saw that it was a week-old issue of the *Haverston Times-Herald*.

Considering that this paper must undoubtedly have come from the house of the cursed Gino, I came to life.

I found the offices of the newspaper in the downtown business section, and got directed to the morgue and thence to an issue of the paper with the missing clipping.

I located the page and sat down to read it. I barely touched the seat, before I was up again as though it had been charged with electricity.

The clipping that had been cut from the paper read:

MORE RED-MARKED RATS REPORTED
TO HEALTH AUTHORITIES

Public Health Officer Bridges today made public that four more of the rats wearing red threads around their necks had been turned in to the health department. This makes twenty-two in all, over a period of five months. Mr. Bridges declared that as yet, there is no solution of how, or why, rats trapped in the eastern section of the city come to be decorated in this unique manner.

He declares that it may be some crank perpetrating a joke,

but that, in his official capacity, he fails to see the humor....

It took me just ten minutes to inquire my way to the Board of Health, and another ten to talk my way into the presence of four dead rats in a brass container in an ice-box.

Each of the four had a bit of red thread, identical with that that was attached to my note, knotted round the neck.

Then I got the monstrous, nightmare possibility.

CHAPTER THREE
HELL'S HUNDRED ACRES

I **ALMOST** ran out on the courteous young man who had been showing me the rats, scurried down the hall—a corridor in the city hall, it was—till I located a phone booth. I called my client's home—and got no answer. I called his office—and cursed through set teeth. He had just gone out—they did not expect him back, in view of the fact that it was now five o'clock, and they did not know where he might be found.

Then I got a real break—and came within an inch of muffing it entirely.

I was standing in the hallway, my hands jammed in my pockets, trying to settle the racing thoughts that were swarming in my head, trying to catch the one among them that would tell me what to do. I was almost alone in the long, dingy wooden corridor.

Subconsciously, I heard the door down the hall open and heard plodding footsteps coming toward me, but it was not till the woman came abreast and I moved aside absently that I saw her face. Luckily, she was absorbed in penciled information written on dirty paper in her gnarled hand.

She was the fat Mrs. Carlucci, the woman who had—at least up till last night—harbored Gino.

After the first start of recognition, I could not see anything in the meeting that was of importance. I knew where she lived. Following her would probably take me there, at this hour, and I could not believe that Gino would be mad enough to return there so quickly, after last night's episode. So I almost dismissed her from my mind. Almost but not quite. Suddenly, I swung round and gazed at the door from which she had come.

I could not see the gold lettering on the door, but a dozen strides put me in front of it where I could. I read: *CITY SURVEYOR'S OFFICE.*

It took me just one second to get conscious. Then I jumped into the office.

Having had a taste of one city department in this cozy little town—the police—I was reasonably sure how to handle another one. Before the weasel-faced young man in horn-rimmed glasses got to me from the other end of the long counter where he was stowing away musty-looking books, I had a twenty-dollar bill on the counter, partly covered by my spread palm.

He looked at it without interest, but kept looking at it while I said: "That old Italian woman that was just in here. What did she want. I want the same information she got."

He licked his lips and mumbled, "I'm afraid—" checked himself and said, "Wait just a minute," vanished through a ground-glass door at the end of the office, came back presently and looked at my tie to tell me: "She wanted a map of a piece of property known as Hell's Hundred Acres—a map of the water mains, the property is now disused but at one time they had water mains—"

"I know," I said. "Where's my map?"

He frowned. "She didn't exactly want a map. She wanted to know the elbows of the mains under that property. We found that there are four elbows and I told her where they were, but I'm afraid it's— You're a stranger here?"

"More or less."

"Well, the only way we could spot the mains for her was to name street corners. Unless, of course, one were to take a set of surveying instruments out and—"

"Well, give me the street corners, damn it!" I said.

"Unfortunately, there are no longer, strictly speaking, any streets. There were only two roads in the whole tract that were paved and they have long since fallen to pieces. The other streets have simply disappeared—completely grown over."

That was a neat stunner. Yet—if the woman wanted them, so did I. I insisted and he wrote out directions—so many yards northeast of the corner of this and that street, so many from this and that street and so on. One direction had to do with a stable.

I was damned if I knew what I was going to with them, but a queer sort of urgency had come over me. Inwardly, I was jumping around like a drop of water on a hot stove. I tried once more to get my client and finally gave him up.

IT WAS dark now, outside. I chased my brain crazy, before I had to admit that I was stumped. Though this much I had: Gino was going to the Hell's Hundred—some time soon. And the woman was now on her way with the information that he needed.

I climbed into my car and, for the second time since my arrival in Haverston, sent it shooting toward the north end of the city, toward the little Italian settlement I had visited the night before.

I was a little groggy at the sudden growing up of this incredible picture. I had come here, twenty-four hours or so before, expecting to find one silly old nut being threatened by another.

And now, I had a murder case—for I was certain now that young Foxglove had been murdered and his body disposed of. There was no other possibility in my mind.

This time, I stopped my car a longer distance from the little colony, and made my way very cautiously on foot.

It was pitch-dark now and I had little trouble. My only fear was that one or more dogs would be out and expose me, but they weren't.

And then I was in a clump of trees, across the dirt road from Carlucci's sagging frame shack—and wondering what in the name of God I would do next.

The last thing in the world I wanted to do was nothing. But that was exactly what I had to do for nearly a half hour. Then Mrs. Carlucci came trudging up the road and I realized that, traveling by trolley and by foot as she must have done, it was not inconceivable that I had beaten her home. My pulse quickened, for I thought she still carried in her fist the slip of paper that I had seen her bring from the city surveyor's office, though in the gloom, even though she passed within ten feet of me, I could not be positive.

But I almost was, when, three minutes after she entered the sagging house, the door opened to let out a ragged, curly-headed boy who took a bicycle from the side of the house and rode off into the darkness.

Nobody would be interested in how I chased after that bicycle, managed to keep it within sound, if not always within sight, while the kid rode squarely into the woods. Fortunately, he did not go far—less than a mile—so when he was at his journey's end, I was no more than fifty or sixty yards behind him.

I saw light flare, in time to keep me from overrunning him and I crouched tense in the bushes.

I heard a man's voice say growlingly, "Didn't she give you any money?" in Italian and the scared voice of the kid deny that 'she' had.

Gino—I had no doubts that this was Gino hiding out—said fretfully: "My God—I've got just about enough gas left in my car to get from here downtown. Well, no matter—I'll get some from your uncle. Tell your mother blessings."

I was not even interested in whether there was more talk after that. I was scooting back the way I had come, as fast as my legs would carry me. If there was to be any going in cars, I did not want to be caught a mile away from mine.

I tried to comfort myself that this was a dead-end section of the city and that if Gino were going to drive downtown, he would have to use the road on which my car was now parked. I couldn't quite convince myself that it was so until I was within fifty yards of my own rented buggy.

Then the chugging on the road behind me became audible. I raced on till the last moment, then ducked into the bush beside my car—as an ancient model-T flivver pumped by. In the light of the dash, I saw the grim, frightened face of the shabby, sinister-looking Gino.

I was into my car and after him, before he was a quarter of a mile away, and it was no trouble catching up to him.

WE DROVE straight to the heart of the city first and again I almost lost him. He entered a smart-looking little one-story brick building on a side street. The building had a black-and-gold sign over its flat front—*Carps and Hogan, Contractors.* Gino went in through an entrance that was in an alley at the side, not through the front door. I parked across the street and it was not till the light delivery truck trundled out and turned so as to pass very close to me, that I realized that Gino had switched conveyances.

I got after him in a hurry, but it was not such an easy job to trail the truck. Its engine was as good as the one in my car, but I managed. We threaded streets in various directions awhile, but presently we straightened out and went east and I felt mounting excitement. We were headed for Hell's Hundred.

The moon was up now—a sickish sort of pale thing—but as we left the street lights behind, it seemed to become more important in the scheme of things. And by the time we reached Hell's Hundred, it was definitely an asset.

The fabulous property was in sort of a valley. I did not know that and when the rough dirt road on which we were traveling suddenly soared me up to the top of a rise, I caught my breath.

It was in panorama before me—the immense, sunken tract. The moon was not strong enough, naturally, for me to see to the edge of the whole hundred-odd acres, but it seemed that I did. Never have I seen such desolation.

Trees were blackened and stunted. Here and there, over the vast expanse, charred, sullen bits of buildings still rose out of the encompassing grass. It was like a battlefield, utterly still and ugly. It gripped at your heart with a reasonless, sick horror. If anyone unacquainted with the facts were told that this had once been a moderately thriving community, including a factory, it would have been impossible to believe. It had the impression of a vast, overgrown field where a few wooden huts had once stood. Even the trees—the ones that had grown up since the abandonment of the tract—looked warped, gnarled, stunted.

The road curved, to lead into the waste—curved and, after a few minutes, was only more field. I had to stop. Running without lights and now in the momentary danger of hitting one of the thin trees, I simply could not negotiate it. I switched off my engine and sprang out.

Ahead of me, I could hear the lumbering of the truck. I ran on, confident that even Gino, who appeared to know this vicinity at least like the palm of his hand, could not make much more speed than my dogtrot.

Nevertheless, it seemed a long, long time till the sound of his motor stopped and another long time till I ran out of a clump of trees, almost into the truck.

He had had time to climb out and was now a good hundred yards away from me. He had a flashlight in his hand and he was walking in erratic, hurried little forays, first one direction, then another, then his light would go close to the ground. Then the process would be repeated.

I watched these little erratic spurts of light, till my eyes ached. In view of Gino's air of urgency, I had thought he knew exactly where he was going. Evidently, he didn't. He must have ranged over five hundred square yards, in short little runs, in which I could see no system whatever.

And then I could. I presently realized that he was narrowing in, was closing in on a point—though what point was a mystery to me.

I suddenly woke up to the fact that the truck might bear investigation. It was no trick at all to step over to it and cover my flashlight with four folds of my handkerchief, give it careful scrutiny while the Italian was occupied.

I FOUND, first of all, a small engine attached to the body of the truck that puzzled me. Presently, I figured it out as something similar to a miniature pile-driver. Then I found other things.

I found a box, half full of sawdust, through which long white sticks showed. It was labeled *Dynamite*. I found a box containing a dozen or more lengths of sectional pipe drill—screw-threaded so that each three-foot length could be screwed into the preceding one. There was a box of fuses and caps. There was a long coil of thin wire rope. And there was a stack of thick black lengths of ladder which I had to puzzle over for a minute before I saw the bottom section.

It was curved over and ended in two long, gleaming hooks. The whole was a scaling ladder—also sectional. And there was a box of white wax candles.

I can't say that I was surprised at any of these. But I was surprised when, almost automatically, I risked a quick peek into the driver's seat of the truck, found that Gino had taken off his coat and laid it on the seat.

I went through it swiftly and got into my hand a thick, legal-looking document and a dirty white envelope, just as the sound of sharp, metallic blows started from across the field.

I took one look, saw Gino, in the beam of his flashlight, driving stakes in the shape of a square, with desperate speed. Hastily, I examined the find in my hand.

I had the deed to a small tract of land. There was nothing in the few phrases that I glanced at to indicate so, but I was sure that this was a deed to Gino's lot in Hell's Hundred. I stuck that back in his coat pocket. I fingered open the envelope—and for a second my head rang.

I had: Item one: the missing part of the torn note which I had ripped from the Italian's pocket the night before. Item two: another note, similar in shape to the first— and bearing the little red thread through its top. But even in that first glance, I felt something wrong—something different about the note. I read—and I felt the blood singing behind my eyes.

The second note read—

> I have at last found a way to get in and out of my prison. But I am not going to leave it, till my business is finished. I have company here now—delightful company. If anyone finds this, give it to Gino, the stonemason and he will understand. If he wants his daughter back, he must find a way to where we are and bring the signed deed to me, with this note. He will know what deed I mean. Maybe his daughter will still be alive, if he is quick enough. Maybe not.

And it was signed by the brother of my client—the man who was supposed to have perished weeks ago in the explosion—Cyrus Lillian!

I fished the torn fragment out of my pocket and matched it with the one I'd just found, raced swimming eyes over the complete note. I read—

> I am trapped somewhere unde rground in Hell's Hundred in an aban doned water main near vein of ballacite. I don't know how long I am here. I thin k Tony Gino, a stonemason from whom I w as trying to buy a small lot became conv inced that I was betraying him to the pol ice for something and tried to kill me b y getting me underground and setting o ff dynamite which completely walled u p my exit. I am in main where there is a nest of hundreds of rats and I have k ept alive on scraps of their stealings. I am helpless to get out myself. Who ev er finds this, please, for God's sake, get to uch with my brother, Beecher Lillian. Te ll him to use dynamite or something to bl ast open this ghastly tomb. Blast near w hat was the Sloane stables, just above a n elbow joint in the main. My head wa s hurt in the explosion that walled me in to this terrible living hell and I think

it w ill not be long before I go entirely mad.

Cyrus Lillian.

I was incapable of feeling any more astonishment. But I was not incapable of thought. And the one thought that struck hard, just as I looked up to see Gino's flashlight start coming quickly in a straight line towards me, was that *the second note had not been written by the same hand as the first!* I was even ready to think that it was an obvious imitation.

Then Gino was at the truck and I had jammed the envelope back in his coat pocket hastily, backed into the bushes. The notes—the torn one and the whole one, I hastily stuffed into my own wallet.

I knew what his next move would be and I was not surprised when he leaped into the truck and drove it, rumbling and bouncing, its headlights picking out the spot where he had driven four stakes into the ground.

I was well out of the way of the headlights when he backed the car around so that its rear was to the little marked-out square. The headlights died then and the flash came into play again as he worked frantically around the back of the truck. The truck's body prevented me seeing much of what went on, but I figured the sudden succession of muffled thumps to be the little engine driving the sections of pipe-drill into the ground. When, regularly, the thumping stopped, then began again, I had no trouble deducing that Gino was quickly screwing on another length of the pipe.

Then I heard what he did—the sudden, startling change in the tone of the thumping. From deep-noted, it suddenly became brassy and I realized that the incredible must be true—he had driven through into a hollow chamber, thirty feet below the surface of the pitted, bleak, rocky ground.

I could see no further point in staying where I was. I began to creep up on him. I heard him muttering, jabbering shrilly, under his breath, almost hysterical, as he yanked sticks from the box of dynamite, fed them down the pipe. My first thought was that the force of the explosion would be directed downwards and I was aghast. Then I realized that drills of this sort are made weak on the sides and agate hard at their ends.

When he lit the long fuse, I hastily darted aside and stretched myself flat. He leaped into the truck, drove it back a hundred yards and cut the engine.

There was one awful moment of silence.

Then the ground belched racking, red thunder. Red and yellow flame mushroomed up out of the ground to a height of twenty feet and dirt and stones cascaded with whistling force in all directions.

CHAPTER FOUR
THE RAT MAN

I **HAD** not moved far enough away. The bushes shielded me somewhat, but the dirt was like a hailstorm even so. It was pure luck that I was not brained by a stone.

I did not move as I heard Gino come running back. When he was at the edge of the crater that I could only see vaguely in the dim moonlight, I heard his broken sob. There was something about the tone of it that told me he had succeeded with the blast—and then he was running back toward the truck again. His flash went on, as he hastily assembled the ladder, but during the long minutes that it took him to do that, I heard something—or thought I heard something—that sent gooseflesh crawling over me. I thought I heard the faintest of faint splashes.

He ran back, panting and tugging the long black ladder behind him. I was on my feet now, torn by indecision—and morbid, horrible curiosity. I could not decide what to do.

He ran the end of the ladder into the hole. Twice he called hysterically, "Maria! Maria!" after he had sunk the deep prongs of the ladder's end into the dirt side of the hole.

He was still crying the name desperately as he flung himself over and began to climb down.

Then he was gone.

I was, momentarily, incapable of constructive thought. My brain was glazed from the thunderous realization that—in spite of what I had been told—Cyrus Lillian had been trapped underground and had managed to exist for weeks, thirty feet below the earth's surface, in a water main. That he had been trapped in a nest with hundreds of rats—and that he had existed on the scraps that this multitude of scavengers had brought home, presumably for their young. It staggered belief. I had heard of such things, but never for a moment credited them. Yet, in all truth, it was not impossible. If there were holes through which rats could enter and leave, then there were holes for air to circulate, even in the bowels of the earth and even if the holes were too small and well hidden for the trapped man to avail himself of them. He was in a water main, in a lime-stone-loaded property with marshes nearby.

Water—if not in the main itself—would filter through the limestone....

And then suddenly, the sound of Gino's sobbing came again and I saw his flash beam appear above the edge of the crater as he climbed desperately up, and I stopped thinking.

I stopped too soon. For the stunner came now—came and was over, almost in one terrible moment.

As Gino's head appeared, a strong beam suddenly sprang from the darkness on the other side of the crater—sprang and slapped the half-mad Italian squarely in his sweating, swarthy face. Beside the blazing flashlight, there was suddenly the shiny barrel of a pistol.

A voice that I recognized instantly as that of my frightened client, Beecher Lillian cried wildly: "Gino! Don't move! I'll shoot...."

But the Italian was beyond reason. He gave a sudden frantic sob and his other hand whipped from his clothes a nickeled gun.

HE NEVER had a chance. The gun in Beecher Lillian's hand exploded—twice. The Italian's nose was beaten into his face—was instantly a bloody, smashed pulp and he was slammed backwards. The hole was too small to admit his slumped, sacklike body to fall down and it jammed there, his head sinking down on his shoulder.

I said, as calmly as I could: "All right, Mr. Lillian—don't shoot again. You've killed him."

He gasped and cried shrilly, "Who is that?" swung his gun in the darkness, tried to locate me. I told him and he almost cried in relief.

"I followed him here, too," I told Lillian.

"He was going to kill me! He tried to shoot me!" Lillian babbled.

"I know. I'll back you up with the police."

I heard a choke in his throat. "The—the police. Oh God, of course! I—shall I go and get them?"

"That explosion and those shots will bring them presently," I said. "Good God, man—if you were there and saw the whole procedure aren't you curious about what's down there? What he was getting at?"

After a second Lillian said huskily: "I—don't care now what was down there."

"You don't? My friend, if I'm not very much mistaken, your brother is down there—alive! He was trapped in an underground chamber by the blast and he has been sending out notes tied round the necks of rats with red thread from his clothing, begging for help ever since. Unfortunately, almost all the notes must have been scraped off by the narrowness of the exit the rats used, but— Come on, let's see."

For a moment, he was utterly silent. I could hear him gasping for breath. Then he croaked: "My—my brother!"

I reached under Gino's armpits to drag him out of the hole. His clothes were soaking wet. He was quite dead. I peered down a shaft just large enough to admit a man's body, There was a faint yellow flicker far below, the oily glint of light on water. Gino had apparently lit some of his candles below.

"Come on," I told my client as I swung a leg in. "I don't know just what I may find here and I want you close."

We went down silently, Beecher Lillian's husky, excited breathing above me the strongest sound in the black shaft. I was listening too intently and when I finally did come to the last rung I didn't realize it. I trod on air, almost went headlong. I flung my hands up, clamped them around my client's leg to save myself. He yelped and I told him, "Steady!" as I slipped my leg through the last rung, hung down—and saw the unbelievable sight.

We were in a water main—a round, fat-bellied tunnel of brick. Water to the depth of three or four feet was flowing slowly directly below me. Three candles had been lighted and they cast a weird glow.

But nothing could add much or detract much from the weirdness of the scene. Rats were everywhere, scampering along the catwalk, yet others—scores of them—lay motionless. The concussion of the explosion had either stunned or killed them.

There was an old, rotting repair raft—the type that workman use when exploring these subterranean tunnels for repair purposes. Two candles were burning on the raft—and a beautiful red-headed girl lay, dripping wet, on the grimy planks. Her eyes were closed, yet her partly exposed, voluptuous breasts were heaving rhythmically. I guessed that she was doped. And I knew, of course, that she was Maria Gino.

But even this faded into insignificance beside the other creature in the chamber. He was a man—but what a man! Ragged, unkempt, unshaven, he stood swaying on the catwalk, staring stupidly, completely oblivious of our presence above him, his eyes foggy on the girl on the raft. He put out a hand to steady himself against the wall—apparently he, too, was just recovering from being knocked out by the explosion. His gnarled, claw-like hand came in contact with a ring in the wall—a ring to which the raft's painter was tied. As he clutched it, the rotten rope parted and he was holding it stupidly.

THEN FOR the first time, as the gentle current tugged at the raft, putting pressure on the rope, he looked up bewilderedly, and my flesh crawled.

For this terrible old creature who had lived for weeks on the food of rats, associated with rats, used rats for his messengers—had somehow taken on the features of a rat.

For all the world, that was my first impression. Then, as he came slowly, unsteadily along, towing the boat, although seemingly still puzzled by it all, I saw that it was mostly a mirage. Mostly—but still not entirely.

Then the raft was passing under us. I whispered up at my client in the darkness above: "Don't move."

The girl floated under me—and I dropped to land just at her feet. The raft rocked perilously. I did not stay on it a second. I leaped off, scrambling onto the catwalk behind the dazed old creature who had been Beecher Lillian, the instant I landed.

Then he was no longer dazed. He whirled on me. His eyes were red and he suddenly raked his claws at me in a movement as swift as light, while from between his bared teeth came a whining squeak that somehow had the volume of a fire siren. I had no alternative. I had to crack him behind the ear with the barrel of my pistol.

Above me, my client cried out in protest. I said: "That won't hurt him. He'll lie peaceful till the police come."

Beecher Lillian seemed to gasp himself to life. His excited husk said: "Shall—shall I get a rope to hoist them—"

"Stay where you are. We don't move till the police come."

He was silent a second. Then he cried out wildly, with surprising strength:

"I won't stay here, doing nothing. That girl—she may be dying."

I swung the nose of my pistol up at him. "She isn't dying. She's doped and she was dropped down this shaft—*after the explosion we just heard!* She may be bruised but that's all. And you are going to stay there, if I have to put a bullet in you."

His voice was suddenly petulant, a little hysterical. "For God's sake—don't do that! I—I didn't know what I was to find here. I—I too brought some explosive—high explosive. It's in my cigar case. If you—"

He suddenly put a hand down into the feeble light, a hand that held a chamois-leather cigar case.

"You see? You see?" he cried crazily. "If you shoot—there will be a third and last explosion that will finish us all. I am going…" and then suddenly he fell silent as what I had just said registered.

"Wait!" he croaked. "Wait! What—what do you mean *the girl was dropped down here after the explosion?* Who— why—"

"Why? That's a little involved, though not too much so. Who? That's easy. You—you damned murderer!"

HE ALMOST choked, then shrilled: "Murderer! You— what are you saying? You yourself saw—you said that you saw that Gino was trying to kill me. I shot in self-defense."

"Yeah. But you didn't kill young Foxglove, the grocery clerk in self-defense. You killed him because he got the first note that managed to reach the outer world from your brother—a note that probably made quite clear that you knew about the ballacite on the property—that you had the best motive in the world for killing your brother—a fortune. Naturally, Foxglove had to go."

"You are mad," he shrieked, "utterly ma…."

"No. But I can imagine you were, when you realized that your brother, instead of being killed by the blast you set off on top of him, had in some miraculous way been trapped down here and was sending out notes tied to rats. That must have been a terrific shock.

"But not half the shock when it transpired that, out of all the people living in this city, the only other note that managed to reach the outer world, had to be found by Gino's daughter. What did he do? Call you up and threaten to expose you if you didn't pay exorbitant prices for his ground?"

I hesitated. There was no answer from above, only that quick, hoarse, animal-like breathing.

"You faced the necessity of finding where your brother was buried—no easy thing even for a surveyor—and completing your murderous work. You were unable to do the task yourself. You could think of only one person who might be able to ferret it out—and a person whom you were going to have to kill anyway. So you tried to find Gino. You pulled a very neat piece of conniving getting me, a stranger here, to find Gino for you. That little gunning show you put on when I left your house last night was not stupid, either. It really had me thinking that Gino was after me. And it was good insurance that I would not listen to anything Gino had to say, if I did come up with him.

"But I didn't come up with him. That is to say, I led you to him, but I didn't capture him—which was exactly what you wanted. You kidnaped his daughter during—or after—the fracas last night, conceived the bright idea of forging one of the notes—and getting it to him—one that his ignorant brain would believe and that would send him in a frenzy to find the underground chamber and open it up. Then you could finish your work of extermination—supplementing it now by killing Gino, his daughter and—I presume—me, if I got too troublesome. Then the ballacite fortune would be yours and no one else would know about it. All you had to do was sit tight and wait a year or so. Oh, it was very nice thinking—you have imagination. But it's too bad it didn't seem to work."

For a second there was silence. Then from above his cold, grating voice said: "What makes you think it did not work, my friend? The end is not yet. I am going up that ladder—"

"And set off your high-explosives? I think not, pally. However if you would like to try it—go ahead. But remember—you may have a chance of beating this rap in court. You have no chance of beating the explosion if you set it off."

"What? Why, I will be miles aw...."

Then he started up the ladder and it was then for the first time, I guess, that he realized he was trapped. He gasped as he grabbed down at his ankle and found my handcuffs there, chaining him securely—the twisters I had snapped on when I pretended to fall.

He took it well, though and did not do anything foolish. He presently had a fit of hysterics and he was laughing crazily when the police came.

TO THE MURDER BORN

THERE WERE ONLY TWO CLASSES
OF SOCIETY IN HADDONSTOWN—
THE STUFFED SHIRTS WHO
LIVED ON RIDGE ROAD AND THE
HUNKIES WHO WALLOWED IN
SQUALOR IN THE VALLEY BELOW.
BUT THE NIGHT GYPSY HAGIN
WAS KILLED THE UNDERWORLD
SWITCHED PLACES WITH THE
UPPER CRUST. WHAT WAS
THE GHASTLY SKELETON IN
ARISTOCRACY'S CLOSET THAT
IMPELLED THE TOWN'S FIRST
LADY TO TURN TORTURESS? WHY
WAS SHE WILLING TO REVEAL
TO A STRANGER THAT IT WAS
RATHER TO THE MURDER, THAN
THE MANOR, SHE WAS BORN?

CHAPTER ONE
MARKED DOLLARS

MAINWARING WAS alone in his spacious, comfortable house, when he received Gypsy Hagin. The establishment's two servants were enjoying an evening out. The hall was lighted and a green-shaded desk lamp glowed in the library, on the desk behind which the snappish, bantam-weight little assistant prosecutor sat grimly waiting. No other lights burned.

Hagin's meaty, solid bulk had barely filled the doorway, before he snatched the cigar from his thin lips and asked sharply: "I saw someone leaving here as I came up. Looked like that pup Burdick. Was it?"

"It was Asa Burdick, the feature-writer. What about it?"

"What was he doing here? You've not given him any hint of what we discussed two weeks ago?"

"Hardly." The assistant D.A.'s sharp little face was expressionless but he could not keep a faintly interested gleam from his gray eyes. "Mr. Burdick was here to discuss you."

"Me? What about me?"

"He assures me that you are the mind behind practically every racket in Haddonstown—including the House of Forty-one Delights. In fact he has written a piece saying so and mailed it to the syndicate he works for."

Hagin's jaw tightened. He eased into an overstuffed chair without taking his brown eyes from the prosecutor. His oddly cavernous, nut-brown face held taut, grim satisfaction. "He has, has he? And he took good care to run out before I got here."

"Maybe," Mainwaring had to admit. "He got a phone call just a minute or two before he left and—rather rushed away. What of it?"

"This of it, my friend. This of it." Hagin's mahogany hand came from his pocket and threw two twenty-dollar bills on the desk. "You recall these bills?"

The cigar exploded with gratifying force and they both whirled as though jerked by strings.

After a minute, Mainwaring said: "I presume they are two of the stack I marked for you, at your request, two weeks ago."

HAGIN SAT back and jammed the cigar in his dark face again. "They are just that. The two I held out from the bundle that you saw me mail. I told you then and I tell you now: those bills will mop up one of the neatest little rackets this town has ever seen—and let you put your finger on one of the slimiest chiselers you've ever been up against."

"Who would be...?"

"This fast-worker that just left here. This guy who calls himself a newspaper writer. Asa Burdick!"

Behind pince-nez, Mainwaring's sharp gray eyes squinted in surprise. "You mean he is behind it—the mind that directed the whole swindle?"

"And why not?"

Mainwaring smiled wryly, leaned back and faced the big man. "This is rather funny. Since Burdick came here three years ago, he's done nothing but smell out one of your little rackets after another, Hagin—and write them up.... Don't interrupt—there's nobody listening.... I know as well as you do that you have your fingers in nearly everything crooked in this town. I also know that you've enough good connections so we can't do much to you. But Burdick's articles have given public opinion a jolt that's hurt you badly and may hurt you worse. Personally, I can't quite understand why you haven't murdered him long before this, except that he may be too clever for you.

"And now you come to me with an accusation that he is behind the Dean Foundation mess. You'll admit that it's rather hard to swallow—coming from you. It would take plenty of proof—plenty—before I'd move."

"Plenty of proof," Hagin growled irritably, "is just what I've got to offer."

Mainwaring said nothing. Hagin leaned forward in his chair. "You may have forgotten that old man Dean and his son made their fortune in mining in Nevada. Well, I know that Asa Burdick worked on a Reno newspaper, seven years ago."

"My God. I hope your proof doesn't consist of such flimsy possibilities as that."

"I'm only showing you that he might have known them before any of them came here to Haddonstown. All right, call it a coincidence. Call it another coincidence that he arrived in town here just about the time they did, three years ago.

"The Dean's—father and son—arrived here, knowing nobody, and without kith or kin. You weren't in the D.A.'s office then, and they retained you as their lawyer—which is why you are in charge of this swindle case now. The boy took ill—some kind of endocrine gland trouble. They flew east, saw a specialist, and the son was cured. They were both impressed—suddenly became fans for this endocrinology. Evidently they found out how little is really known in that direction and how much research has to be done before the medicos know where they really stand.

"The old man made out a will, leaving his fortune in trust—the son to get the income during his life and the principal to revert to a certain Foundation when he, in turn, died. This Foundation was to be a research clinic for endocrinology. It was to be under the absolute direction of a Doctor Ullman, and was to be administered solely by him. All right. The old man *and* the boy were killed in an airplane wreck and suddenly you, as executor, had over five million dollars to hand over to a 'Dean Foundation' supposed to exist under the direction of this Doctor Ullman.

"It was several days before you could even find Ullman. Then he arrived—from Nevada. At least *a* Doctor Ullman did."

Mainwaring said: "If you are attempting to imply that Doctor Ullman was a fraud of any description you are wasting your time. I satisfied myself that he was an unusually brilliant doctor, who had known the Deans in their home state."

HAGIN SHRUGGED. "All right. Say he was. But this much you won't deny. In the two years since Ullman has been in charge of outfit, he has calmly milked the place of eighty or ninety thousand a year. The Foundation has never done any real research work—merely built a building and put up a front. Hell, all this is in the John Doe indictments you've got out against the place. They got around legal investigation by pretending to buy a lot of equipment in Canada. On the other side of the ledger, vast sums were charged off to breakage. The payment, you found out, was sent to Canada in solid, cold cash—untraceable.

"A month ago you got tipped off that Ullman was on the run, that something was fishy. Presently, the newspapers came out with the truth about it—that the supposed firm in Canada was merely a post-office box—that the whole setup was merely a matter of milking the five million dollar fund quietly and systematically—and that, from all appearances, the whole thing from start to finish had been merely created to jump on that loose five million. There was no Dean Foundation for the money to go to, so some wise bird quickly concocted one, located a Doctor Ullman who could act as a front—and went to town. All that, you practically admitted when you went before the grand jury for your indictments.

"Since that time—a month ago—you haven't been able to find hide or hair of this Ullman. He's vanished! Well, you'll probably never find him. He's probably under six feet of earth now—in a spot where he won't do any talking and involve the real brain behind him—the real crook who thought up and worked out, this scheme."

"All of which," Mainwaring said wearily, "doesn't involve Asa Burdick one whit. As a matter of fact, if I were to assume that all you say is true, do you know who would be my choice for this hidden master-mind?"

"Me, I suppose."

"Exactly. I can't imagine you letting anyone else get away with a plum like that, in your town."

Hagin jumped up. "Now sing me the old song. Burdick is a University man—he wouldn't be mixed up in things like this. He has *breeding*. Bah! That's what's the matter with this whole damned town, if you want to know. We're too near Boston—and Cambridge. There's a layer of snobs and a layer of hankies and nothing in between. Oh, I'm not kicking—it's meant a fat living for me. But I'll be damned if I'll listen to that stuff now—as regards Burdick. He went to University—with our best people, sure. But he's a worthless, dissipated, unscrupulous, lying soak now, scratching out a living by lying about his betters.

"Maybe, as you suggested, I could kill him—after this furor dies down. But it'll give me a thousand times the satisfaction to see him sent to the pen where he belongs— and see his fine-feathered friends trying to explain away why they were palsy-walsy with a swindler. They'll be sweating on Nob's Hill and here on Ridge Row, when he stands in the dock and gets his sentence—and that'll give me more satisfaction than a trunk of gold. And get this: this is one prosecution that isn't going to be hushed up, smothered. I've had to get a little political power to operate my business. Now I'm going to put the pressure on to have this rat convicted. And you can take it and like it."

Mainwaring's eyes were dull and uninterested. "I'm appointed, myself, not elected," he said. "Better sing that to my boss. And, if that's all you've got to offer in the way of proof against Asa Burdick...."

"All? I haven't offered any yet. But I'm going to. You remember, two weeks ago, I brought four thousand dollars in twenty-dollar bills in here and had you mark them. I made up a bundle, right here on your desk, stamped it and addressed it to the Dean Foundation. All right. I told you then that the crook behind the place wasn't scared—hadn't run away, as you thought. I told you he was just lying low, taking his time, trying to figure a way into the clear again. He knows—or did know—that you had nothing on him. Well, I walked with you to the mailbox and we mailed that bundle of cash. I knew damned well he couldn't resist putting it in his pocket. And he didn't! He's walking around with some of it on him right now. He spent two marked bills in one of my spots tonight!"

"Who did? Burdick?"

"Do you think I've been talking about Nathan Hale?"

THEN—FOR THE first time—Mainwaring suddenly began to wonder if, after all, it was possible that Asa Burdick could have slipped into the morass of crookedness.

For just a minute he hesitated, then said with decision, "All right, Hagin. We'll have a showdown," and picked up the phone.

When he laid it down, five minutes later, Haddonstown's forces of law and order were looking for Asa Burdick.

Mainwaring said grimly: "Well—do you want to hang around here till we locate him?"

"No," Hagin said. "But don't try any fast ones. I know he has that marked money on him—and I've ways of finding out if it's taken off him when you pinch him. Don't forget that."

"How do you suggest that he got the money after it was delivered through the mail to the Dean Foundation?"

"That, my friend, is up to you to explain. I know there are two coppers on duty at the place. And I also know that Burdick has been in and out. You've all been fooled because he wrote that original expose of the place. Why he wrote it, I don't know, frankly. When we get hold of Ullman—or if we do—he can probably make it clear just what sort of inside monkey-business there was. Maybe Ullman decided to give Burdick the push and Burdick couldn't do anything about it so he turned on the heat. I don't know. But mark this: Burdick has had the run of that place since it was closed, but nobody else has. Ask your coppers. Ask them who—except this Asa Burdick—had the opportunity to pick up a stray piece of mail."

Mainwaring sought for words to express his vague distrust of the somehow specious-sounding trap that Hagin had apparently closed on Burdick, but there was, in truth, no logical objection he could put his tongue to. He accompanied the big racketeer to the door.

The peculiar location of Mainwaring's home was important in view of what followed.

Haddonstown was in a narrow valley, between two towering mountains. Its east end ran almost to the side of the mountain. The city's largest park was, literally, in the shadow of a sheer rock cliff, a hundred feet high. However, even at this hundred-foot level, there was merely a set-back—a little notch just large enough to contain a road. Straight up from the road, another ninety feet, the cliff continued, to flatten off into a rocky plateau.

Along this plateau some of the 'first families' of Haddonstown resided, overlooking from vast height the little shelf that was the road and, below that, the expanse of Kemmerer

Park. The plateau was practically the only spot in Haddonstown which escaped the sweltering heat the rest of the valley city suffered in summer. In view of that, this portion of the town's aristocracy was willing to undergo the heavy climb from the roadway to their respective domiciles.

Each plot-owner along Ridge Road had an ample piece of frontage. Not more than thirty families lined the slightly rising road, from the point where it lifted out of Haddonstown proper, to the spot where it ended in a sheer, blunt-nosed precipice. Just about halfway the length of the ridge, the city had constructed an interminable, wide, cement stairway that led from the edge of the road down into the park, far below.

Directly above this stairway—a matter of some seventy or eighty feet—was Mainwaring's rambling establishment, set in a clump of pines. The walk that led from it down to the road zig-zagged sharply, back and forth across the face of the hill, to ease the sharp grade for a climber.

Mainwaring stood at the front door as Hagin started down the path. The big, dark-skinned man turned back to ask: "Will you let me know when you pick him up?"

Mainwaring said he would and went back into his hallway. He turned on an amber floodlight which lit the slanting face of the steep grade down the road, and—inasmuch as it could be turned off from an upstairs switch—went slowly to his second-floor study, troubled.

HAGIN WENT down the uneven gravel pathway, his attention completely occupied in maintaining his footing.

Then the slaughter that shook Haddonstown.

No one knew from just what direction the shots came. The first one caught Hagin high in the left side and he gasped, shrilled a vile name as he staggered. The second shot got him in the thigh, tripped him, and he cried out in fear; the third hit an ankle, crossed his legs and half-spun him; the last got him just under the ear, choked the scream in his throat as he found himself hurled forward on his face, over the sheer, precipitous brow of the hill.

His first dive took him forty feet down before he landed, somersaulting wildly. He rolled over and over like a flung side of beef. He hit the road almost squarely on his head, and such was the terrific momentum that he was cata-pulted straight across it. He bounced off the iron railing, lit on the eighth step and went flapping, hurtling, slam-ming down the flight of steps that dropped sheerly into Kemmerer Park.

After the second shot, Mainwaring had raced to his upstairs window. In the glow of his floodlight he had seen Hagin shot down, had seen him pitched down the hill. He ran downstairs—in his stocking feet, having been in the act of changing into slippers—and the moment he stepped on the sharp gravel of the driveway he was made conscious of the unprotected condition of his feet. He ran back inside, hastily called the police, got his slippers and ran out again. It took him the better part of fifteen minutes to reach the bottom of the huge cliff, and the mangled, sickening thing that had been Hagin.

Police from the park were there before him, so in a matter of minutes, he had a whole corps of police swarm-ing over the grounds of the houses adjoining his own, searching for ejected shells or some definite evidence as to the direction from which the shots had come. Though they searched for nearly three-quarters of an hour, they turned up absolutely nothing.

And just about forty-five minutes later Asa Burdick was picked up in a cheap saloon, half comatose—or pretending to be so—from poor liquor. In his pocket he had upwards of a thousand dollars in marked bills—the marked bills that the racketeer had used to bait his elaborate trap. Burdick could not account for his movements during the time since he had left Mainwaring's house, nor for the money in his pockets. He told a confused, rambling story of having visited several saloons which he could not identify clearly and in which he was not known. As an alibi it was purest drivel.

A raid—personally conducted by Mainwaring—turned up the murder gun in Burdick's cheap room, at the bottom of his laundry bag.

Asa Burdick had undoubtedly shot Hagin, either in a fit of anger at being exposed as a criminal, or in pursuit of some obscure train of thought which told him that the murder would prevent such exposure. He was not the first murderer to be attacked by a brainstorm upon completion of his deed and to collapse emotionally, either with or without the added fuddlement of liquor.

This was the assistant district attorney's story, and I was stuck with it—plenty. I could see just exactly no chances of getting Burdick off.

CHAPTER TWO

D.A. RUN-AROUND

I TOOK a last suck of my cigarette and dropped it in the cuspidor at my feet as McDougall finished telling me the story. The D.A. was an odd-looking duck who might have stepped out of a Currier & Ives print— long frock coat, wing collar and black stock, handlebar mustaches and piercing mouse-gray eyes that matched his mathematically parted mouse-gray toupée. I would have bet his cuffs were detachable.

I said: "So you think Burdick is the master-mind behind this Dean Foundation scandal? You think Hagin found a way to trap him into exposure? And that Burdick killed him either in anger or to prevent, somehow, that exposure? Pretty thin evidence, if you ask me—considering that it was Burdick's own articles which started investigation of the Dean thing. And that Hagin, a known racketeer—or vice king, if I get this House of Forty-one Delights right—cooked up all the evidence against him on that angle to begin with."

McDougall cleared his throat importantly. "Oh, we have other evidence which we are not at liberty to disclose just yet."

Mainwaring—the assistant prosecutor in front of whose house all this had taken place—came in then, with a sheaf of papers for his chief to sign and I was introduced. The D.A. had already forgotten my name, but he had not forgotten that I was from the Acme Life.

Mainwaring, an alert little bird-dog of a man, fastened sharp eyes on me. "Acme Life? What's the matter—don't you believe Hagin's dead?"

I said I was an investigator, not an adjuster.

"Oh," he snapped. "You think we need help in prosecuting the murderer—is that it? Well, you can rest easy. Haddonstown juries have a lot of respect for a gentleman—but not when he makes a cad of himself, turns his back on his birthright, as this Burdick has. We'll have no trouble in getting a conviction, never fear."

A D.A.'s office is no place for a man working on the defense to find aid and comfort. I got up and wandered to the door, before I said that that was what I was afraid of.

"What?" they chorused at me.

"I said that was what I was afraid of. It wasn't Hagin's life that Acme insured. It's Burdick's. If you hang him, it costs us a hundred thousand dollars maybe."

McDougall exploded: "Why—you damned impostor! You told me—"

"I didn't tell you anything," I expostulated.

"It doesn't matter," Mainwaring's slaty voice cut in. "Take warning, Mr. Investigator—if we catch you interfering or conniving in any way to free this man illegally, it will go hard with you. Furthermore, I think we shall keep careful watch over your movements while you're in Haddonstown."

He spun on his heel, walked out. As the door closed behind him, McDougall's mouse-gray eyes looked at me mournfully. "Why don't you go back to New York?" he asked me. "We really don't need you and you look like you might be about to obstruct justice, any time."

"This is splendid," I told him sourly. "This is what I like—real cooperation."

I left abruptly. I had boned a pass to see Burdick in the local gow—boned it at the beginning of the interview, before McDougall had found that my interest lay in getting the newshawk free—and I wanted to get over to the jail and use it before it occurred to the muttonhead to rescind it.

I EXPECTED a stinking, dingy old jail and I was not disappointed. I was directed to the waiting-room on the third floor, where four cops clustered around a fifth—a fat man with a perfectly square pink bald head and little brown bug-eyes. He leered at my pass, then at me, then said, "Samson," and one of the cops went into a whispered conversation, vanished through a swinging-door beyond which I caught sight of a corridor of barred doors. In a minute he was back, and I took a jerk of his head to mean I should follow him. Presently I was standing in front of Asa Burdick's cell.

The news-writer was in shirt-sleeves, lying on the narrow cot. His well-cut tweeds hung loosely about his slender legs. He was red-headed and at one time must have been gently handsome. Now, dissipation lined his face. His candid, bright blue eyes regarded me with the expression of a swimmer peering over an immense wave. I found out that this was perpetual with him.

He, too, made the mistake of thinking I was working to convict him. He drawled in a lazy, cultured voice that was just taking on the resonance of the confirmed rummy: "So Acme is after my hide, too."

I set him right: "If anybody gets your hide, it costs Acme fifty thousand—maybe a hundred, if it can be called accidental death."

"What's this?"

"You have a fifty-thousand-dollar policy on your life, friend. Did it slip your mind?"

He wrinkled his forehead. "*I* have?" Then he recalled it and laughed loudly and mockingly. He swung his legs over and sat up, fumbled in a breast pocket for a cigarette. He smiled a sardonic smile. "Well, well, well—aid from Sir Hubert."

I didn't catch that, but I didn't waste time saying so. "Did you kill this Hagin?" I asked.

"I don't think so."

"You what?"

"I don't think so. Somewhere, I collected a hell of a load, and I don't remember much after that, but why would I kill him? I hated the louse but I had him on the run."

"Where did you get that marked dough? They told you about the marked dough?"

"Yeah, they told me. I haven't the faintest idea where I got it. It was planted on me—either in some joint, or by the bulls when they took me."

"Did you have any piece of that Dean Foundation racket?"

He shook his head, lit his cigarette. "Don't be like that."

"Do you think Ullman, this missing doctor, was the head man or do you think he had a boss—as yet undeclared?"

"I think he had a boss. I don't think he has now."

"You mean Hagin?"

"Who else?"

"You think Ullman shot Hagin?"

"Maybe. Though trying to single out the people in this town who'd have liked to shoot that rat is a man's-size job.

I hesitated. "You know your old friends are going to turn against you."

"Are they?"

"Sure. Hoity-toity people take sort of a masochistic delight in bearing down on pals—when the pals are back of the eight ball. It makes them think they're punishing themselves for having associated with him. Or something."

"So you're a psychologist."

"Whatever I am. I'm about the only guy you can depend on."

He thought that over and said reasonably: "You may be right. What you mean is, I should tell you everything. The hell of it is—I have already—everything."

"Where did you go when you left Mainwaring's last night? And what was the phone call that you took at Mainwaring's house?"

He grinned, his swimming eyes reluctantly admiring. "Well, you're the only guy who had the sense to ask me that. I'm sorry as hell I can't tell you. I mean about the phone call. All I can say is that it had nothing whatever to do with Hagin's death. When I left Mainwaring's, I headed for a tavern about eight blocks away and had a couple of quick ones. Then I stopped at another, a half mile or so further on and had a couple more. That's the last I can remember."

"If you can name the joints, there may an alibi."

He grinned wryly. Don't you think I have a lawyer? He went over the ground this morning. Neither of the places remember me and if they did, it still wouldn't add up to an alibi, on account of the time element."

After another minute I said glumly: "You'd better tell me about the phone call, if you expect me to get you in the clear."

He shook his head slowly. "The phone call is out. It wouldn't help. As for putting me in the clear—I don't think that's a productive line. Now, if you follow me closely, I'll give you another better one. Hagin didn't shoot himself. Somebody shot him. It wasn't me. Question: who was it? Now, if you could find out who *did* shoot him...."

He broke off and looked down the corridor. I did, too. The swinging-door at the end was open and a huge Irish warder was striding towards us, his face red. He bellowed at me, "Get out, you!" but my attention was on the held-open door, behind him.

A LITTLE old lady stood in the door-way, flanked by bowing cops and flunkies. She was a fragile piece of old Dresden, in black and white, long white gloves covering her tiny hands and arms, which were clasped before her. Her age-penciled little face was lovely, pink-and-white, her kind blue eyes bright and cheerful under the veil that dropped from her pert little black hat. Her hair was pure silver, charmingly arranged in the fashion of forty years ago.

I did not realize that the warder's bellow had brought reinforcements from the other end of the corridor till they closed in behind me. I looked at Burdick and his face was pale, his eyes worried.

He flung at me in a swift, urgent undertone: "Good Lord—I don't want to see her. Keep her away from me, pal—will you?"

I said, as one burly fist twisted my collar and a knee drove hard into my rear: "Sure, I'll use my influence." Then they were giving me the old heave-ho.

As they wafted me past the old lady on the run, she looked disturbed and said, "Oh, dear," in a frightened voice.

"Don't worry, Mrs. Steadman, ma'am," a cop told her. "Just some guy sneaked in here which the D.A. doesn't want him in."

My companions didn't let loose of me, till we had ridden down the elevator and were on the front steps. I had been kicked out of better jails than this, so I was quick enough on my feet to avoid the barrage of toes that came my way. At that, I lit on my face on the sidewalk, to the amusement of the swarm of passers-by.

I picked myself up and walked away. Then I walked back again.

My attention had been taken by the Rolls-Royce that stood gleaming at the curb, directly in front of a fire-plug.

It was about twenty years old and even those expensive imported cars change styles a little in twenty years.

My escorts having vanished back inside the building, I leaned against the steps and watched it, mentally noted the license tag—no hard job, as it consisted of just two numbers.

I saw a stocky man in conventional black suit emerge from a nearby store. He had a chauffeur's cap on and he was testing the bristles of a new whisk against his glove. He opened the tonneau and began to whisk out the old Rolls-Royce.

I debated engaging him in conversation but he didn't look very pleasant. He had a face like dark stone—thick and forbidding—and utterly cold, expressionless slate-gray eyes. The lobe of his right ear had somehow been sliced off squarely. I figured my best bet would be to attempt to brace the old lady herself. If she were a friend of Asa Burdick's she should be sympathetic toward me, and if she knew anything to help the news-writer she ought to give.

I had neglected to consider the obvious prestige of the old lady. When she emerged, a few minutes later, there were three cops with her, including one with gold braid, and I had about as much chance of getting near her as if I'd been a leper with a bell.

But I did get one surprise. As they escorted her across the sidewalk I glanced automatically at the chauffeur's seat, cursing myself for a fool for not having dickered with him. The chauffeur was gone. He was nowhere in sight and, apparently, he wasn't expected to be. A copper ran around and held open the driver's door and the old lady stepped gracefully into the driver's seat, which was obviously built up with pillows. She settled herself, thanked them all with a smile, calmly pressed the starting button and, after gunning the ancient motor once or twice, bobbed her little old head and drove off.

I WAS off down the street toward where my rented car was parked before she was away from the curb, and out in the stream of traffic up the city's main artery almost as soon as she was. Her car was not hard to spot—a big, open job—and she did not drive fast. I figured out, presently, that she was heading toward the north end of town where there were two or three suburbs which qualified as Gold Coast, and I took a look at my city map. It was not hard to keep behind her, till she wound out of the north end of the city and turned onto a stretch of wooded, country road—narrow, winding, with thick trees encroaching right to the shoulders.

It was so narrow that once, spinning around a bend, I almost piled up with a long back sedan parked at the roadside. In avoiding it my fenders scraped the trees on the wrong side of the road. Presently, the road started on a long bend, and I estimated that we must be skirting a large thumb-shaped private estate which my map showed to be plunked down squarely on the right of way.

It was just as we started this long detour that I jumped alive to the fact that the black sedan was slipping along behind me. I started slowing, then accelerating—and within a mile I was satisfied that the big car, for some reason, was following me.

It had six times the power of my rented hack. Suddenly it came from behind like a streak and rolled along beside me. I glanced over and saw the twin barrels of a shotgun resting on the sill of the open window nearest me. There was only one man in the car—a man with a face vaguely reminiscent of the old lady's chauffeur—save that it was smaller. He was nattily dressed and wore a peaked cap.

I tried to jam on my brakes, but he was ahead of me. His bumper slammed into my running-board, crumpling it, and my car was bounced sideways, hurled straight toward the giant bole of a tree. I had enough presence of mind to whip my wheels hard over and accelerate. Metal ripped and screamed, but I succeeded in turning our locked front ends in the other direction, so that it was the black sedan's nose that ploughed across the road and crumpled into a tree-trunk. By that time we were moving comparatively slowly and after the ear-splitting crash, neither of us were shaken up much. Miraculously, the shotgun did not go off.

He switched his own ignition and roared at me from the side of his jaw: "Cut your motor or I'll blow your damn head off!"

I reached down and cut it. Our front wheels were tangled up but my bus had slued around enough so that there was space for him to open his door. The shotgun never wavered from my face as he stepped out.

One look at his beady little brown eyes and I began to be concerned about my own safety. I was not foolish enough to take my hands from the wheel, but I could pull my foot up from the clutch and put it on the door handle of my door without his being able to see me doing it. It was a desperate expedient, but I didn't know what kind of a spot I was in and anything looked good.

He snarled: "Get out!"

"I can't," I told him. "My doors are jammed."

"Yeah?" He stepped closer. "What's your interest in the old lady?"

I let him have it. I drove the door open with all the power of my foot, simultaneously throwing myself down sideways to slide under the wheel.

The sharp edge of the door caught him squarely in the forehead, slashed a vertical crimson line. The shotgun roared—above my head—and then I was out feet first, whirling like a madman to dive under the gun as the thug staggered back. I ripped an uppercut to his jaw that sent him slamming back against his own car, bounced him off flying sideways, to land on his back. He was half stunned, but his hand dived inside his coat. I aimed a kick at his half-drawn gun. It missed and drove into his jaw, almost knocking his head off, and I dropped on his chest with both knees to snatch the blue pistol.

A voice behind me said: "Move so much as an eyebrow and I'll fill your back with lead."

CHAPTER THREE

A COUPLE OF ROCKS—A COUPLE OF BREAKS

I **DIDN'T** move a muscle except to clench my teeth till the voice said: "Spread your arms out and get up." I got up and turned to face the dark-faced, gray-eyed gent in black clothes who had been whisking out the old lady's Rolls in front of the jail. He wore a black fedora now; the chauffeur's cap was gone.

The other yegg was moaning and groaning on the ground. He sat up groggily, blood streaming through the fingers he held over his face. He put one hand down to prop himself and his glassy eyes fastened on my shoes without comprehension. Then, as they gradually crawled up my legs, the glassiness began to fade.

The dough-faced pseudo-chauffeur said sharply, "Milt! Are you O.K.?" and the other came back to his senses.

He saw me, winced back—then suddenly sobbed and red fury jumped into his beady eyes. He sprang up, stumbled back against the car, flaming eyes on mine. He located the shotgun, dived for it.

The other said: "Hold it! Are you crazy?"

The thug I had beaten gasped through clenched teeth: "I'm going to blast his belly through his spine."

"You are not! Drop it!"

The other straightened, the gun held slanting across his body. He brushed blood from his eyes and cried hoarsely: "You—you're a hell of a brother. Where were you, while he was—"

"You damned fool, I told you to stop him a hundred yards further on. I had to run like the devil to get here before he polished you off entirely. You—" he snarled at me. "Who the hell are you and why were you following—"

The wounded thug had a one-track mind. He blurted in a savage, pumped-up voice: "I'm going to kill him. Look at what he did to me."

"Yeah? And who are you going to blame for it, you sap? We're on a spot here. We've got to get back to town on this one road and we'd be lamped sure. If a corpse turned up here, our records'd sound nice wouldn't they? For God's sake use your head. If you want to kill him, do it later when you're not stuck for the job." He swung his voice back to me. "Well? I asked you a question."

"I don't get it," I told him. "I wasn't following anybody."

His flat gray eyes grew darker. "Oh, you want we should beat it out of you. What's your racket? Who are you?"

"I'm an insurance adjuster for Acme Life," I told them. I figured they were going to look at my papers anyway and it was barely possible that they might skim over them and be fooled.

It was a mistake. The one I'd hit suddenly howled: "Ha! This is him! This is the dick who blew in this morn—"

The gray-eyed gunman said shortly: "Shut up! What sort of shape is your car in?"

The other hesitated, then walked around to look. I heard him curse petulantly. "The wheel's smashed to bits and the radiator's a mess. We can't drive it."

"All right. How is his?"

After another minute the wounded one said sullenly behind me: "His seems to be all right. The running-board's gone, and a fender, but we can drive it, I think."

"You think! Well, dummy, start thinking what would have happened if you'd shot this jobbie. We would have arrived back in town in *his* car. Wouldn't *that* be nice? Get going and separate those bumpers." To me, he said through set teeth: "You get a break, gumshoe. But I'm giving you fair warning. Get out of this town—and stay out for twenty-four hours. After that, you can have a field day. Before then, if we run into you just once, you're going to have about six slugs in your back.... This for a sample." He stepped forward and slashed me suddenly across the temple with gun and I went out.

THEY HAD laid me out near the wrecked sedan, so that when I came to I was in the right position to have been pitched from the car. I sat up dizzily in the pitch dark. There were a few minutes when I didn't feel like moving. Then I got stiffly to my feet, felt my head gingerly, fished for a cigarette.

I tried anxiously to shake kaleidoscopic thoughts into place, but they wouldn't shake. Particularly the gunman's terse warning that, for the next twenty-four hours, I stood in momentary danger of a bullet from the dark. Why twenty-four hours? What grim work was being scheduled for that time-span—and in what possible direction could I look for it?

By a miracle my pencil flashlight had not broken. I got it out, played it quickly over the battered black sedan. No incriminating or illuminating information had been left behind in the car, save the license plates. And the sedan would not go, could not be made to go.

I leaned against a fender and sucked my cigarette. I was a little astonished that no cars had passed me, even in the few minutes I had been conscious. I got a lot more astonished as minutes passed and I became aware that this country road was practically disused. No cars passed in either direction. I became very unhappy at the prospect of walking back eight or nine miles in the half-giddy trance in which I found myself—and then I got a weird break.

From a point some distance ahead I suddenly heard the steady hum of a motor. After a minute, broken flashes of light came through the trees as the approaching car rounded the long finger-like detour. I ran as fast as I could, managed to put a good hundred yards between me and the wrecked sedan. It was well off the road and trees might screen it from a car approaching from the direction this one was. It was in my mind that I was getting in too deep— that I had best get myself down to headquarters and put in some sort of explanation of this little party—one that wouldn't pile-up on me later on. And one that wouldn't embarrass the Acme. If I were to do it at all, I ought to do it as quickly as I knew how, and if the oncoming driver did not see, or connect me with, the wreck, why I would save just that much time.

I stood out in the road, waggled my flashlight on the little shield Acme gives us, and the car came to a halt. It was a sleek streamlined sedan, moderately expensive and almost the latest model.

I walked out of the glare of the headlights, around to the side door, saying: "Sorry to bother you, mister, but could you give me a lift into town… before I saw that I was not addressing a mister.

The driver was the bonneted and gloved little old lady who had, three-quarters of an hour before, been driving the Rolls the other way along this same road, presumably to her own house.

She said, "Gracious, officer…" and then, to my further surprise, "Why—it's the insurance young man. How fortunate. Do climb in."

I was surprised that she knew me, but I let it go. "Why fortunate, ma'am?" I grinned as I accepted her invitation. "That is—except for me?"

"I was wondering where I could find you," she said. "I have a message for you"—shifting gears postponed the rest of her speech until we were scooting along the road at a good pace—"from Asa Burdick. Just hold this wheel a moment—there—"

While I steered the car, she picked up a beaded handbag, snapped it open and took out a little sheaf of cards. She peeled one off, put the others back in the bag and passed the card to me as she took up the driving again. It was an unusual oblong gray card, carrying her name, *Mrs. C. Bullock Steadman* under a simple fattish crest in bright blue. Across the card, in spidery tiny handwriting was the name, *Joe Harris.*

"Asa Burdick wished me to tell you that he thought of something after you had—left this afternoon. Something that he wished to tell you. He has entrusted the secret to that man there, who, he wished me to inform you, has sandy hair and a limp. He is an attendant at the jail and will communicate Asa's message upon payment of five dollars."

I thanked her and pocketed the card.

She said: "I do hope you are making some progress in your efforts to help that poor young man."

"I could make a good deal more and still not be satisfied," I told her. "You're a friend of his?"

"He was at school with my grandson," she said. "Naturally, we want to do all we can. It's absurd to think a chap like Asa would commit murder."

I DIDN'T think it would do any harm to worry her. She might possibly put in a little weight on the right side of the ledger if she got anxious enough. I said: "Well, the evidence against him isn't the strongest in the world but, after all, it's a jury that has to consider it. And I've seen so-called black sheep up against an aristocratic jury before. He doesn't get much of a deal."

Her blue eyes flashed me a side-look—faintly curious but a little annoyed. "What in the world are you talking about?"

I shrugged. "I suppose I mean that the blue-bloods of the town will be against him, too—as well as the hunkies—and that he'll have a time getting a fair break."

"Gracious! What on earth makes you think that?"

"My experience with so-called 'nice people' is that they are pretty stiff-necked when trouble comes. Apart from an incomprehensible idea of their own importance in the scheme of things, there isn't much to them. They're like a pack of wolves when one of their own kind goes wrong—publicly."

"You haven't met nice people, then, young man."

"Maybe not. What's your definition of 'nice people'?"

She drove us in silence a minute then, "Well—the leaders of the community—the families whose outlook is broad enough to fit them to make decisions involving others."

"That's scarcely a definition."

"No, it isn't. I—I don't believe I have ever been asked to answer such an extraordinary question before. On thinking it over, it boils down to people who live broadly—who live by standards and who consider standards more important than self-interest. People who try to adhere to their ethics, at whatever inconvenience to themselves. People who try to set an example of unselfish and gentle living to the masses."

She was way ahead of me, by now. But I'm always interested in people's viewpoints. I prodded her gently with: "Most of them that I've met are much more concerned about hushing up their manner of living."

She did not seem upset, nodded gently. "Sometimes that must be done—for the sake of other members of a family. Scandal and disgrace are indiscriminate—they shake confidence not only in the scamp who gets into trouble, but in all his associates—or at least his family."

Then we were coasting to a stop in front of the jail.

I sat in my seat with my hand on the door and said: "Mrs. Steadman, you may find more trouble in all this matter than you dream of. Won't you oblige me by letting me get you a man to accompany you if you're really going to chase around alone at night this way."

She smiled. "I have already taken that advice—from Asa...John!"

A gun was pressed against my cheek. A man's hearty chuckle sounded behind me from the dark tonneau of the car. I turned my head and saw a capable-looking hand holding the pistol—a hand with a red-eyed snake ring circling its third finger.

A reassuringly tough male voice said: "I'll look after Mrs. Steadman, never fear."

I couldn't think of any more to add to that so I got out and thanked her for the ride.

She leaned down a little from her throne of pillows and bobbed her little head like an elder promising a child reward for good behavior. "A little later, I may have something to help you," she confided. "Something to help you help Asa Burdick. Where can I find you—say at ten o'clock?"

It was then about seven. I said: "That's hard to say, ma'am. I couldn't call you?"

She thought that over a moment, then said: "Would you do this? Would you go to—or call me at—my grandson's apartment? Doctor Ralph Steadman, in the Hartz Towers? It is not so very far from here. I will call him and tell him to expect you, or your call. He will be in his apartment on the eighteenth floor."

I said I would, and she drove away.

I LOOKED at the police station—it was directly across the street from the jail—and then I looked at the jail. I decided to squander a few moments trying to contact this warder who had Burdick's message before doing my stuff with the cops.

I went over and asked the elevator man where to find this Harris and he went up after him.

Harris turned out to be a sandy-haired, glum-looking Scotchman. He walked away from me when I told him who I was and I followed him down the hall into an alcove. He looked both ways before informing me—as he took my five—that Asa Burdick seemed to have remembered that he might have been—some time during the preceding night's liquor fog—in the House of Forty-one Delights and that the certain thing we had discussed might have happened there.

It did not take me long to figure that he meant to convey that the marked money might have been planted on him in the establishment with the suggestive name.

I thanked Harris and walked over to police headquarters and into the motor-vehicle-bureau office. I went to that department because I figured there was less chance of my friends in the D.A.'s office having soured things up for me there. In that I was wrong.

Captain Oliver, the spare, gray-eyed, gray-haired officer sitting with his hands clasped on the desk in front of him surveyed me with keen interest and, what was more surprising—with some hospitality.

He said: "So you're the gent that's trying to obstruct McDougall's office's idea of justice for young Burdick."

I tried a grin and it got some response so I eased into a chair and popped off with my story about my car. For a minute I thought he was going to get hard with me, but he finally shrugged and called someone on the phone, more or less repeated what I had told him, and told the party to go out and bring in the wrecked sedan.

"As to your thugs," he said when he had hung up, "I don't recognize them. You want to look at the gallery?"

Since this was exactly what I did want, I assented in an offhand way and we went down to the identification bureau.

Half an hour later I was back in his office with the knowledge that the two who had crashed me were named respectively Milton and Charles Rothenberger, alias, Rock.

These prize specimens had both served terms for armed robbery and had a string of arrests against them for everything from gun-toting to mayhem. They were at present resting up from a pinch for the murder of a baker, presumably in the course of some racket activities. The charge had been dropped for lack of evidence.

I played it safe with Oliver though: "I didn't seem to recognize any of your collection." I offered him a cigarette and he took it. "Say, what kind of town is this, anyway?" I asked suddenly as I held a match. "I can't figure just where I stand. What are the cops like, for instance?"

HE LOOKED at me steadily, for a full minute, with disillusioned gray eyes. Then I found out the basis for his cordiality.

"I used to be a New York cop myself," he said slowly. "I quit because it was too grafty and came back here—my home town. What a fool I was."

"I get it," I said, "and thanks for the warning."

"I don't think you do get it," he said with a sudden bite of bitterness in his voice. "But this much I'll tell you right out. If you've got any information that a crook might want—don't whisper it around this building. Some crook will be paying cash for it within minutes."

After a minute, I said: "You're a good guy. Would you like to see me break this case?"

"Why not?"

"It might stir things up a little—get the citizens to thinking, or something. What's your personal angle? Do you think Burdick did it?"

"I do not."

"What about the evidence?"

"Framed by that rat, Hagin."

"The gun that killed Hagin wasn't planted by him."

"No. But the killer evidently knew that Burdick was being framed for one thing, so he just added this to it. No, I know young Burdick. He'd be a pretty decent guy if he didn't live so wild."

"You think this Ullman did the killing?"

Oliver shrugged, put his hands behind his back and leaned back in his swivel chair. "Ullman—or Ullman's boss, if there is such a person. Sure. He had a good racket. Hagin wanted to cut in. He tried, and put on too much pressure. The other guy lost his head and—well, I'm glad I'm not on Homicide."

"What do you know about the House of Forty-one Delights?"

His gray eyes narrowed. "Nothing more than you do. It used to be run by a Chink but Hagin shot him up and took it over. You don't need any diagram to know what kind of a joint it is, do you?"

"No. How can I get into it?"

"You can't."

"It seems like I've got to."

He hesitated a long minute, in deep thought, then he said: "That's on the level? It's really important?"

"Plenty."

After another minute he pushed a button and when a uniformed cop came in, Oliver told him: "Go down to the tank and bring Richard Roe in here—that is, if he's sober enough to talk coherently."

Five minutes later a battered-looking athlete in a rumpled and ripped dinner-coat stumbled into Oliver's office. With some astonishment, I recognized him as rather a prominent boxer who was due to fight in Boston three nights later—an important bout.

"Well, Slapsie," Oliver said. "I've decided to call in the newshawks and let them spread your condition all over the papers. Think it'd hurt the gate for the fight?"

The boxer winced, and his bloodshot eyes dropped to the floor.

"Unless," Oliver said, "you care to give my friend here all the information necessary to get in to the House of Forty-one. And don't tell me you don't know either."

Five minutes later I stood on the sidewalk outside, repeating the meaningless phrases that were supposed to be the open sesame to the establishment in which the marked money might have been planted on Asa Burdick.

I looked at my watch. It was not quite eight yet. My date with the old lady was at ten. I decided to go to the House of Forty-one Delights and have a look.

I walked down the main drag until I located a small shop that sold tricks and novelties. I did not expect to run into any mammoth brains on this quest and simple gags are usually enough for simple minds. I did not kid myself that I might not be running into a peck of trouble. I was just trying to prepare a slight break for myself in case I did. I had made use of one of the simplest gags in the world before, to give me all the edge I need when the trouble starts.

I bought some trick cigars.

I was within walking distance of the slum street on which the place I was seeking stood. I stopped in a drug store, two blocks away, begged a cardboard carton from the clerk and transferred the contents of my pockets, including my gun, to the carton. It was a cinch I would never get past the front door with anything like that on me. I gave the clerk a dollar to tie up and check the box till I came back, promised him another dollar when I returned, and went out.

CHAPTER FOUR

THE HOUSE OF FORTY-ONE DELIGHTS

THE STREET was dark and so was the towering old-fashioned house that I found at the address Oliver had given me. It was of brick, had once been a mansion. Brick cupolas and turrets showed high above me against the faintly starlit sky as I stood at the foot of the entrance steps. I closed the spiked iron gate behind me, making sure it did not latch.

Getting in was nothing. With the required number of rings, I brought a Filipino with a thin black mustache to the door, and with the meaningless jumble of words I had memorized, he let me into a long hall. I handed him a hundred-dollar bill as I had been instructed, and wondered grimly whether I was going to get that back on my swindle sheet.

There were four doors down the hall. My guide preceded me to the one at the end. I noticed that the third door was open a crack, and I lagged a little. As I came abreast I took a quick peek. A man was kneeling by a safe, with things scattered on the floor around him.

I leaned against the door. The hall was dark enough to make it a fair bet I could get away with the gag. I fell heavily into the room, landed in a comedy fall and gasped.

The man in the corner—a big, meaty, red-faced bruiser with bad teeth—leaped to his feet, his hand under the armpit of his dinner jacket. The things on the floor around him he did not touch and I had one swift glance at them.

Some were piles of checks, some were pictures—and one pile was cards. They were very special cards. Even from ten feet away and in the split-second that I had to survey them, I saw what they were—gray cards with bold little blue crests in one corner—Mrs. Steadman's calling cards—the kind on which she had scribbled the jailer's name for me.

Then I was pushing myself erect, looking stupidly around the room. I growled petulantly: "Wha's idea? I fall through the wall."

The Filipino and the others exchanged disgusted glances and I figured I had gotten across. I stumbled to my feet, giggling a little, they helping me. The room contained nothing but a flat-topped desk and the safe. I weaved, found the door and went out.

The Filipino closed it behind me and took my arm in the hall. "Look, chief—aren't you a little bit tight?"

"A little," I admitted, "but not too drunk. You needn't worry."

He looked at me a long, worried minute, shrugged, went to the door at the end of the hall and knocked three times. Then he pushed it open and stood aside for me to enter.

It was a magnificent, stately, old-fashioned room, done in maroon and silver. Columns were silvered, huge mirrors maroon-draped, thick maroon rugs underfoot. In one corner a little incense smoke floated up. The furniture was real Queen Anne. But I was hardly aware of all that.

Three girls rose from chairs as we came in—rose lazily and unhurriedly. They were in evening gowns.

My guide mumbled in my ear, "This is Diane," and I saw a perfect full-breasted blonde—young, with transparent rose-petal skin, her blue eyes deep blue, her hair fluffy, behind shell-pink ears. She wore pure, clinging white.

The Filipino muttered, "This is Estrellita," and a China doll stood before me. She wore a Chinese dress—black, with embroidery at her throat and sleeves. It went up to her chin. The sides were slashed from waist to ankle. Her figure was a perfect little hour-glass, her skin the most delicate blush. She was utterly Oriental, save for brown eyes that were no part of the Far East. Behind lashes an inch long, they smoldered with a strange fire that was half impish, half maddeningly provocative. Her eyes caught and held mine and a tiny, understanding smile curved her vivid, perfectly outlined lips.

The guide said somebody or other was Suzanne, and in a vague way I was aware that a green-eyed girl with dark red hair and a green gown was staring at me through the smoke from the end of a cigarette in a holder. But I kept my eyes on Estrellita and the other two smiled at me and at her.

Then the jarring note.

IT WAS the swift whine of the opening door that brought me instantly alert. I had my lighter snapped aflame and was touching fire to one of my cigars by the time the hoarse, snarling voice said behind me: "That's him—that's the damned insurance snoop!"

I turned and laid the cigar on an ashtray, slowly turned to face the meaty, red-faced man—over his blue pistol. I folded my arms. The girls were running swiftly through a door in the back of the room, picking up their skirts.

"So what?" I inquired.

The Filipino's eyes were worried little sharp daggers. He had a hand on his hip but he had drawn no gun. I swaggered around and sat on an chair-arm, my brow furrowed in annoyance. Then they both had their backs to the smoldering cigar.

The meaty man closed the door through which he had entered. "So what do you want, wise guy?" he demanded. "What do you come here for?"

"A ton of coal," I sneered. "What do you think? Can't a guy in my racket have a little relaxation?"

"Can it. Wake up to the fact that you're going out of here feet first—if you try to play clam. We don't have to take chances here."

"Not even with your head man dead?" I said innocently.

The man's lips tightened and his eyes got narrow. "Not even with our head man dead," he said after a second. "Spit it out—what's your game?"

The cigar exploded, with gratifying force. They both whirled as though jerked by strings. I was on the back of the Filipino like a leaping cat, whipped him around, even as I jerked the gun he had instinctively drawn from his hip. The meaty man, upset, fired—and the Filipino screamed, sagged, clutching at his side.

I fired and the gun flew out of the meaty man's smashed fingers and he clutched his wounded hand, his face a mask of agony.

"All right," I said. "Are you using your head yet—or do you want more of this?"

When he did not answer, merely clenched his teeth and let sweat run down his red face, I followed with: "I don't want any trouble with you. But I'll kill you, and like it. I want that stack of blue-crested calling cards in your office safe—and I went out. Further than that, you can all go to hell for all I care. Do I get what I want?"

For a whole minute, his pain-reddened eyes searched my face. He gasped: "Good God—I don't want them cards!"

"I do," I said, and slashed the Filipino suddenly behind the ear, dropped him to the thick rug. "Let's get them—and then we're quits."

I pocketed them in the office and warned him: "Now I'm going out. That is—I'm going out if you're going to keep on living."

"All right," he whined reassuringly. "I—I don't want no more of you. I'll be damn glad to see you go. What t'hell you going to— What do you want them cards for?"

I was damned if I knew, but I let him assume what he could from a grunt, and pulled him close to me, kept one hand hooked in his collar as we went out into the hall.

He called into a perfectly empty corridor: "All right. Go back to your places."

I wondered if this would work—if it were possible that I could get out alive after what had happened. If a dozen of his henchmen were not already taking a bead on the back of my neck.

Apparently they weren't for I got out.

At the door, he growled: "I hope to hell I don't find that you're putting a fast one over on me. If you are—you won't live twenty-four hours, I promise you."

"That's fine," I said sourly. "You're the second big-mouthed that's promised me I won't live another day."

I considered the matter, then whacked him unconscious as he opened the door, wiped the gun on my cuff and dropped it beside him as he fell. Then I was running—for all I was worth.

No lead shower followed me. No one, apparently, even had any interest in me. A block away I slowed to a walk, straightened my clothes.

CHAPTER FIVE
LITTLE OLD LADY

IN **THE** drug store, I got back my belongings, meanwhile raking my brain to try and figure what to do next—something that would make my visit to the House of Forty-one Delights productive. I looked at the cards. I had acquired at such risk and apart from the fact that I had seen their twins in the handbag of that determined aristocrat—little old Mrs. Steadman—they meant nothing.

Then I called Captain Oliver at police headquarters. He nearly burned my ear off with his shout. And he nearly stood my hair on end with the words he spouted. "Damn you!" he roared at me. "Why didn't you tell me that sedan had killed a man—that there was a dead man practically under the wheels! Good God, am I in a mess, now! I said it was reported by a friend of mine. Homicide wants to see the friend!"

"Where is the corpse now?"

"It ought to be at the morgue, any minute—"

"Meet me there in five minutes!" I snapped at him.

I was there ahead of him. The morgue attendant made no bones about letting me in, nor about showing me the latest corpse. The drawer had not yet been closed.

The head of the man on the slab had been beaten in—literally to a pulp. He wore a plain gray suit. A red-eyed snake ring circled the third finger of his right hand. He was Mrs. Steadman's erstwhile bodyguard.

I raced for a phone, called Doctor Steadman's apartment in a fever of fear. The old lady was not there, but her grandson said he'd been talking to her within the past five minutes. The car had developed a knock and she had sent it with an attendant, to a service station while she completed her errands on foot. She would probably be, the tired young man's voice assured me, in his apartment very shortly, and if I were the insurance man, she trusted that I would be there to meet her.

I hung up absolutely at a loss how to figure what had happened. That the old lady was alive and phoning within the past few minutes certainly seemed to mean that she had not yet come to harm. Yet the lad who had been driving her car had been taken, killed, and planted at the scene of my little imbroglio with the Rock brothers, all in a matter of less than an hour—it was not very much more than that since I had seen him.

Conscious of the urgent necessity of getting to the old lady I almost forgot Oliver. We plunged into each other as I was going out the door. He looked plenty worried.

"This thing has started to pop," I told him without permitting him to speak. "You've got to play along with me—not drag me down for explanations that don't explain. I haven't a second to spare—if I'm going to stir up this man's town like I think I am. For God's sake, hold them off me for a little while longer. Where can I get a car?"

"On the level," he bit through clenched teeth, "have you got something? If you have, I'll string along with you. But for the safe of your health, don't bluff me!"

"I've got something—if I can get a car fast!"

For another second he hesitated, then said "I might as well be hung for a sheep. Take mine—it's at the curb. But if you flop—start running. That's all—start running!"

ALMOST BEFORE he had the words out of his mouth I was whirling crosstown, toward the Hartz Towers.

I noticed the car was radio-equipped. The Haddonstown police force had achieved two-way radio, and there was even a miniature mike through which the occupant of the car could broadcast back to headquarters. I turned on the police calls, half fearing to hear an alarm out for myself any minute.

It had not come by the time I was shown into Doctor Ralph Steadman's eighteenth-floor apartment in the swanky, modernistic skyscraper apartment building. I told a faintly disapproving butler that I would keep my hat.

He announced me and I walked into a white-and-gold living-room. Four people were playing bridge in front of a wood fire. They were all in full evening dress.

Young Steadman got up and came over. He was a surly, impatient-looking youngster, for all the world like a head-strong, handsome, spoiled, erratic boy of fifteen, hiding in evening clothes. He ran a feverish hand over his dark forelock, introduced himself and the rather pickled-looking, ancient pair he was playing cards with—a Major and Mrs. something—and then to the girl whom he called his fiancée.

Her name was Mary Conant and I did not have to be told that she, too, was one of the best people. If I hadn't heard the Conant money ranked with the ten largest fortunes in America, the girl herself would have convinced me. She was a tall, stately blonde, with an absolutely perfect figure and no more fire in her than so much marble. She gave me the merest excuse for a nod and loathed me with her pale blue eyes. It was the same look aristocrats usually use when gazing upon my humble carcass so I was not put out.

I insisted that they go on playing and sat on the sofa, my hat in one hand, an unwanted whiskey and water in the other. I felt like a fool—yet what could I do?

I stood it for just about half an hour, then I got up and asked if I might call Mrs. Steadman's own house.

Irritated, and not bothering to hide it, young Steadman said: "Oh, yes. The phone is in the hall. If you want to know Grandmother's plans, ask for Harry at the gate. He is the only one who would know."

Harry, at the gate, told me: "Mrs. Steadman arrived home no more than fifteen minutes ago and is at present in the hands of her masseur. She will be available for telephone calls in thirty minutes or so."

I became insistent on talking to her, told him who I was. Then I thought to ask: "Did she bring her own car home?"

"No. It had engine trouble. She rode home in a taxicab. May I ask you to repeat your name?" And when I did, "I say, are you at Doctor Steadman's? For Mrs. Steadman left a message that I was to call you and urge you to come and see her immediately."

"How can she see me if she can't talk on the phone?"

"She will no doubt be able to interview you by the time you arrive."

I THINK my first suspicions of the old lady began at that point. As I raced through the night in Oliver's car, I was beginning to realize that, under her charming dainty gentleness, there was a streak of something hard and inflexible as tempered steel—but I couldn't quite understand what it was.

I had one moment of panic as I flashed by the spot where my little act with the brothers Rock had taken place that afternoon—fear that a police detachment might have been left at the spot. But the place was deserted, the car gone.

Then I was around the turn and, half a mile ahead, I saw the blue light that I had been informed marked the entrance gates of the old lady's modest country house.

Somehow, as I coasted in toward the high, spiked-iron gates that bounded the property, I felt that the payoff was at hand.

I stopped my car with its nose against the gates and a man stepped out of the gate house. Light glinted from brass buttons, on a trim semi-uniform coat, visored cap, and something steely in his hand. I called, "Harry?" and identified myself by name.

He stepped out and touched his cap, asked respectfully to see my papers.

I, like the veriest green fool, reached for them and undid the door on his side, so that he might examine them in the light from dash.

To show how utterly unsuspecting I was, even in the moment that he peered thoughtfully at my stuff, I calmly did the thing I had been vaguely planning ever since I got in the car. I turned the dial that controlled the wave-length on which the car's occupant could broadcast—turned it till it corresponded with the wave-length on the loud-speaker dial—the wave-length over which broadcasts came *from* headquarters. Then I clicked the switch that shut off the power from the entire apparatus.

I say I did this while he was examining my papers. If he had had any knowledge of radio at all, it would have been my finish. But he didn't.

The first warning I had of my disastrous blindness was when he slid into the seat beside me. Then I jerked erect. His gun covered me. He thumbed back his cap and looked at me with a dull, fishy look. He was Milton Rock—the one who had held me at the point of a gun beside the wreck, after I had downed his brother.

"Just drive on," he said dully. "The gates will open as you push them."

I clenched my teeth, but I was trapped, cold. I had no alternative but to obey. I let the car nudge open the gates and we went up the drive.

I said: "So you do tricks with coats as well as hats. What's the racket?"

"Save your lip," he told me. "Drive round to the back of the house and stop."

I did. He climbed out, still covering me carefully. The younger brother, Charlie, suddenly opened the back door and stood there, gun in hand.

"Get out," Milton told me.

I got out. The last thing I did before I left the car was to get my knee against the switch that controlled the radio. Somehow I managed to turn the power on again, unnoticed.

"Get inside," Milton snarled at me, "and keep your hands up. Make it snappy."

We went into a kitchen that was neat as a pin. Charlie, the one I had mussed up, told me through gritted teeth: "How I'm going to hate this."

I was propelled into a scrupulously neat little living-room and was barely inside when Charlie, from behind, drove a rocklike fist under my ear, cursing viciously as it landed. It sent me sprawling into a corner with a crash that shook the house.

"Well, where's the picture?" he shouted.

I sat up, shaking my head to clear it.

"Come on, come on," Milton chimed in. "Get it up."

"Behave," I growled. "I don't know about any picture."

Milton cursed in his throat, snarled, "Hold the gun on him, Charlie!" and came over and knelt beside me, went through my pockets, being none too gentle about it.

He got everything I had, but he didn't get any pictures, naturally. I couldn't even guess what picture they might be talking about.

HE GOT up and stood over me, thinned eyes measuring me. The impulsive Charlie came and stood over me. He blurted: "We're going to pistol-whip you within an inch of your life, till you cough that thing up."

Milton said: "It'll have to wait, Charlie. I've got to get back on that gate, till the boss gets here. He'll know what to do." And, after another second of quick thought, "Throw him in with the old lady, meantime."

I was driven up three flights of stairs. A locked door was thrown open and I was kicked inside. I sprawled on the floor, on an old-fashioned rag rug, in an old-fashioned little upstairs sitting-room, and the door was slammed behind me.

I picked myself up and faced the rosy-cheeked old lady, Mrs. Steadman. She had a huge sewing-basket beside her on the sofa and she was placidly knitting. Only someone who knew her very well, or a trained observer, would have noticed the taut, strained lines under her jaws. On casual inspection, she was still the twinkling-eyed, serene little old pastel.

She said in her delicate, silvery voice: "I feared that they were planning to capture you when they forced me to phone my son. I am terribly sorry—terribly."

"Think nothing of it," I reassured her. "We're not dead yet."

She looked at me a little wonderingly. "You—you mean you have a plan to outwit these terrible people?"

"Give me a chance, lady. I just got here."

Her knitting needles had ceased operations. Now they click-clicked again and her face lost a little color. Behind her spectacles her eyes seemed a little more intense. "I—am afraid you don't understand. They are going to kill us."

"What does that get them?"

"They are in hopes—they are in hopes that they will draw—certain information from me."

I looked at her sharply. "Wait a minute. What information?"

She compressed her velvety little lips. "Information that will free Asa Burdick from this terrible charge. Information that I got tonight at a photographer's—after I saw you. They—they were waiting for me when I came out of the shop. They had overcome Frank, the guard I had hired. Fortunately, I saw them and threw all the pictures but one into a stove and I—I was able to conceal that one. It means ruin for them and they know it. They will try to get it from me and—they sha'n't."

"I don't get this," I told her. "What is this picture?"

Her bright eyes met mine a little impatiently. "The picture I took from the man Hagin, as he died."

My hair stood up. "That you what? Good God, you don't mean that you killed Hagin?"

Her eyes put me in my place. "Don't be absurd. I happened to be in the vicinity of the prosecutor's house—in fact I was going down the steps into Kemmerer Park last night—when Hagin was shot. I did not realize that his body was falling down the stairs behind me, till he crashed into me, knocked me down. When I got up, I had this picture in my hand—he had somehow jabbed it at me—he must have died with it in his hand. Naturally, I had no wish to be involved in what seemed like a scandalous mess, so I hurried away. I didn't really realize I had the picture, till I was across the park and in a taxi."

"You mean these thugs came after you for that picture? Good God, did they see you there?"

"No. I rather imagine they traced me through my spectacle lens. You see, I have a very special prescription for my glasses. And one of the lenses was knocked out of its frame when this—this happened. They have as much as told me that they traced me through that. And they want the picture."

"What in God's name is this picture? Do you mean you have it with you?"

"The picture," she assured me, "is of one Doctor Ullman, a friend of my grandson—the missing head of the Dean Foundation. And it shows, I believe, where Doctor Ullman is now. Where he is being held prisoner."

"Where is that?"

She looked at me grimly. "Turn your back, young man."

For a moment, I could not guess from where she was taking the picture and then, by sound, I realized that she must have concealed it under her bridgework. When I turned back, she was dabbing at moisture on the edges of a tiny—Leica-size photo. She held it up for me to see.

IT WAS a picture of a lean, gangling man with an almost bald head and cavernous, hawk-like features, an unusually clear print. The man lay on a couch to which he was bound, with wire I assumed, almost from head to feet.

His eyes were closed. There were dark splotches all over his face—blood, I presumed. His feet were bare and the picture was such that they were not properly foreshortened. They loomed out of the picture horribly. They were hardly the shape of feet any longer and were covered with huge blisters. There was a small tin of canned-heat on the floor under the feet, and a faint flame wavering in the tin.

Thought of the torture this poor devil must have taken put sweat beads on my forehead. I said: "You got this from the dead hand of Hagin?"

She nodded and put her finger on a wall telephone that showed in the print. "I thought that possibly I could have this enlarged sufficiently to make out the number on the mouthpiece of that phone. That was what I was doing at the photographer's. If we knew the number we might be able to locate the room—"

"You didn't get it?"

"Of course I got it," she told me and turned the photo over. The back of it was covered with tiny, spidery handwriting, so small that I had to squint to read it.

"They left me in this room with a pen and ink," she told me proudly.

I read—

> This picture is of Dr. Ullman, the missing head of the Dean Foundation. He is confined in a room where the telephone number is Wabash 6547. If the police will go to that number, they may be in time to find him alive. Undoubtedly he can reveal the name of the man who is—or was—the real head of the Dean Foundation.
>
> I am at present captive in the hands of criminals. I have overheard their conversation. The truth behind the death of the man Hagin is that he attempted to force the proprietor of the Dean

Foundation to share with him the money that was being stolen. When the man refused, Hagin threatened to expose him. He had word taken to Asa Burdick, the news writer, who investigated and wrote the expose. Hagin, hating Burdick for prior exposes of Hagin himself, saw an opportunity to involve him, and conceived a scheme which he outlined to the District Attorney's office.

In other ways, Hagin put pressure on the man who was behind Ullman. That man shot Hagin. I do not know his identity, but if you can find Ullman alive, he will be able to name him.

Priscilla Steadman.

I whispered: "Gentle Annie! You've got it, lady."

"You think that will free Asa Burdick?"

"If it reaches the right cop."

I should have been warned then. An almost fanatical look came into her old blue eyes. She quickly lowered them, knitted swiftly. "Then that is all I care about—freeing that poor boy. It may seem queer to you—but I don't mind what's coming much. I am an old woman—I have, lived out my life."

"Don't talk like that." I said. "We still have a chance."

"What chance?" she asked me and her voice was lower now. "Tell me, if you really see any chance. My mind is not old, like the rest of me, young man. I have considered our predicament and I am not blinding myself by foolish optimism. Certainly they will kill *me*. I do not expect my heart will stand much of what they will do to me to try and extract the information from me. And if they kill me you can hardly expect to have them let you go. What possible escape have we? I know that the man behind them—the man from whom they take orders—the man behind all this horror—is on his way here now. If you see any way of escape tell me now. I must know."

I was getting the willies. "Don't worry, lady—"

"Then you *have* no real hope. There are bars on these windows, felt covering and shutters. We just cannot escape."

"Why be so morbid? I've been in jams—"

"Because we must face the situation. We are going to die. If we accept that and prepare for it, we may be able to—"

I made an impatient slashing gesture. "If I'm going to die, ma'am, I won't accept it till the slug is in me."

She was silent a minute, her rose-petal lips compressed. Then her needles clicked furiously. Her voice was weary: "I knew—knew that you—"

It was at that moment that something else occurred to me. "Listen," I said. "Just what were you doing alone on the stairs leading down to Kemmerer Park last night? You didn't come there by accident."

"I was doing nothing," she told me calmly, "that was any of your concern."

More light jagged into my brain. "By the Lord Harry! You're the one who phoned Asa Burdick—phoned him at Mainwaring's house—phoned him to hurry away and meet you! That's it—isn't it! It has to be it!"

She said: "Really, must you be so absurd…?"

I blurted, as the inevitable line of logic opened up: "But you didn't walk to Ridge Row! And there are no street cars. You must have taken your automobile up there—yet you walked down that interminable flight of stairs. Why? Because you had turned your car over to Asa Burdick and he—or, my Lord, I get it now. You sent him—"

She was suddenly on her feet, her apple-cheeks burning. "Please—I have no time to discuss such vaporings." She swayed a little but there was intense determination on her kindly little face. She hurried on, almost breathlessly: "Young man, what I am going to do may be wrong, but God help me, it is the only thing I see to do. And, remember this: I do not believe that we will lose anything by it. You have admitted that you have no plan of escape. Now—you must leave it to me."

CHAPTER SIX
TO THE MURDER BORN

I LOOKED at her bewilderedly as she fumbled in her sewing bag. Somehow, I was coming to have an unholy respect for her—for her shrewd old mind, for her ruthless will and her utter lack of selfishness save for her own caste. I didn't have any clear idea or plan in my head, admittedly and—she, apparently did.

I stood unmoving, while she popped something into her mouth. Simultaneously, she took one of those egg-shaped dingusses with a handle on it—the kind women use for darning—from the bag. I should certainly have been warned, I suppose, by now. But the truth was that my mind was unable to catch up to her. I was involved with the sudden string of revelations that were still glowing in my mind. Though maybe there never was a time at which I could follow her lancing, cold line of reason.

Before I could divine any part of the shocking thing she was driving at, it was too late.

She tottered across the room so quickly that it was unbelievable. Before I knew it she was hammering on the door with the egg-shaped thing, raising hell.

Presently the door burst open. And I had never seen such acting on any stage.

Somehow, her cheeks were flaming scarlet now. The door framed Milton Rock and, behind him, Charlie. They both had their coats off and sleeves rolled up. The hall behind them was in blackness, save for a faint filtration of light up the stair well. Milt bellowed: "What the hell is wrong with you?"

She drew herself up, trembling, her eyes flaming behind her spectacles and threw the words out of her. "I will not stay in this room with this person a minute longer. I will not be forced to listen to his filthy talk!"

Milt snarled: "Oh, nuts, lady. You won't have to listen to it much longer. Go on back in and can that row or the boss will—"

"I care nothing for your boss. I simply will not stand his disgusting blasphemy and slander. He should have his mouth sewn up, so that he can never speak again. I—if I had the materials from my grandson's fishing-tackle box, down in his room, I would do it myself!"

Milton made a disgusted slash with his free paw, sneered and half turned away.

A soft voice behind him in the hall said, "Take the dick, Milton," and somehow, the big thug moved with a speed that was too much for me.

Before I knew it, he had leaped across the room and his gun smashed into my face, knocked me to the floor. I lay there, my head filled with shooting stars, while he crouched over me, panting.

"All right boss—what now?"

I tried to sit up groggily to see out into the dark hall. Milt's gun whacked my nose and I groaned and fell back flat. Over Milt's shoulder, I saw Charlie's face, and in his eyes hunger for a crack at me. I lay still.

The soft voice in the hall said: "You were saying, Mrs. Steadman?"

She said in a prim, sharp voice: "Come in here, where I can see you!"

"That will not be necessary," the voice chuckled, "but I did hear you say something that sounded most entertaining. Would you mind repeating it?"

She took a long breath and said: "Simply that I utterly refuse to stay in this room with this revolting person. I have never heard such foul and disgusting slander in my life. He is not fit to be allowed to speak."

"And," the voice prodded gently, "you thought that something might be done to prevent it? Didn't I hear you say something—about the catgut your son uses, probably for making dry-fly leaders and such?"

It was then that I realized the incredible, mad thing at which she was driving. I don't think I should be blamed for not seeing it earlier. It simply surpassed all the bounds of sanity. But the realization came too late—far, far too late.

Her voice took on a viciousness—rather, the shadow of viciousness—for nothing in the world could make that soft, sweet little old voice truly vicious. Yet there was no hesitation whatever in her instant reply: "I said I would like to sew up his mouth—and I would!"

For just a second, there was silence in the hall. Then a soft chuckle. "Why then, lady—since we all owe this gentleman a little something—you shall indeed!"

I tried to yell, tried to leap up. A smashing, blinding blow caught me in the forehead, knocked the senses out of me—and then there was blinding, maddening fire tearing my lips.

THERE IS no description for the excruciating riot in my brain as I came to myself. First, the terrible agony in my lips drove everything into a red blaze. I looked up into the leering faces of the sadistic Rock brothers. They held me, on either side, my head fast on the old lady's knees, looking upwards. Her face was a wax mask. From underneath I could see the ghastliness—but it was still a mask. Save for her utter pallor, had I been five yards away, I would have sworn she was enjoying the hellish work she was doing. And what she was doing was slowly sewing my lips together with a length of catgut and a darning-needle.

I wanted to scream, but the slightest motion of my lips or tongue told me the story agonizingly—that half my mouth was utterly closed now. And then I got the rest of the story—the utterly unbelievable thing to which this astounding old lady had nerved herself.

For there was something in my mouth—a little something, slick and crackly—and for an instant I forgot my pain as my startled brain leaped to figuring what it was. And then I knew.

It was a tiny oilskin pouch—I had seen half a dozen of them, holding small needles in the old lady's sewing-basket. And inside the tiny pouch was something that crackled—the tiny photograph.

Determined that we were to die, she had thought out the only—to her—inevitable solution, ghastly and terrible as it was. She was sewing the evidence into my mouth—the evidence which would clear Asa Burdick—the evidence which the police would undoubtedly find when my dead body turned up!

Somehow, she had slipped the little pouch, without their noticing it, into the one place where nothing on God's earth would ever send them searching for it. For she would not tell them—not after this. Undoubtedly she knew what was in store for her—but she was prepared to face it. Doing this to me proved it.

I was bathed in sweat. I writhed with the agony of that piercing needle—but my two grinning captors held me as though I were clamped with iron hands.

I was cursing myself frenziedly—cursing myself for not having really believed that the old lady had meant literally every word that she had said—cursing myself for not telling her of my one ace-in-the-hole.

And yet—even realizing that seconds seemed years—screaming agonizing years—even so, the dreadful fear began to be borne in on me that my ace-in-the-hole must have failed me—the one thing I had counted on so confidently to give me a break, had collapsed—that we were doomed....

Then the doorbell downstairs rang sharply.

That it was totally unexpected to the others gave me my one spark of hope. The voice in the hall said curtly, "Wait a minute!" and everything stopped. The voice continued: "Milton, you fool, I told you to bolt those gates! Damn you...."

Milton's gasp told me he had forgotten. The man in the hall said: "Charlie—keep a gun on the dick. Come on, Milton—get that chopper. We won't give up now—for anybody!"

They ran out.

Charlie jumped away from me, the muzzle of his gun trained on my face. In my feverish, pain-fogged state, I still could think a little bit and I let my head roll limply, closed my eyes, simulating a faint.

The hall door was open. I could see Charlie, from under my almost closed lids, aching to run out and see what was going on. I tested my position. I was a little too far down on the floor for a spring. Gradually, with the patience of Job and the deception of a sleight-of-hand performer, I eased myself till I was sitting up a little straighter.

And in that minute, Milton's sharp yell came from below: "God—the cops!"

Then the cold, bitter voice of the other man floated up. "Get down on those stairs! Turn that chopper on the door—and let them have it when they come in. Remember this—if we win, I can square anything! Anything, understand? If we're taken—we all hang!"

ALL THE time he had been speaking, there had been heavy pounding at the door, constant ringing of the bell. As he finished, there were three booming shots from below—the police shooting at the lock.

For the first time, the nervous Charlie Rock could not control himself. He swung squarely toward the open doorway.

I sprang.

I had no chance to get away with it scot-free. I knew that before I did it. But I knew also that we were facing our last and only chance to get out of this thing alive and I did what I had to.

Charlie's gun exploded almost as I sprang. But he had whirled too quickly, fired too quickly. I felt the sickening tear of a slug through my side and I wobbled, but my mind was hurling my body. I closed with him, ripped a vicious jab up under his jaw and that sent his second slug into the ceiling. Then I had both hands on his gun. I dropped to my knees, throwing myself around to bring his arm over my shoulder.

Shots were still hammering at the door below as I threw my whole weight on his arm. It cracked like a rifle report—and then I had the black automatic. I flung myself toward the door. Below, I heard three shots fired—fired from *inside*—clearing the sub-machine gun.

I hurled myself to the stair-well, looked down. On the lower flight, facing the door, stood Milton, the sub-machine gun in his hand, his teeth bared. The minute that door caved in, I knew death would spray the police like an attacking barrage. For they were unprepared. They had not come here after murderers. They had come here simply and solely because of the way I had tuned the radio set in Captain Oliver's car—tuned to the same wavelength as the official headquarters broadcasting station.

I had known from long experience, that radio experts would recognize the interference for what it was—and that they would instantly send out technicians to correct it. By orienting on the direction from which the interference came, I had known that they would sooner or later arrive at this house. That was what the bluecoats below were here for—to stop radio interference. But having found an empty police car, they were warned in some degree, but by no stretch of imagination could they know what was awaiting them behind that door.

I simply threw down on Milton below and pressed the trigger of the automatic. My gun jammed. Nothing happened.

My hair stood straight up. I flung a quick look at the second-floor landing—at the slender, crouched man in dinner clothes—Milt's boss. I could not see his face. He had a black slouch hat on.

The door below began to give.

I swung myself over the banister, got heel-hold and dived—squarely at the shoulders of the man in the black hat. I remember the ghastly, frantic feeling in the instant it seemed that I had missed—that I was going to jackknife my throat over the banister—for I almost did just that.

If he had not been standing close to the railing, leaning down to watch Milton, I would have been done for. As it was I lit with my waist across the banister—but my eager arms snatched his head to me and I dragged myself over. I drove lashing, frantic rights to his face as we collapsed in a heap. He writhed and shouted as his gun went skittering across the floor. Our arms and legs flailed and I hit him—a thousand times it seemed, before he slumped.

Then I dived for the pistol he had dropped, flung myself back over the banister and took careful aim. The door went down with a crash as I fired.

I shot Milton through the top of the head, before he had a chance to let out so much as a single shot. He simply stood up, turned a little sideways and pitched down the stairs, the machine gun clattering ahead of him.

He lit at the feet of a band of police led by the white-haired Captain Oliver.

I made the best shouting sounds I could with half my face closed. They ran up and I raised my hands as a precautionary measure. Oliver burst out crazily, when he saw me: "Good God, what—"

" 'Nother upstairs. Cut m' free!" I croaked:

He gasped but roared orders, among them one for an emergency first-aid kit. Racing shouting bluecoats filled the house.

When I could, I spat a mouthful of blood from my mouth—and the little oil-silk packet. I ripped out the picture, mouthed at Oliver, "Find house address this number," and he sent a man running toward a phone.

DON'T ASK me why I did it, but I did. I said to Oliver: "Old Mrs. Steadman is upstairs. We must get her out of here—the papers mustn't know a woman like that was involved here."

Upstairs, Charlie was unconscious with a gash in his skull inflicted by the blackjack of one of the officers who had gone up. And—somehow this seemed all wrong to me—old Mrs. Steadman had fainted. By the time she came out of the faint, I guess she was halfway to her son's house.

I had almost forgotten the man in the black hat. We ran out of the upstairs sitting-room as I remembered him.

From above, I saw him just regaining consciousness. He shuddered, then raised himself from the floor, looked around. By some miracle he was alone on the landing, although cops swarmed above and below him. Oliver, hearing of the radio interference, had guessed close to the answer and had brought three squad cards to my rescue.

The killer who had caused all this got to his feet, thinking he was unobserved, and started for the stairs.

I called down: "Don't try it, Mainwaring. You're through."

He looked up, and for a second his little terrier face was a vicious, frantic muzzle. Then he sprang at the banister, intending to dive over and finish up his troubles, I guess. I stopped that by shooting a leg from under him, sending him sprawling on his face. "No, no," I rebuked him, "you've got some hanging to do."

Oliver roared beside me: "Good God—did you say Mainwaring? Is that Mainwaring, the assistant D.A.?"

"Who else?"

A cop ran out into the stair-well on the ground floor and called up: "Hey, chief—that phone number—what do you think? It's on the attic floor of the House of Forty-one Delights."

Oliver looked at me and I nodded. His voice roared: "Handcuff Mainwaring and take him to the hospital with these others. Halloran, you take them down. The rest of you, come on—we're raiding the Forty-one joint."

But we didn't. We found it utterly empty, no sign of life in it. The rats had deserted the sinking ship.

In the attic we found one corner of the place walled off, plaster over steel. The door was steel and all over it were signs of heavy battering—even a smoke-seared place where an explosive had been used. But the door had not been opened. There was neither key nor lock nor handle to it.

"Hagin was the only one who could get in here—a secret button to push or something," I told Oliver as we waited for acetylene torches to be rushed to us. "He kidnaped Ullman—single-handed—after trying to muscle in on what he thought was Ullman's graft. Ullman couldn't put anything out, because he was under the thumb of his own head man. Hagin brought Ullman here to torture the name of the head man out of him.

"Then he took a picture of him, all tortured to hell, and went to see Mainwaring, whom Ullman had named. That interview last night was nothing at all like Mainwaring cooked up. Hagin went there to demand a cut and showed the picture as proof that he actually knew what was what and that Mainwaring had better cut him in or else. Mainwaring shot him as he was leaving the house—and then concocted that crazy yarn to involve Burdick. He had these two hoods—the Rock boys—working for him. He was probably holding a murder charge over their heads—maybe that baker they were jugged for killing the last time they got let out. He had them arrange to plant the dough on Burdick and he, Mainwaring himself went to Burdick's room and planted the gun when he pretended to lead the raid in which it was found. Ullman will fill that story in."

The torches arrived and presently we were inside. Ullman was barely able to talk, but he was still alive.

"Mainwaring framed me," he gasped out. "When Dean died and there was no place for his legacy to go—no hospital run by a Doctor Ullman—Mainwaring decided to produce one. He found me, God knows how, and sent for me. Somehow, after I'd been here about two hours, I found myself in a room with a girl who had just died from a criminal operation. My instruments were all over the room, bloodstained. Mainwaring had a dying statement from the girl that I had operated on her. I was done for—trapped. I had to do as he told me. He set up that fake Foundation, drained it of money. When Hagin came—"

"We know that part," I said.

Outside, Oliver said to me: "Where does the old lady come into the picture?"

I said innocently: "She was just helping her grandson's school-pal, Burdick."

BUT THAT wasn't what I said to Burdick when he came to see me in the hospital. When we were alone I growled at him: "So you and the old lady were willing to get us all killed, rather than tattle on young Steadman."

He said surlily: "I don't know what you're talking about."

"Oh, no? Suppose I call in a couple of other newshawks and explain to you all."

"Don't be like that," he said after a minute. "We—well, we couldn't foresee that things would go to that limit."

"No, but at any time during the proceedings, either you or the old lady could have admitted the truth and got us all out of the spot."

"What truth?"

"That the young blue-blood went on a bender and wound up in the House of Forty-one Delights. That the old lady got wind of it and called you in a panic to get him out of there. That you left Mainwaring's house in a rush, took her car and lammed over to the joint and got him home."

Burdick's dissipated face winced. "My God—do you realize that old Mrs. Steadman put damn near every nickel she had in buying a fashionable practice for the kid? That her sun rises and sets over him. And that if it were known that he was in a spot like that—blooey! They'd run him out of town—his friends I mean."

"A great pair," I grumbled. "Rather than let you come out with the truth—that you were dragging him out of there at the time of the murder, thus giving you an alibi, they were willing to let you take the rap."

"You think so? You're crazy. You don't know how these folks' minds work, gumshoe. According to my lights, I did the 'right' thing. And now, are you going to tell me that the old lady laid down on me? Hell, by your own admission, she was willing to die of torture to make sure I was acquitted—and acquitted *without* her grandson's ruin."

"Well," I growled, "you're all a bunch of mugs. I'd spill the whole works to the newspapers, except for one thing."

"What thing?"

"That you, being the worthless, pubwalking degenerate that you are, probably know where we can get hold of that Estrellita."

He thought that over for a minute and then said: "No. But I can locate Diane."

"Maybe," I pointed out, "Diane would know where to get in touch with Estrellita."

"Maybe she would," he conceded.

MURDER FOR NOT MUCH

IN ALL THE YEARS THAT HARD-
AS-NAILS INSURANCE DICK HAD
BEEN INVESTIGATING INDEMNITY
FRAUDS FOR ACME, HE'D NEVER
RUN ACROSS A KILLER WHO
CANCELED HIS VICTIM'S POLICIES
JUST BEFORE MURDERING
HIM. NEVER, THAT IS, UNTIL
HE STARTED TO UNRAVEL THE
DAYON CASE—AND WOUND UP
MASQUERADING AS A CORPSE
WAITING TO BE BUMPED OFF
TWICE IN ONE EVENING.

THIS DAYON was under forty, a big, husky fellow with a shock of tawny hair. But he had worry lines in his face, and his eyes were bloodshot. The last rays of the setting sun just got through the windows of the frame shack that was the office of the lumber yard as I told him: "Don't get me wrong. I'm no salesman. Like my card says, I'm an investigator, but the Acme Life hasn't any agents on Long Island, and I had business in Montauk. They asked me to stop by and see you. Let me get it over with and I'll be on my way."

"Get what over with?"

"This stuff that they gave me to tell you." I had anchored myself across the desk from him in a chair and the desk-top concealed the little slip of paper I cuddled in my palm. "The boss—not my boss, see, but the salesmanager—thinks you're making a mistake about your policies. He wants I should point out better things to do with 'em."

HIS BADGERED eyes were muddy. I exuded more embarrassed sweat and squirmed in my chair. "First—you got an endowment policy—ten thousand bu— dollars. Then a straight life the same amount. You been paying on them eleven and twelve years respectively. Take out new ones today and you'd have to pay double the premium."

"My God, I know that."

"Please," I begged him. "Let me get this out. I told you I'm no salesman and I don't care what you do—only I got to spout this stuff. I—" I felt my ears getting red as I glanced at the next note. "If your action is caused by economic distress"—imagine some squirt of a salesman saying that to an established business man—"the boss says you may have overlooked—"

His face was red, too, now, but with anger. "What the hell are you talking about? Go back and tell the fathead that sent you here to mind his own damn business. Every penny I've borrowed on those policies is legitimate and if he's got anything to say about it—"

He screamed as the truck thundered into the light car.

"No, wait—" I said, and tried to find where the answer to *that* was in the notes. There wasn't anything about it. "Well, hell," I said, "it don't—doesn't say anything about loans here. I don't know about that."

"Well, for the love of God what are you talking about? There are no premiums due for two more months—"

"Premiums." My finger found that. "Yeah, that's right. That was one reason why the salesmanager couldn't understand your canceling them now. Matter of fact we *can't* cancel 'em except on a premium date. Also, you've been paying on them so long, it seems a pity to let them go—"

His eyes were feverish, utterly exasperated. "Who the hell said anything about letting them go?"

I had the answer to that one. "You did," I told him, "in your letter last week."

"My what!"

"Your let—" About this time it began to occur to me that maybe there was a hitch here somewhere. I dug the letter they'd given me from my pocket, opened it up. It was clear enough and written on the letterhead of the Northaven Lumber Company, Northaven, L.I. It said simply to cancel policy numbers so-and-so, but it did add—which I hadn't noticed—*on the next premium date.* "Oh, yeah," I said. "You did specify—"

"Let me see that thing!"

He took one look at it and his eyes bugged out. He bounced out of his chair and roared: "I never wrote this letter! I—" He raised a shirt-sleeved arm—then groaned suddenly and sat down, clutching at his left side. I jumped up. His face was wrung with pain but he bit hoarsely through clenched teeth: "Sit down—just one of my damned boils—under my arm. But I never wrote that letter!"

That woke me up. I began to feel thick-witted. In a quick backward flash I remembered the long nose of Preeker, the head of Acme's Investigation Department and my boss, poking into that letter. I wouldn't bet a dime that he hadn't smelled trouble in the first place.

So the letter canceling Dayon's policies was forged. That put it squarely up to me—and for once it got my curiosity. Why would anyone want to cancel another man's policies? How could anyone expect to profit in any possible way?

I started to say: "There's no sense…" and the phone on the maple desk rang. He snatched it up—all his movement were little jerky ones—and snapped on the desk-light.

"Yes?… No. I don't know…. Yes, sir…. No, a very funny thing's come up. I—" He cupped a hand over the phone and asked me quickly: "What will you do about this?"

"Do? Find out who sent this letter, of course—and why, if there is a reason."

"You mean you'll do it now? Stay in town and—"

"I certainly will."

He turned back to the phone. "I'm sorry, Dad, I'll be tied up. I'll tell you, supposed…. All right. That'll be fine. I'll drive by after dinner and see you for a minute." He hung up, his eyes asking me questions.

I was staring at the letter again. In ten years snooping for Acme, I'd had some funny ones, but never one that made as little sense as this. I wasn't even sure it was a criminal act. Certainly, there could be no profit motive in it for anyone.

I asked him: "Do you know anyone who might have a grudge against you—someone petty enough and ineffectual enough to do this out of spite just to cause you small annoyance?"

"No," he said disgustedly. "What sort of idea is that?"

"It does happen," I defended my perspicacity as a sleuth. "Is there just one typewriter in this office?"

"Yes." He jumped up, and led the way out to the outer office. "You want to see if it was written on our machine? Is that it?"

"Yeah."

THIS LITTLE building was a simple board shack, divided into three parts, plus a washroom. There was a large office into which one went from the front door, and two private offices at either side of the outer one. There was a stenographer usually at work in the outer office and, I presumed, Dayon's partner, Leany, usually in the other private office. I had arrived just after the stenographer had gone home.

I took the cover off her machine and sat down. Dayon said, "Here," and hastened to get me a letterhead. Before I was a third of the way through copying the letter, I knew the forgery had been written on this machine. I finished it and handed it to him. "Sign it—your usual signature," I said. "This machine wrote the letter all right."

I broke off as the door opened. A small girl stood there. I mean a small big girl. I couldn't call her a woman, yet she was over twenty. She was tiny, beautifully made, with immense, long-lashed dark eyes—shy eyes. She wore a simple, brown peasant dress that clung loosely to her dainty figure. Her hair was a fluff of dark brown around her head, with curls at her soft, white nape. She had little black gloves in her small white hands. She edged in, waiting to be spoken to.

Dayon said: "Oh. Lola. I—I'm afraid I won't be home for dinner." He looked at me, sort of in half-question, but I didn't have any answer to it, whatever it was. He fished in his pocket, was lucky enough to find my card there and introduced me to the girl. She was his wife.

She acknowledged the introduction in a barely audible voice. "You—what's happened, Charles?" she found the courage to ask faintly.

He told her in clipped, fretful phrases, ending with, "find what weak-minded half-wit—" and his lips suddenly clamped.

This was all over my head, until I noticed that the door of the other private office—the one with *Mr. Leany* on the door had opened.

A pale young man with a black, pointed mustache, carefully waxed, came out. He was elegant in Panama hat, chalk-striped gray flannel suit, blue shirt and blue silk tie, and he carried gloves and stick. He did not even glance at Dayon, but walked straight to the door. He bowed, lifted his hat and the frightened Mrs. Dayon slipped quickly aside, her lips shaping something that she didn't put voice to. The door closed behind Leany.

Dayon said: "You run along home, Lola. I have Dad's car here."

She made me a shy bow and slipped out, not giving me a chance to get in the customary pleasantries.

Dayon was looking at the palm of his calloused hand. His jaw was clenched. He was taller than I, by an inch or two, but I realized now that his clothes were too big for him. He had a razor-keen, sharply-chiseled face and his blue eyes would have been electric if there were any fire in them—that is, any fire besides that slow gnawing fever. He said through tight teeth: "That was my partner, Leany."

"Not particularly civil, is he?" I groped.

"We're not on the best of terms," he informed me in a tired voice. "He knows nothing about this business. It's his money—or rather his father's—that's in here. His father used to own all this part of Long Island. Harold seems to think I'm personally responsible for our not doing so well these last few years. Well, what now?"

I didn't know what now. I said it was up to him to think of someone who might be pulling this insane gag on him. It was dark now so he suggested dinner at the town's only restaurant. His car was out in the sprawling enclosure behind the office—the lumber yard. As we went out, I saw a few lights in the various yard buildings. One came from a driver backing the last of four ten-ton trucks into a shed-garage. One was a small high-powered bulb outside the shed where the checker had his headquarters.

It was in the outer fringe of this light that I saw Joe Moench.

YOU PROBABLY know Joe better as 'The Goose.' He was just an East Side package thief, till prohibition, and he didn't ever seem to fit in anywhere even during that lush period. But he was never in jail and he always lived high. Repeal didn't seem to disturb him and he continued to live on the fat of the land. He was at least part Italian and had a long, sallow face, shrewd little brown eyes, black hair and black sideburns. He got his moniker from his long, reddish-smooth neck. Somehow he seemed to dress in the most extreme Broadway fashion, with a tight, soft collar and a spurting tie—almost as though he were deliberately courting attention to his long neck. He was a puzzle to the New York cops, as he was to me, though he seemed to be in the dough, always. At least he always had permits for the two guns he carried and I heard one pretty shrewd cop class him as a merciless killer. I hadn't heard anything about him lately.

He was in the edge of the arc of illumination that the high-powered bulb threw on the gravel outside the sheds. It was almost as though he were waiting for us to get near enough so that he could see who I was—or who we were—before he melted off into the blackness.

I yelled, "Hey!" at him, but I had not recognized him until the very instant that he vanished, and my running after him did me no good.

Dayon was even more strained-looking when I came back, cursing. "What—what was it?"

"Saw a bird I thought I knew," I said. "You haven't anybody named Moench working around here?"

He said he hadn't and apparently had never heard the name before. By now I was anxious to phone in and get a little more explicit orders from Preeker, my boss, so I hurried the jaunt down into town.

It appeared that the lumber yard was on a little plateau, at the top of a hill. The village of Northaven was between this hill and Long Island Sound. For my dough, the hill was a mountain, as we turned out of the grounds and started down a perfectly straight road, thickly lined with trees. There were no street lights and the road was so narrow that I could not see how two cars could pass if they did meet, and my heart was in my mouth as we plunged in what seemed almost a perpendicular dive, down the side of the hill and into the business section. This was one street of stores and shops—maybe twenty-five establishments altogether.

Dayon parked his—or, rather, his father's—ancient sedan in front of a remarkably decent-looking little English-style restaurant. I recalled that Northaven's three thousand population was swelled in the summer by another thousand or so New York folk, out for the hot weather, and understood how the town could support such a place. I wolfed as fine a steak as I have ever tasted, hammering at him between bites for some lead on this funny business, and waiting for my call to go through to Preeker in New York.

We didn't get very far. He seemed absolutely sincere in his protestations that he knew no one who would fit the picture of a spite gesture of the kind we had run into. In fact, he could not think of anyone who bore him any ill-will of any sort, though he seemed very anxious about it all.

When the phone in the pay-booth rang, and a waiter came towards our table, I half got up, but it seemed the call was not for me but for young Dayon. He went away and returned in a minute looking pale and worried. "My God!" he burst out. "That was my dad. Some woman named Helen just called there and wanted to know if I was there."

"Who was the woman?"

"I don't know. I don't know anybody named Helen. She said she'd call back."

"Let's go," I said quickly, forgetting my own call. It came in, however, as we were getting our hats, but I didn't get much help from Preeker.

"I knew it," he said. "I knew there was a sour smell. Well, use your own judgment. If we can't depend on you we can't depend on anybody." That was all he had to contribute.

BACK IN the ancient sedan, we drove three blocks up the main street, then turned back toward the direction of the lumber yard.

As far as I could see, we were climbing straight up the hill again—but our headlights played on a solid phalanx of trees. There seemed to be no road. That was explained when we had driven about half the distance of a block.

The road made a right-angle turn to the left, then almost immediately, another right-angle turn to the right again. Recent heavy rains had caused ruts to form in the road so that our tires were spoke-deep in the now-hard clay. There were comfortable little houses all around this section, half hidden by trees. Where Dayon brought our car to a stop was at the exact bottom of the straight road that led almost perpendicularly up between two solid blocks of trees. I was out, almost as soon as he had stopped. His gesture to check me came too late, after I had already slammed the door.

"No," he said. "Wait." He looked over the iron-picket fence that bordered the road, and up a flagged walk to a small, pleasant house from which light shone brightly, forty yards back. "I—that is, my stepmother and I don't exactly get along. Dad'll be out."

He tapped the horn three times gently. As we waited he explained, in answer to my prying, that his father had been a fairly good surgeon. He had retired, ten years back, and bought one of the town's two drug stores to occupy himself. Prior to that, however, he had married for the second time. Young Dayon had been greatly attached to his own mother and had been in a frenzy of rage at his father's remarriage, had made certain inexcusable and inerasable remarks and it had been impossible ever to restore harmony. Just one of those embarrassing situations, he assured me, with no great ill-will on either side, at least after this long.

I lit a cigarette and stood with one foot on the running-board. A man came out of the front door of the house, came slowly towards us. He was a splendid-looking old gentleman, older than I had expected, with a mop of pure silvery hair shining above a kindly, patrician face. He had a short white goatee. He used a thick cane as he walked. It was my impression that he must have been a more than ordinarily shrewd and sympathetic surgeon. He had the same bright blue eyes as his son.

I heard a faint clicking sound up in the brush above us, as he fumbled with the latch on the fence gate. Even as young Dayon introduced me to the approaching old man I took a quick glance over my shoulder, puzzled. I could see nothing at all in the blackness.

The old man came through the gate and latched it behind him, made me a little bow. His anxious eyes turned questioningly to his son in the driver's seat. "Charles— this woman—" He coughed a little, looked at his palm in a gesture that was so identical with the one the younger man had used in the office that I smiled.

"I don't know any Helen," the other said fretfully. "My God, what is going on here? Do you know what's happened? Somebody's written my insurance company, forging a letter to cancel my policies."

I heard that clicking sound above us again, took another sharp glance into the solid rising wall of blackness, as the old man said, "Well!" in a surprised voice.

I turned to ask the old man if he had been about to say that the woman had called again. Something jerked my head back, toward the now loud clicking sound. It saved my life.

The horror burst so fast that it was all over while I was still gasping for a single breath.

Two dull eyes suddenly caught the light from our head-lamps—two dull eyes that were no more than twenty feet from me when I saw them fling at me from the blackness. My heart froze and I dived, yelling, "Look out! Jump!" as I realized what the clicking sound was—one of the mammoth ten-ton trucks from the lumber yard, plunging at us so fast that its wheels rocked in the deep ruts.

As I flung myself through the air, I caught one glimpse of the contorted, terrified face of Dayon in the dashlight's glow, as he grabbed wildly at the car door. Then the truck thundered straight into the light car.

MY EARS were tortured by screaming metal, by the detonation of the terrific impact. Our car had been parked, just at a slight angle across the road. The truck seemed to blast up the nose of the machine, shear through it, bounce it high in the air and fling it over on its back with a crash that was an earthquake. I heard Dayon scream. The truck, rocked a little sideways by the impact, seemed to hesitate, then charge ahead once more. There was another rending, grating sound—but this time the truck hit obliquely. It was caromed across the narrow road, bounced back from the sheer, tree-studded bank—and sent slamming over on its side, still sliding down the hill, till it brought up thunderously against the bole of a huge tree.

I caught my breath, leaped up, yelled at the old man, "Call an ambulance, quickly—for God's sake!" and plunged at the overturned old sedan. My heart was in my throat as I flung my flash beam on the crumpled, distorted mass of metal. Then I heard a whimpering groan—not in the car, but along the ditch a few feet further on. I jumped for it—and saw Dayon. One leg was under him and he lay on his back. His face was a mass of blood, his leg obviously broken. God only knew what else was wrong with him. He was unconscious, of course.

The old man flung himself down beside his son, his face a stricken mask. I saw the door of the house fly open, saw a woman's body framed in light. I roared at her "Phone for an ambulance—and the police!" and she had enough sense to run back in the house.

She didn't need to put in the call for the police. The town evidently had an alert, if miniature, force. Even as I spoke, a siren was wailing in the main street below us. I heard the old man blurt brokenly, "Oh, God," as he felt the body of the prone lumberman and there was raging fury in my heart. I swung round, raced toward the truck. I think it was in my head to stomp the mad driver to death. I make no apologies for the fact that my brain was a little numb. There is no sound quite so horrible to me as the wrenching metal of colliding cars.

There was, of course, no driver. The truck had been set at the top of the hill, its wheels in the deep ruts of the narrow road, and, when our car was firmly parked, the truck had simply been eased over the brow of the hill and allowed to hurtle itself down.

The police car screamed around the corner then. Doors all around bloomed with light. People came running. There was an hour's nightmare while I explained myself to the police. Both I and the old man fairly screamed at them not to touch the broken body of the still breathing Dayon. They were all for picking him up and loading him like a sack of meal into the car, regardless of his condition. The old man stood up to them like a white-faced general, however, and they, remembering that he'd had medical training, took orders. Even the ambulance internes, when they arrived, did what he told them to, up until the time they finished the wild careening ride to the hospital. I rode in the police car that thundered ahead, clearing the way. There the old man's authority ended.

The surgeon he'd told his wife to summon—sometime during the mêlée, I don't know when—met us at the emergency door of the hospital and, after one look at the stricken old man's face, gently barred him.

Then we were all in the waiting-room, frozen, silent, while they rushed Dayon to the operating-room. I divided my time between answering the questions of the harassed police sergeant, who was trying every possible way to avoid the cold staring conclusion of murder, and trying to flog my brain into telling me what to do.

I was in a spot all right. Supposedly a prize gumshoe, I had had warning of funny business in the wind, then let a client be killed under my very nose. There were going to be some frozen faces in the offices of the Acme when they paid out forty thousand dollars—double indemnity, of course—on Dayon's policies. I swore a hot, grinding oath that I would nail the person who had done this, and that I would leave just enough life in him so that they'd have something to burn in the electric chair.

SO I sweated there in that waiting-room, burning to get out and get to work. I hadn't mentioned the Goose to the police. That was my own private business, at least for the time being. Dayon's wife, the little shy-eyed girl, came in, driven by the dead-pan, elegant Leany, if you please. Her face was like chalk, but it had no more and no less expression than when she had been in the lumber office earlier. Her dark eyes seemed larger now, pools of fright.

Dayon's stepmother, a charming, though firm-chinned woman of fifty-five, arrived. Consistent to the last, her worry was about the old man, who sat sunk in the corner of the divan, one hand shading his eyes. Any talking was done in whispers.

Then someone sent for the police sergeant and he passed through the door that led to the operating-room corridor. I don't think any of us breathed while he was gone. When he came back, we were around him like a swarm of automatons. He had good news.

The operation had been successful, as far as it went. Ribs had pierced Dayon's lungs, but they thought that had been taken care of. Internal injuries were critical, he had a fractured skull, his leg was broken in four places—but he was alive, and fighting for his life. He was not conscious, of course.

I told the police sergeant as I snatched up my hat: "If he gets conscious, try to get a statement. I swear he knows what's behind this."

I HAD to call a cab to get back to Northaven this hospital was ten miles away, in Huntsville—and it dropped me beside my own car at the gates of the lumber yard, in fifteen minutes.

Queerly, there was not a soul in sight at the lumber yard. Either the entire police force of Northaven was busy elsewhere, or else they could not think of any reason to check on the truck that had been the instrument of the attempted murder. Come to think of it, I was a little stuck myself as to what I expected to find, in that direction, in the lumber yard.

I drove down to look at the truck. It had been taken to a garage as had the ruin of the old sedan. I drove to the top of the hill and looked over the spot from which it had started down.

From the many tracks in the layer of dust at the dry top of the hill, I guessed that the police had examined the place thoroughly. I stood there and sucked a cigarette. Who had run the truck out here and pushed it down? Who had been standing here, looking straight down at us from the blackness, when we drew up in front of Dayon's father's place?

For a moment I thought of his stepmother, but she was out. She had appeared in the doorway of her house too promptly after the crash. It would have been impossible for her to have been at the top of the hill, aiming the ten-ton projectile, and then to have reached the house within a minute of the time it struck.

Who then? Leany? I picked him mostly, because he seemed to be a precious sort of rich man's son—the kind that might be capable of a petty trick like sending in that letter canceling the insurance policies. Oh, yes, I was quite certain now that the same person who had sent that letter had planned and practically accomplished, Dayon's death. Surely, it could not be the doe-eyed little girl who was his wife. That seemed ridiculous.

Why had he been murdered—or nearly murdered? One thing seemed paradoxically certain at least. It had not been for the insurance. Or had it? Could it be that the person who had concocted this whole scheme had shrewdly reasoned that the policy would still be in force at this point, but that the police would be thrown off the track *because* of the letter? It was not a bad idea.

I was out of cigarettes so I rode down: the hill to the town's main street, found a drug store. I put in a long-distance call for Preeker before I realized that I had chanced into Dayon's father's store.

It seemed a typical small-town drug store with modern soda fountain and great display of general merchandise. I could have improved on the lighting. I had to wait for the clerk to get through fixing up a package of ice-cream with dry ice for an Italian customer before I got my cigarettes. Drug-store clerks know everybody's business in small towns. I was trying to shape up some inquiries to make of this one, but the phone rang and it was Preeker.

I didn't give him any of the gory details. All I asked was, "Who is the beneficiary on Dayon's policies," and got the answer that they were made out to his estate.

I made another call, to the Criminal Identification Bureau of the New York police and got hold of Harry Skidmore.

To my surprise he said grimly: "I can tell you exactly what Goose Moench is doing these days. He's getting smuggled heroin into this port and I'm damned if we can figure how."

"Tell me more."

"Some fed got a tip from a stool-pigeon two months ago that New York was full of the stuff, and that the price was coming down. That meant a lot more than usual was coming in. The feds have a slue of men here. We're watching every boat like hawks—but it still comes in. Moench's name came along with the tip."

I said, "Thanks. Maybe I'll be some help to you," and hung up. The whole thing seemed suddenly clear.

I HURRIED back to my car, hailed the Northaven police car that was just coasting by. The sergeant informed me: "No change. He hasn't regained consciousness yet. His wife and his partner have gone home. The old man is still sticking."

I sent my car shooting back to the lumber yards.

There was a break, of course—in the matter of time. Yet, at that, I don't know if it was a break for me. I was not prepared for the little tragedy to run out so quickly.

I had barely parked my car, vaulted over the fence that surrounded the lumber yards and landed in the blackness, when I heard a sound. Don't ask me what it was—just a sound in the pitch blackness ahead of me somewhere—a soft muffled sound—but I knew I was not alone in the yard.

I crept down the gravel, my gun in my hand, and almost tripped over the rails—evidently this was also a private siding from the railroad. Most of the lumber sheds were along one side of the property, with coal elevators and the garage on the other. I chose the lumber sheds. There were six of them. I stole along, stopping to listen at every one.

I caught no more sound, no repetition of the first noise I had heard. Then I was at the fifth shed—and there was a soft sound of two pieces of wood hitting together. I wasted a lot of excitement and nervous energy before I found it was the unlocked door of the shed, gently banging. I wasted more before I got round to peeping in, aided by a squirt of light from my flash.

It was a bare, looming shed—not a scrap of lumber in it. I went noiselessly in. There was the usual trellis-work of beams, providing space for long lengths of lumber to be stored, but there was no lumber. I could not make up my mind if that were queer or not? Should a lumber yard have lumber in every shed?

I stood in the blackness, trying to figure how to discover the secret I knew was around here somewhere.

Fortunately, I was standing facing the door—or I would have died right then.

I can't say that I saw the door open—it was as dark outside as it was in. But I will give myself credit for what amounted to split-second judgment.

The electric torch blazed at me from the doorway. I saw the muzzle of a pistol under it—and realized the light had been turned on only to help someone shoot me. I fired instantly.

I hit the flashlight, exploded it into a thousand pieces. A stab of orange thundered at me and I felt my hat flick from my head. The gun blasted again—but I was already a yard to the left, leaping up to catch a rafter in one hand. With wrist and hand I wriggled up—thanking the builders for making sturdy beams that didn't creak. From the doorway there was silence.

Then a hoarse voice, "Come on out—and you've got a chance. If we have to burn you out—you won't get out."

I knew that was a bluff. They might gun me in safety— we were some distance from Northaven and sound might not travel, but a fire could not get under way without help coming.

I put my hand over my mouth, turned my head toward the rear corner of the building and said sneeringly: "You better start making tracks Goose. Your racket's flopped. Dayon spilled everything."

There was a second's silence. Then, "Maybe he spilled where the stuff was, then, wise guy."

"Maybe," I said, and threw my cigarette case across the shed to find out where I stood.

Nothing happened. No shot came. There was silence from the door. I was scheming, figuring how to make sure of blasting this bird—or birds, for I had the impression of two people—before they got a chance at me.

I wasted a full minute at that stupid effort—and then I heard the car, somewhere outside, grind into life.

I suddenly realized the bloomer I had made and dropped down, sprayed light. No one was at the door. I ran out to hear the exhaust of the car just vanishing through some unknown gate far at the rear of the yard.

I knew from their direction that they would have to take Highway 25—or else a back country road. I tore towards my own parked car, knowing that I could cut a mile off the distance by taking 25-a. My motor, still warm, caught at the first touch of the starter and I wheeled round, went down the suicidal hill with my heart in my mouth, hit Main Street and raced on till I whirled into the highway. Then I put my throttle to the floor.

On the way I figured out a plan.

WHEN I flung up in front of the hospital I did not even bother to park. I left my motor running, directly before the steps, went up them five at a time.

It was when I hurried into the waiting-room that I got my first hunch of what had happened. The old man—Dayon's father—was no longer there.

An interne checked me, just inside the door of the corridor leading to the rooms. I snapped at him: "Mr. Dayon?"

His lips were tight as he said: "He died five minutes ago. I was just going to notify—"

"Where's his room?"

"You can't—" Then as I flashed my badge, "Oh. Twenty-seven—just down there." He pointed to a closed door and I jumped for it. For just a second, I hesitated, then I went in.

The old man was standing there, with his chin up. There was a nurse in the room. She was drawing the sheet over the figure on the bed.

I swung out, beckoned the interne and rattled words in his ear. He gasped—then ran for more internes.

In three minutes flat, they had wheeled the dead man out of the death room, and into a vacant cubicle, had wheeled another bed in, and four internes were working feverishly on me. My clothes were being put in a closet by the nurse. Bandages were being whipped round my arms, my hands.

A good imitation of a plaster cast was being jammed on my foot, and suspended by a pulley from the ceiling. The internes were young, and cooperative, and had entered into my plan with grim enthusiasm.

And then, suddenly, I was alone. My bandaged arms and hands were outside the counterpane. I lay back, my eyes closed, feeling like a mummy.

After five minutes, I began to feel like a fool. Not a damn thing happened. The corridor outside was silent as a grave.

I began to curse myself as the conviction grew that I had made my second fool miscalculation of the evening. And this time it was disastrous. I felt the agony of the too-smart guy who has outsmarted himself—and then suddenly there was the faint creak of hinges at my door.

I lay still and let Death flirt with me.

For a minute there was no further sound, except the door whooshing closed on its patent arrangement.

Then a soft voice said: "Dayon."

I contained myself. After a long minute, I said thickly: "Wha's matter?"

I let my eyes open the narrowest slit and got a glimpse of the two pasty-faced, dapper rats against the door. One was the Goose, the other a Philadelphia gunman named Bragdon. I could not, for the life of me, recall his first name. Two pairs of shining eyes regarded me. There was a bulky object, wrapped in flannel, in the Goose's arms.

The same soft voice—the Goose's—asked: "Where did you put the two cases of stuff, Dayon?"

"Where?" I mumbled. "Lemme think. You mean the two cases"—all this was in a mouthed mumble—"you brought it in your speedboat, from where the liner had dropped it overboard with a buoy on it?"

They seemed a little at a loss, but finally said: "Yeah, that's what we mean."

I tossed a little, muttered wearily: "Lots of stuff—months and months—use my lumber sheds for a drop—run it in across Queensboro bridge—fool federals...."

Something—an electricity in the air—got me. I had said something wrong. I knew instantly what it was. I should not have used the word 'drop'. Dayon would not have used it. Light suddenly glinted on two blue-steel barrels. The flannel was slipping from the object in the Goose's arms and I realized that he held a submachine gun. I heard the hiss of whispers.

And then it was touched off.

The fool nurse—oh, I had told her to keep out and all that, but apparently she had thick brains—suddenly popped into the room through the other door—the one into the adjoining room. As if she had not done enough damage by that, the fool broad piped out, "Oh, Mr. Detective—" and then froze, one hand flying up in horror as she stared into the muzzles of two guns.

I had no choice—if I were to save her worthless life. I whirled up and fired—fired the gun that was concealed by the bandages on my right arm. I got the Goose squarely through the throat.

He staggered back as I screamed, "Down!" at the nurse, but she hadn't the brains of a gnat. She simply backed. But the other thug's gun was swinging toward me—not her. Fire and flame belched from it—just as I spun myself in bed—the only way I could get out of that damned pulley-and-weights business in a hurry—and his slug whizzed over my head. I slammed down on my face, fired along the floor and almost mowed one of his feet from under him. His screamed curse blued the air—and then he was wrenching at the door.

I FLUNG myself up, clawing the bed. The damned cast on my foot nearly sent me headlong, but I scrambled my way to the door, hopping, throwing myself.

I burst out into the hall, just as the fleeing thug was yanking at the door of the hall—the door that led out into the waiting-room and safety.

I steadied against a doorsill, drew a bead on the back of his head and blew his brains out.

I turned back as he went down. A dozen internes were running out of rooms, faces aghast. One grabbed me by the arm and blurted in my face: "The old man—Doctor Dayon—he won't stay down there where you told us to take him!"

"He can come up now," I said. "I'll be glad to see him. He deserves an explanation if anyone does. Leave me alone with him for ten minutes. That one"—I pointed my gun at the prone gunman—"is plenty dead. And there's another one in the room you can drag out any time. I'll see Doctor Dayon in here—and give me a cigarette."

I was smoking it when he came in. His eyes and distinguished old face were haggard as he saw me on the bed. He winced as he recognized bandages similar to those that had clothed his dead son.

"The case is all closed up," I told him. "Your son fell into a tough situation."

"What?" his voice was almost inaudible.

"The lumber company was on the rocks. He went for a proposition from a couple of New York gangsters—a proposition to use his shed as a halfway station for a smuggling-ring."

"No!"

"Yeah," I said. "I think that's why he was killed. Or was it?"

His mouth opened, closed. He croaked: "Are you asking—asking me why he was killed?"

"Who else would I ask?" I said casually. "You killed him. You set him up in front of your house on that narrow rutted road. You had a truck up at the top of the hill. You kept phoning him every few minutes—even making up a phony dame named Helen to confuse the issue to keep your time element right—and you were the only one who had access to the murder weapon."

"Wha—what?"

"As I figure it there's only one way that truck could have been left at the top of the hill, timed to come down at a certain moment—timed so that you would have an alibi. Shall I tell you what it was?"

His eyes were ghastly. "I don't know what you're talking about."

"Sure you do. You know I'm talking about a couple of chocks of dry ice under those wheels. It evaporates straight into the air, leaves no trace—and it furnished you with a beautiful alibi. Using it in your drug store, you no doubt knew to a second how long it would take a certain size block to evaporate, and—well, it was a nice idea."

He said nothing, licked his gray lips, stared at me hollow-eyed.

I LOOKED at my cigarette tip. "There isn't any question in my mind as to how it was done. The only question is—why? Tell me—beside what dough was in the business, had your son borrowed any money from that sweet partner of his?"

The old voice was like chalk. "Yes—yes—I believe he had—a few thousand."

That made things clearer.

"So the only thing left in the estate for his wife is the insurance—the *double indemnity insurance.* Right?"

His lips shaped, "Yes," but I could not hear it. I was up on my feet, eyes boring into his.

"That wife of his—a sweet kid—helpless, eh? Couldn't make her own way? Would starve to death. Your wife wouldn't let *you* support her? Dependent on what her husband left her, eh? And if he had died in the ordinary course of events, his life insurance would have been gobbled up in debts! Only the double indemnity business makes it so that she *gets* something. That's it, eh?"

He did not answer. One skinny old hand was crawling toward his throat.

I drove on: "I can't say I blame you. She's a sweet-looking jane. But by God, I can't fathom a man who would kill his own son, simply to provide for his widow. A man who would carefully concoct a phony letter to the insurance company—a letter designed to throw the insurance dicks off the trail and nothing else—and calmly do his son to death. I—by God, I can't understand! I—wait a minute! I'm getting a little light here now. You did it because you found your son was going wrong, was in with smugglers of narcotics. You found the two cases that were stored in his shed—found them and took them away. You felt you'd rather have him dead than in such a racket. That it?"

He looked at me from a thousand miles away and said in his hoarse croak: "I don't know what you're talking about."

And then it hit me like a thunderbolt. I blurted: "Holy Hell! The boils!" I grabbed him by the arm. "Those boils that he had—you treated him? Nobody else treated him? How long had he had them?"

He swallowed, didn't want to tell me, then husked out: "Two—two years—more or less."

I blew out breath. "And I'll guarantee you wouldn't let him go to any other doctor! That you handled them yourself—even, maybe, did a little operating on him from time to time?"

His old legs gave way and he dropped into a chair, let his face fall in his hands. He was licked. He cried from the depths of his heart: "Good God, are you a mind-reader?"

"No," I said, "although I'll admit that last was a guess. So it was cancer. He was due to die before very long anyway. You arranged the truck death to collect double indemnity and at the same time spare him the agony of cancerous death...."

He nodded. Through his fingers he pleaded with me desperately: "I—I know it's a futile thing to ask you, but—couldn't you forget you work for the insurance company—just for once? It isn't going to do you any good to—to report the truth now. And she—the little one—for all her shyness—she wouldn't touch a penny. All my frightful torture and risk—it will be in vain if you insist on dragging this to the surface. I—I'll kill myself, if you'll only—"

"Tut, tut, Doctor," I said after a minute. "I don't know what you're talking about. Your son was killed by the two heroin dealers that I shot in the hall here ten minutes ago. As far as I'm concerned there's nothing more to it. It's murder for not very much, but I'm not the guy to crab a party that's cost a nice gent like you so much grief. I can handle my office, if you're sure you can handle the girl."

"I—oh, she will never suspect—" he cried, springing up. Tears were running down his face.

I handled my office. Yes, I did! They scorched the ears off me—but they still don't know the inside. The feds nearly kissed me, though.

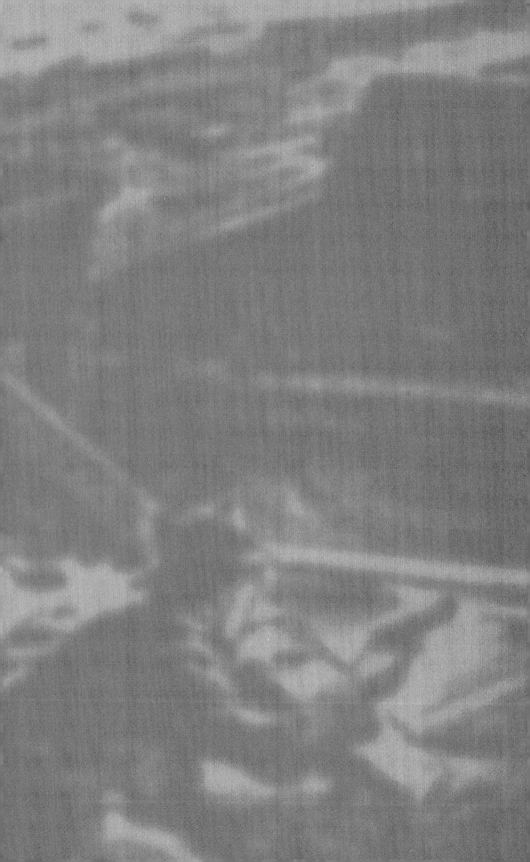

GREEN EYES FOR THE CORPSE

THAT HARD-BOILED INSURANCE OP HAD FALLEN FOR A PAIR OF SPARKLING EYES MORE THAN ONCE. THE LAST TIME IT HAD BEEN BLUE ORBS IN A BLONDE— THE TIME BEFORE THAT BROWN IN A RED-HEAD—AND HE'D GOT SLAPPED DOWN BOTH TIMES FOR GETTING FRESH. HE THOUGHT IT'D BE SAFE ENOUGH TO FOLLOW THE COME-ON WINK FLASHED BY THE GREEN ONES IN THE SIGHTLESS SOCKETS OF A MOULDERING SKULL BUT THEY PROVED TO BE DEADLIER THAN ALL THE REST. ALL HE GOT THIS TIME WAS A SLIGHT CASE OF MURDER AND A CHANCE TO WALK HOME FROM A RIDE IN A GARBAGE SCOW.

I DIDN'T think he'd lie to me—not Klein. We were by way of being friends. Not a week before when he was getting his lumps at headquarters over a missing sunburst, I had—in an offhand way—scoffed the cops out of really giving him the business and he knew it. He was the sort to appreciate little kindnesses like that—or so he said.

He was a greasy little article in his gray shirt—maybe it was once white—his sagging gray vest and pants, the wisp of sorry red string tie that hung away from his collar. His whole face seemed to have been warped, just slightly to the left, and then squeezed to a sharp edge. He had merry little grape-blue eyes that squinted in the dim glare of the one bulb that burned feebly in his filthy bedroom.

HE WENT on thanking me for going easy on him in the cellar at headquarters. "Them lousy cops—a bunch of sadists," he complained. "If you hadn't of been there, they would of beat me to a pulp. Your going easy on me, and kind of hinting around that you didn't think I had the lousy sunburst—"

"That's all right," I assured him. "I know who did fence it."

He looked at me, pain and surprise in his eyes. "And you stood there and let them cops—"

"Behave," I said. "I'm trying to buy the thing back for my company. The fence that took it in is too cagy. If I tipped the cops, they'd never get it—and my insurance company would be out a fat chunk of dough. I had to keep quiet."

"Oh." That cleared it up and he seemed quite happy.

He leaned forward on the edge of his doughy bed, shook a clawlike finger at me.

"All right then. Now I'll show you old Klein is a man that pays a favor for a favor. About a year and a half ago you was down in Messanah, wasn't you?"

"Uh-huh."

"You was looking for a little mother-of-pearl skull, with two juicy, drop-cut emeralds in it for eyes. Belonged to a rich party named Munday. Or am I a liar?"

I assured him such was not the case.

"You didn't find it, huh? Give me the real dope on how it was—and maybe I can see something hot in what I heard."

I shrugged. "There wasn't much to it. This dingus—the Green-eyed Monster they called it—was insured with the Acme for fifty G's. The grandfather Munday had it made when he first got rich. When he died, it went to his son and so on, till the last death left it as part of the estate that came to this widow Munday who insured it with us."

"And?"

"And nothing. It was turned off."

"You didn't suspect nobody? How was it turned off?"

"She has a big estate there, sprawls all over the place. Regular Southern mansion stuff—and a handful of servants. No guards, no locked doors, no nothing. She kept the damned thing in a safe that a baby could open with a sticky finger, in her bedroom. She had a couple guests there and she took the lot of them to the races at Louisville one

Three figures in the scow ahead
covered me with shotguns.

week-end. They were away two days and when they got
back the skull was gone. No fingerprints, no nothing. The
box was so old-fashioned that you could open it by listening to the tumblers falling."

"Didn't you suspect nobody?"

"It's a cold day when I can't suspect somebody. I
suspected nine servants and the entire population of the
town of Messanah—about sixty thousand folks."

He leaned back and sniggered. It was a gruesome sight.
Then he leaned forward and said: "Well, maybe what I got

to say don't help much. You never got trace of this here skull?"

"Not a smell."

"Well, whoever lifted it must feel it's cooled out by now. I got a roundabout ask for a price on it, this morning. Naturally, I ain't telling you how or where, but—the little item is going on the market and, as I understand it, it's still in Messanah. It'd be worth something if you could turn it up, even now, eh?"

"To me, plenty. I'll remember you if—"

"Naw, naw," he corrected me. "I don't mean that. A favor is a favor—for old Ike, anyhow."

"Well, thanks a lot," I told him. "I appreciate it."

He followed me to the door, fingering my sleeve with his filthy claw. Just as I was about to step out, he checked me and coughed apologetically, looking at the weave of my coat critically.

"A nice piece of goods," he decided absently, and coughed again. "Eh—now about this sunburst. You're sure you know who took it in? You're sure you know where to go to buy it back for the ten percent—"

I groaned sheepishly. "A fine monkey you've made of me. I must be slipping. O.K., Ike. Our negotiator will give you a call tomorrow."

ACME DOESN'T mind its sleuths fooling around with the red file—the jobs that have had to be settled—in their spare time. I'd even trained them—after twelve years with them—to hand out expense vouchers without my hiring Samuel Leibowitz to plead my case.

Preeker, the head of the investigation department, and my boss, undertook, reading from the file I shoved on his desk, to analyze the case for me.

"Now there's that Englishman that was one of the guests," he said. "Aha! He was poor. A fortune-hunter!"

"He wasn't a bad guy," I said. "A little on the haw-haw side, but he could have made a monkey out of us. We cabled London and from the dope they sent us, we might have thought this Doodlebug—"

"Droodingham," Preeker corrected.

"—was a rich man. Good family, and all that. If he himself hadn't taken me aside and told me that he didn't have a penny, we never would have known it. Besides that, he was getting ready to marry this widow—he's done so since—with a couple million at least coming. He wasn't the sort to get into any blackmail trouble—not the type at all—and what in the world would he steal a fifty-thousand-dollar bauble for anyway, taking a chance of losing all those millions?"

"*Hmmmm.* Nevertheless. Ah! The son! That's it! The son got into some trouble that he couldn't tell his mother about. Some girl trouble! You know these Southern adolescents. The hot climate—"

"Behave," I said. "With the best intentions in the world, he couldn't have got any girl in trouble. He was twelve years old."

Preeker peered closer. "Oh. It looked like twenty-two here. Why don't you learn to write? I'll wire our broker there that you're coming."

"Nuts. I don't like that guy. He was a sap ever to write the policy in the first place without seeing that some locks were put on. Furthermore, he got under my feet all the time—"

"Nevertheless, my friend, he assumes twenty percent of the loss—that's our agreement with him—and if we deceived him, he might have grounds—"

I WENT to Messanah the day following, arriving the night after that.

The town was not far enough south to get into the you-all belt but it had chain gangs working on the roads. There was just enough of the rapidly fading light left at eight o'clock when I dropped off the Limited to show the end of one of those weary processions winding out of sight a half-mile away.

I was hoping that Preeker would at least have omitted to tell this Manson—that was the insurance broker concerned in the job—the exact time of my arrival. He was the son of one of the impoverished local aristocrats. For my dough, he only got by because of tapping the friends of his parents for business which they couldn't very well refuse. He was a lazy, pale-faced, dark-eyed good-for-nothing, about forty years old, and, as far as I was concerned, most of the help he had given me on my original investigation consisted of ogling Mrs. Munday, the widow, or any of her female servants that he could approach out of the lady's sight. I wanted a day—or at least an evening—to look around without having him trailing me.

Evidently, I was to have no such luck. As I started toward the row of ancient-looking hacks at the platform's edge, a thin, meek-voiced youngster with a chauffeur's cap over his eyes sidled up with what I guess he thought was smartness and stood at attention, speaking my name.

I stopped and growled, "Yeah?"

"Mr. Manson's compliments," he said. "He was unavoidably detained but he has made reservations for you at the Premier and will call you there within an hour."

I resigned myself and told the redcap to put my bags in the shiny black touring-car—not more than a year old it wasn't, either—and I climbed in beside the driver.

It had not been my intention to get in touch with the widow—Mrs. Munday. Or I should say, now, Mrs. Droodingham, since she had married the Englishman. This kind of tip was something that called for nosing about in the underworld—not in the upper crusts. And Messanah had an underworld—make no mistake about that. Sixty thousand people practically all making a living one way or another out of the world's leading soft-drink factory, and not more than a very few of them ever touched a soft drink—at least not after nightfall.

Nevertheless, when I walked up to the desk I was handed a key and a note. The note said that Mr. Manson had informed Mrs. Droodingham of my arrival and, as she presumed I wished to see her on whatever nonsense had brought me here, would I be so kind as to either call before ten or after twelve. Between those hours she would be away from home. She urged me, however, to do what I had to do that night, as they were all driving over to the state capital the following morning.

I could not figure what to do about that, so I let it lay while I was ushered into the elevator.

Getting off at my floor, I almost barged into a man waiting to go down. He was a fattish man, though he didn't look flabby. His big face had queer little ridges of flesh under the eyes, and he was as bald as a billiard ball.

I had seen him before. I could not think where, but I knew I had seen the face somewhere. I stood a moment after the elevator door had closed on him, wrinkling my forehead, but I could not remember where.

When I walked into my room I got a real shock.

The bellboy had turned on the light and was standing blinking at the bed. On my nice clean pillow there was a nickel-plated pistol.

I won't say that the pistol conveyed any exact meaning to me. It was not an underworld symbol like putting a nickel in a dead man's mouth or cutting out a man's tongue or that sort of thing. Nevertheless, I knew of a New York racketeer, seeking to engage a leading comedian for a stage production which the racketeer was backing, being refused because the comedian was tied up with Hollywood contracts. The racketeer's gun—nothing else—was mailed in a carton by return mail. The comedian arrived in three days, via plane.

The gun on my pillow, at any rate, didn't mean that anybody was particularly welcoming me to the city.

THE FACE of the baldheaded man popped into my mind. I left the stammering bellboy and turned and ran down the hall, dropped to the lobby in another elevator. The fat man was no longer in the lobby. I ran to the street but he was not in sight there either.

Coming eventually back to the elevator, I spotted a city detective that I knew—one, in fact, who had worked on the job originally with me. His name was Sands.

I went over and caught his arm, hastily exchanged greetings and described the fat man.

"I know the face but not the name," I said. "He just went through here—I thought maybe you might have seen him."

"I didn't, but I think you're talking about Albert Heflin. And you didn't see him but you might have seen his brother Tiny—they look alike. Albert just got out of Leavenworth a month ago, and his brother—Hey! Now I get it! Albert was in the gow the last time you were here. They're a scummy pair—cheap bootleggers, peddling policy slips, even I wouldn't be surprised, reefers—always in some dirty little racket. Though they're never big enough fish for the state's attorney to take seriously.

"Tiny was pinched—I remember well—the day after they discovered those jewels of Mr. Munday were heisted. You were down at the gow with us talking it over when somebody brought Tiny in for selling reefers. He's doing a bit right now at the county farm."

"What's his brother doing?"

"God knows. Hiring out to anybody that wants any piddling little rottenness done, I suppose. He's got a job as bartender out at Hart's Tavern—a cheap little roadside dump on the Missassauga Road. Why? Why are you—"

"I guess I made a mistake," I said. "Thanks for the dope."

He wanted to know what I was doing in town, so evidently news of my arrival had not spread all over the city. I stalled him off, promised to go stepping with him when I should find a free evening, and hurried back up to my room.

The bellhop was still standing there, running his finger inside his collar.

I gave him five and told him: "I'll be here three days or less. If I find you haven't opened your yap about this by the time I leave, there's another sawbuck in it."

WHEN HE had gone I examined the empty pistol. It was a cheap, nickeled, mail-order item, untraceable.

I began to get puzzled. It occurred to me that news of my coming might have leaked through Ike Klein back in New York. Presently, I called him up to bawl him out—also, maybe stumble onto some lead as to how the information would have leaked to these underworld scavengers.

I got more puzzled.

The man at the other end of Ike's phone turned out to be Simmons, a detective-sergeant of the headquarters squad in New York. He informed me that Ike Klein had disappeared. That his little jewelry shop had not opened for business this morning and that he was nowhere to be found. I scoffed that these Bowery joints did that all the time, but he said they had some sort of a tip that he was in trouble.

I hung up and took my own gun out of my suitcase, looked it over to see that it was in working order and stuck two spare clips in my side pocket. On second thought I took two more for my other pocket.

I sat down to think and sucked a cigarette. This wasn't right. The bauble of my company's client coming out on the market shouldn't, in the ordinary course of events, cause any such stirring and smoldering as there seemed to be here. What could....

My phone rang. A muffled voice—talking through a handkerchief—and I could just see the fat, bald-headed man behind it—said: "This is a friend. A certain party told me to tell you that if you went down to the docks at the river, at twelve midnight tonight, you'd find something you wanted very much."

The receiver clicked. I began to get irritated.

Obviously, something was coming off at midnight—something not at the docks by the muddy creek they call a river here. I looked at my watch. It showed nine o'clock.

I TRIED to irrigate my brain with a hooker of Scotch, but it would not irrigate. All I could be sure of was that too much activity was going on. My coming here in a simple effort to nose into—maybe recover—jewels insured by my company, should not have stirred up anything in particular—but it certainly smelled as though it had.

I tried to look up Hart's Tavern in the phone book but it was apparently so far on the outskirts of the little town that it was not listed. I decided I would have to seek information from the bell-captain and had my hand on the phone, when there was a tap on my door.

I opened it, to find Manson.

He was in white dinner jacket, black trousers, his sullen, pale, thin face irritated-looking. He had, he informed me, as though I were some sort of extremely boring form of lower life, come to take me to the Droodinghams'. He reminded me that their time was limited and since he thought it only courteous to conform to their wishes because they were after all not obliged to take any time for me, etc.

I had only one question that I wanted to ask the Droodinghams, but I could hardly do it over the phone, so I went with him.

The stately, Colonial house, set far back from the road in a mess of cypress, magnolia and honeysuckle, had the nostalgic look that anything familiar would have. The family—the three of them—were waiting under the portico on the porch when we got out. Mrs. Munday Droodingham looked a little—and not too little—like Queen Mary of England. She gave me a distant and faintly impatient nod, as though hoping I would come to my point as soon as possible and let them get on with their packing or whatever it was.

The boy, fourteen now, was bigger, but just as silent and big-eyed as ever. He stood against the wall, his dark eyes looking at me with calm intensity. The little bright-eyed Droodingham, about forty-five or fifty, short and chunky with a red face and thin sandy hair high on his red forehead, tried to do the honors. His mouth watered with perfectly meaningless British phrases.

I said: "I had no intention of troubling you all tonight, but since I have the chance I just want to ask you: have you had anybody approach you and ask if you wanted to buy back your Green-eyed Monster?"

They hadn't. They all looked at me with bright expectancy as though this was the prelude to something interesting. Unfortunately, I couldn't think of anything else, so I exchanged good-byes—their's rather baffled—and Manson drove me back downtown.

He started to say in a long drawl: "You know—the way I would go about this thing—"

"Yeah," I said, "I know. Tell me tomorrow," and climbed out in front of my hotel. "Good-night."

He sat looking after me with a faint scowl on his pale, dark forehead.

I went in and got my information as to the location of Hart's Tavern from the bell-captain. He gave me a kind of funny, pitying look for asking. I looked out a lobby window to be sure that Manson's blue car had pulled away. Then I found that there was a car-renting agency just down the street and started out of the hotel.

I was passing a narrow alley at the edge of the hotel when a dark figure lounging there, said: "Hey mister! You dropped something!"

I didn't *know* he said this, because, as luck would have it there was enough noise going on to drown out his actual words. They have a vicious siren in these towns that lets go whenever a prisoner gets loose on the chain gangs and this one had gone off at exactly the moment he tried to speak to me.

I turned back and shouted, "What?" saw his finger pointing at a black seal wallet on the sidewalk, and started to bend over for it before I got my wits about me.

I snatched at the gun in my pocket, but he swung faster than I had any idea he could and his blackjack got me along the jaw. I went to my knees, still unable to get the gun out and he whacked me again and I drew a blank.

I WOKE up to a dank smell of garbage. Fortunately, I have a head about two inches thicker than it should be. It's fooled a lot of people. If I hadn't wakened up when I did, I would have been thirty miles down the river where they dumped the tow's garbage. Yes—I was on a garbage scow, being slowly tugged down towards Eastfolk.

I sat up and started to raise hell. I was on one of a string of scows—about the third—and I was the only one on it. I yelled till I was blue in the face, but there was a wind in my face that blew it all back in my throat. I shot my gun—I still had it—and that got me nothing. Finally, I got mad and started aiming it at the tugboat that was pulling the scows.

I must have pegged something important, because it wasn't long before lights started coming back towards me and hoarse voices called on me to surrender. Three dark figures finally grouped in the stern of the scow ahead of me and pointed shotguns at me, demanding that I give myself up.

It would be just my luck to have a convict escape their damned road gang—the one the siren I had heard earlier was announcing—at this point, and they were positive it was me. It took me plenty hoarse shouting, sweating explanation, pleading, promising, to get them to realize that I was myself—and then they were disappointed. Seems the law pays all of twenty-five dollars for an escaped convict.

I played on that angle—the angle that they seemed interested in money. I finally—after plenty more argument—got them to agree to send me back in the scows' tender—a fishy-smelling motor launch that ran on two cylinders and just about broke the current.

It was while I was trying to urge this hopeless craft onward by straining my body that I thought to look at my watch—and I sweated plenty. It was five minutes after eleven.

It was twenty to twelve when we finally chug-chugged into the stringpiece of the pier and I paid off, started running up the pier toward a lone rack of taxis.

Five minutes took me to the rent-a-car place and two more fixed me up with a car.

Even after I was in it, I did not know where to go. All I knew was that I had to go some place—fast. Irrationally, I found my mind aiming at the Droodingham place—and I gave in. Don't ask me why—a weird hunch.

It was ten miles or more and for the first part traffic was thick. I sweated, cursed, while my heart climbed up and down my gullet a dozen times.

Then I was in the clear and sending the car over the road, my foot to the floorboards. My clock said eleven minutes to twelve.

I started sighting familiar landmarks soon and was less than a mile from the Droodinghams'. I suddenly remembered that their sprawling acres had a road running through them that was about as far behind the house as this main drive was in front. I almost ran past this side road in the pitch blackness, but finally got around into it on two skidding wheels, took a chance on cutting my lights down. I had to estimate about how far I was, but presently the long grass dropped away on either side of me and I swung my car into the road that ran beyond the house.

I stopped, almost immediately, was out in a hurry and hastening toward the house. I could see the sparkling lights of the mansion through the trees. I was no more than a couple of hundred yards away at the most.

I almost ran into the car that was parked forty feet ahead of where mine was.

The blackness was so intense that I was inches from it before I noticed it. I caught my breath, stopped.

I went around it like an Indian, breathed again when I saw there was no one in it. I felt the radiator and it was piping hot. I risked a squeeze of my flash and my eyes widened. The car was blue. It was Manson's, the insurance broker's.

While I was recovering from that shock, wondering why he, a friend of the family, would park furtively in this God-forsaken spot I heard the rustle ahead of me.

It was some one treading on a stick, and it jerked me upright. It was very close to the house, though I couldn't see a wisp of movement. That did not mean anything—it was black enough save where the light chinks came through, for an army to move invisibly.

I SLIPPED around the car and eased into the long grass, and then into the thick trees. I went forward, stopped—did it again—lashing my brain the while to try and make sense of this fantastic business.

Then I saw the glow.

It was the size of a pea, and it was on the ground, twenty yards ahead of me. I was now no more than forty yards from the house.

I went down on my hunkers, edged forward, gun ready, handkerchief-veiled flashlight ready.

I spurted faint gleam, caught my breath, leaped up, dived forward, sprayed light freely.

Manson, the pale-faced insurance broker lay on his back unmoving. Fresh blood was cascading down over his collar and shoulders from a wound in his neck. An ice pick had been driven up under his chin, driven up so that the haft was tight under his wattles and the point in his brain. He was still alive—but not for long.

I dived for the house. I saw Mrs. Droodingham in an upstairs window carrying dresses across my line of sight. And as I ran I looked along the upper story and saw the Englishman, also placidly folding clothes.

I was almost at the back door when the figure rushed away from the blackness in front of me.

I still was in pitch blackness, despite the lights in the upper part of the house, but this unseen man whisked away, not more than ten yards from me, went darting, racing through the trees. I whirled automatically, ready to shoot at him—but I could not see a thing. I danced on hot coals, finally felt a stone underfoot and snatched it up, let the blighted Englishman have it straight through his window.

He bellowed in surprise, came a little apprehensively to the window and I roared: "Manson is lying outside here stabbed—murdered. He's still alive. Get a doctor as fast as you can!" I heard him gasp and then I was off after the fugitive.

I raced straight for the road. I knew the man ahead of me was not going to run around in circles and that he would have to hit the road sooner or later. When I got gravel under my feet I stopped to listen.

Directly ahead I heard him run ten steps and stop. I flew back toward my car, skidded to a stop beside Manson's as I went by. I yanked open the door and switched on the headlights.

They were powerful and lighted up the road for a hundred yards ahead.

For just an instant, a racing figure was outlined ahead of me squarely in the middle of the road and the figure—fat, short, squat—was clad in the prison stripes of the chain gang!

I had run into the escaping convict! And so, apparently, had Manson. I fired instantly—but the convict had cat-footed off the road before I could wing him.

I started after him, then ran back instead and got my car. I sent it shooting forward, whirling around Manson's. From the corner of my eye as I shot away down the road, I saw lights coming from the main house, flashing, rolling around.

I slowed down, started idling my car along the road. I had no idea what kind of country this was, but I was sure now that the escaping convict was unarmed and that all I had to do was patrol the roads till the police cars started arriving and I would have him held here.

And then things started to happen. I suddenly got my numb brain to work and astoundingly figured out who the convict must be! Like the curtain going up on a play, the whole weird sequence suddenly dawned on me. Tiny Heflin's brother, Albert, the cheap gunman who had been arrested the day after the original robbery of the emerald skull! This then, was why his brother had been so anxious to get me out of the way! Tonight was the night of the big man's prison break! My presence in town, unexplained, had alarmed the brother and he had jittered around trying to put me out of the way, thinking I might have learned about—and be a menace to—the escape business!

But why was the escaped con in the grounds of the Droodinghams? And why had he knifed—or rather ice-picked—Manson?

Even as my flaming brain tried to fit this together I saw him again.

I CAME driving through what I thought were thick woods—and suddenly was between open fields on both sides. They opened in a fan-shaped fashion, V-ing out back of me, and I saw that the last fifty or sixty yards of trees that I had driven through were no longer forest, but only a thin line along the road.

Even as I stopped and looked back, I saw a flashlight glow and against its faint ground-light, spotted the fat body of my man going hell-bent away from me, up the slight rise of the field.

I was out like a flash—but so was his light. I started to shoot, held my fire, dived after him instead. In open field, he could not keep away from me for long.

I raced up the rise and then, to my astonishment, was suddenly at the top and standing on a long ridge.

The rise I had come up was ten times as long as the short drop on the other side. It fell straight down to a road, and even as I checked myself, an automobile came shooting along the road and I saw that it was a highway.

I could not see my fugitive. I did not need to see him. Sixty feet north and across the highway a red neon sign glowed over a ramshackle bar and grill. The neon sign said—*Hart's Tavern.*

I ran... and as I ran, I saw a figure break away from the roadside, almost to the few trees that surrounded the ramshackle shack. I fired once—and the figure was gone among the trees. I put on a burst of speed, raced across and found that I was diving for the side door of the tavern. I could see movement through the window, but I did not check myself.

I went in like a football player.

The face turned toward me, from behind the bar, was that of Albert Heflin. The back was that of his brother, Tiny, in stripes. There was not a soul in the bar but the two of them and I interrupted wild motion.

Albert, behind the bar, was whipping a gun from a drawer with one hand, jabbing a second at his brother's grasping fingers with the other. I saw a flash of something red on the bar—and then guns roared. Mine put a bullet through the fat bartender's left eye. His slug ticked my shoulder. I never could quite explain the incredible swiftness of this big lug.

I was slammed back against the screen door. It didn't stop me and I went head over heels through it, landed on my neck on the veranda. I shot at the ceiling through my flying heels, and at the door as I came down. I heard a groan, heard the bar mirror smash as I whirled myself frantically together, plunged—then leaped aside as two booming shots slammed lead at me.

For just an instant I hesitated. Then I heard racing feet and a front door slam.

I dived in again and took a split second to fling a quick look around.

I had killed the bartender. He lay, unmoving, half covered with popcorn, behind the bar, still bleeding from his gone eye. His gun was a foot from his hand. I hardly had eyes for him. I was looking at the item on the bar.

The mother-of-pearl skull, with one of its emerald eyes fallen out was standing on the red-flannel bag it was habitually kept in. I gurgled, snatched it up, brushed away the flakes of popcorn—one of my shots had exploded a bowl of it and it was everywhere—and flung myself on.

I did not have to go far this time. As I burst out the front door I heard my man crashing through bushes along the roadway and caught a faint sliver of light.

I set my teeth and went after him. Brushes raked and scratched my face, but these were only bushes, no trees. The light ahead grew stronger and I saw a frame shack, evidently a cottage for the operator of the grill. I heard no more crashing ahead when I stopped to listen—but I heard no door open either.

Both of us had come to a standstill, I decided. I crouched down trying to get my breath back, hastily stuffing the skull and the loosened eye into the red bag. I had what I had come for—but I never even thought of it in that moment. I wanted revenge for the crack on the head and the ride on the load of garbage—and I had to bring somebody in for the murder of a man right under my very nose.

I STARTED to inch forward. There was no sound from the man I was chasing and I suddenly wondered if I had hit him with one of my wild shots and he was quietly dying.

Then I was almost within arm's reach of the lighted cottage, but not, unfortunately, exactly opposite a window.

I didn't have to be.

A face suddenly appeared at the window and I almost strangled.

It was the sharp, twisted face of Ike Klein, the New York fence who had tipped me to the thing in the first place.

For just a second I simply could not figure it. And then it dawned on me. The dirty little rat had coolly and calmly used me to knock down the price on the hot article! He had been—my God!—I began to see the whole story now!

Tiny Heflin, in the clink, had arranged his break! But Tiny Heflin had had the Green-eyed Monster safely cached somewhere—cached where he and only he could lay his hands on it! He—through his brother—had started negotiations for a quick turnover, the instant he got out, to provide a getaway stake for him to flee the country!

And Ike Klein, the wily, insolent fence had deliberately turned on the heat, so that he could take it at his own price! The heat being me!

White-hot fury got my head—I admit it. I rose up in my wrath and charged for the house. If Tiny Heflin had been lying low with his gun he could have put a bullet through my foolish face like shooting fish—but he wasn't.

I dived at the door. I knew one little rat of a fence who was going to be beaten within an inch of his life right here and—

I kicked the door open and Ike Klein whirled to face me. He was not armed—he was not the type of criminal that chances being caught with a gun.

He turned three shades of green when he saw me. His Adam's apple bobbed up and down.

"Oh—uh—"

"I'm going to tear you up in little bits and make you eat—" I began.

An automobile started, hastily jammed, screeched into life fifty yards further down the road and my words stuck in my throat. I heard the car scream, in second gear, through brushes, bump out onto the road, roar away. The ex-con had not been ex—long enough to drive very well—but he could drive and he was away.

I groaned, half jumped after him. I remembered a phone back in Hart's Tavern and raced for it. I had to turn a handle and I turned it till it fell off. It took me—I swear—five minutes, to get the operator.

I roared for the traffic division of headquarters and railed at them: "Your escaped con is on the Missassauga road, driving a car toward town. He's within a mile of Hart's Tavern right now. Can you bottle him up?"

The voice laughed at me. "We got a flash coming in on the other wire now—he ran squarely into one of our own patrol cars, stripes and everything. Wait a minute—yeah, he was subdued without undue vio—"

"Bring him over to the Droodinghams' house at once," I begged them. "You don't know the half of this yet."

"Huh? What—"

"Murder!" I let him figure that out and flung away.

My head wasn't tracking very well or I wouldn't have run back to the cottage where the little fence had been. I don't know what I expected—maybe that he'd be sitting calmly in a chair waiting for his beating. He was gone, of course.

I didn't waste any worry about him. I would attend to him in New York. You think I wouldn't? That he'd duck out? Don't be silly. Little rats like him, with jewelry shops that could be bought for next to nothing admittedly sleeping in greasy blankets in unwashed, unventilated stinking Bowery rooms—and making just about the income of a top steel-company executive—are not going to run out of their soft spot just for fear of a beating. He'd be there all right when I went after him.

I RACED back over the ridge I had covered. I was spinning in the head as I realized the mad way this whole thing was shaping up. And I knew the toughest part was still ahead of me.

Tiny Heflin—this was the ironical part of it—stealing the bauble under my arm—and then being arrested and thrown into pokey the next day *for something else!* What a crazy sequence of circumstances—but even then, I knew that it would not be as crazy as the one ahead of me. I raked my brain, trying to jockey up the solution of the still untold mystery—and then finally it dawned on me.

I caught my breath as I saw the whole incredible picture—and then I was running across the road, while police cars were arriving by the dozen, it seemed.

There was a huge searchlight focused from the side of the house making a weird circle in the clearing where Manson lay. A score of people were standing around. I burst into the circle along with three cops, just as a doctor got up from one knee and said: "He's quite dead."

And then a siren screamed on the road—a siren that evidently was unexpected by the cops around me, for they all turned and looked surprised.

I said to the world at large: "That would be Tiny Heflin, your ex-con. I asked Traffic to get him and bring him here."

Some big lieutenant barked, "What? Who are you?" and somebody told him in an undertone. Then he said in a more conciliatory voice: "Well, what the hell? Was it Heflin that did this?"

"I chased him from here within minutes of the time it was done," I said.

"Oh!" They turned and started down the hill.

"Wait a minute," I warned them. "Have them bring him here."

Then Tiny Heflin was standing there, surrounded by cops, breathing hard, a huge apelike figure in his stripes, blood and hair all over his face.

Droodingham's hoarse voice suddenly said to his wife: "My dear, you must go inside."

I said: "By all means, but I'll need some help from you, Mr. D."

He said he would be right back, and I started answering questions. "Sure. Tiny stole this jigger a year and a half ago. He hid it somewhere, till he could find a market—and then was suddenly squeezed for something else in the meantime.

"Tonight, when he made his break, he had it all planned with his brother—" I went on to explain about the New York fence that was involved and his being on hand to supply cash in exchange for the skull instantly. "So that Tiny could get away—probably by motor," I finished.

"Why did he kill Mr. Manson?" one of them snarled.

"Mr. Manson was a blackmailer."

"What?"

"It doesn't figure out any other way," I assured them. "Mr. Manson must have gotten wind of the truth on the original robbery. I can see now that he did—he certainly got in my way enough and messed things up for me when I was investigating. He got hold of the truth—and he didn't fool. He waited his time—planning to shake the criminal down for the whole boodle—when the time was ripe."

"What the hell you—" Tiny roared suddenly and went down cursing as two police fists smashed into his mouth.

"Keep quiet while the gentleman's talking," one of them said. The worried Droodingham came hurrying back.

A COPPER did not let me get away from my main story. "Just how did Manson know that Tiny would come here?" he wanted to know. "Wait—you mean the loot was cached right on the property? And Manson knew about the crush-out and was waiting... Hey, what the hell! If he knew where the cache was, why didn't he take the thing himself instead of waiting to squeeze it out of Heflin?"

"Don't run off at the mouth," I advised him. "The stuff wasn't cached here—or maybe it was, I don't know. But—Heflin didn't come here to dig it up."

"What for then?"

"Because this slippery fence from New York had driven the price down so far that Tiny was desperate. He was so desperate that he was willing to take a chance and try and sell it back to the original owners. The poor lug came here to try and see if he could strike a deal with the owners—not knowing any better, having never touched anything with more than thirty cents in it in his life.

"And right there is the nub of the whole thing. How in God's name would a cheap crook like Tiny have the imagination—"

"Hey!" the forgetful big man in stripes roared, and went down again.

"—to cook up a robbery as big as this?" I asked. "Answer—he wouldn't. He was hired to do it—but immediately it was done, the person who hired him regretted it and told him to keep his mouth shut and keep the thing."

"What?" they yelled.

"Sure," I said. "Manson was here to blackmail the party behind Tiny—not Tiny himself. It was neat justice that Tiny wound up on the same spot, at the same time—or almost at the same time—as the original party paid off

Manson in the one coin that always settles blackmailers—four inches of steel."

"Who? Who is the... they chimed. I guess this was the town force's glee club, they worked so well together.

"Who? Why—think it over. Or no—I guess you don't really have enough information. You see—a certain party came here to marry Mrs. Munday. At the time I was here, he didn't think he was going to win out. He'd blown every dime, trying to make the grade and he was desperate because he thought she wouldn't give. So he fixed up this little plan—had the skull stolen, while they were all off on a three-day jaunt to Churchill Downs—and in that time found out that he'd doped the situation wrong—that Mrs. Munday *was* going to marry him.

"What could he do? When he got back to town, the thug he'd hired was already in the can for something else. He got word to him to forget the whole thing. Naturally, he didn't want—"

I whirled around to where Droodingham was standing—only he wasn't there any more.

I saw him then, diving into one of the police cars, far down the road. I yelled, "There he goes—" and pointed him out with my pistol. I wasn't really aiming. Trying to shoot down a slant at a shadowy figure moving at full speed, in the almost pitch-dark, is about as silly a proceeding as I know of. But I gave the trigger a touch anyway.

Flame spurted—and Droodingham screamed, fell straight over backwards into the road and lay there.

I said in a bored voice: "He's all yours, gentlemen. Excuse me while I phone an alarm for a certain rat in New York. I want to have a nice reception committee ready when he gets home."

THE JUDAS TOUCH

THERE WAS A KING NAMED MIDAS ONCE, AND EVERYTHING HE TOUCHED TURNED INTO GOLD. DANIELS DAHL WAS A KING TOO, AFTER HIS OWN FASHION, AND HE MADE PLENTY OF GILT WHERE NONE HAD GROWN BEFORE. BUT THOSE ON WHOM HE LAID HIS BLACKMAILING HANDS TURNED CROOKED THEMSELVES BEFORE HE'D FINISHED WITH THEM. HE'D ADDED A JUDAS TOUCH TO THE MIDAS TAINT—AND THE GOLD THAT POURED FORTH WAS CRIMSON—FOR HE BLED HIS VICTIMS WHITE, EVEN AFTER DEATH.

CHAPTER ONE
MURDER AT THE
MONTFALCON

IT GAVE Broadway a wallop—but hardly a surprise.
It had been cooking for a long time. And something
pretty spectacular was always expected of Daniels Dahl.
Reports of the incident began to leak out just as the night
spots were filling for supper. They rippled up and down the
section and everybody seemed to know all about it, within
minutes. Folks celebrating after the theater had it served,
piping hot, with their first drink.

I got it that way myself.

A hack driver, it seemed, had set Daniels Dahl down
in the Grand Central zone, a half-block from the Hotel
Montfalcon, at twenty minutes to eleven.

The fat little gossip-columnist was freshly barbered,
scented, manicured, the ends of his tiny black-gray
mustache carefully waxed. He was carrying a black walk-
ing-stick and gray gloves and was, apparently, making a
half-hearted effort to escape recognition—keeping the
collar of his gray topcoat up around his chin, his rakish soft
gray hat pulled low. This did not confuse the hacker. He
was a Broadway veteran and perfectly familiar with Dahl's
fat little egg-shaped body, his sharp pink nose, his pinpoint,
greedy little pale-blue eyes and boneless pink hands.

Moreover, after he had set him down, the hacker took
time to watch him walk. There was light—a cold moon,

almost full, rising low in the sky, flooding the bare street with blue glow. It was impossible to mistake Dahl's gait and certainly no one could imitate that knock-kneed, wobbling little trudge. The hacker sat watching—after the scandal-writer had thrust a bill at him with a high-pitched "Keep change," and set off—watched him cover the few rods to the niche-like little side entrance of the Montfalcon. He watched until the fat little gnome had scampered up the stone steps, pushed through the revolving door and into the side corridor of the hotel.

No one, apparently, noticed Dahl in the long corridor as he walked down it, to the main lobby, but he was spotted by the headwaiter of the Sunset Room as he sailed out into the open.

This was the famous Victorian lobby—New York's latest and gaudiest. It was vast, the winking green lights of the service desks set far back from the main entrance, leaving an acre of cream tile dotted with maroon carpets—huge ones, but looking like so many scatter-rugs—holding cozily grouped lounges. Fat-bellied cream pillars rose from lobby level, towered three stories up, to be lost above the brilliance of the gigantic crystal chandelier.

The Sunset Room's arched entrance was close to the staircase that led up to the mezzanines and Dahl, after a glance at his watch, slowed a bit, but came straight toward the headwaiter—and those stairs. He glanced up, at the two mezzanines girdling the vast walls, one above the other. Quiet, dim retreats, lined with luxurious lounges, reading lamps, little rows of writing desks, phone booths, darkened shops—these on the lower balcony only. The lower mezzanine was practically deserted at this hour—the top one completely, on the word of the house detective who

The creeper skidded across
the floor and my feet went
out from under me.

was coming down from there at about the same moment
Dahl neared the foot of the dim, carpeted stairs.

The Sunset Room's headwaiter assumed a quick smile
of greeting and stepped forward as Dahl came abreast—
but got only a cold-eyed stare as the little fat man waddled
hastily up the dim stairs, vanished.

He passed the house detective at the turn of the stairs
on the lower mezzanine. The sleuth, oddly enough, did
not know Dahl by sight, but he gave him a careful, inclu-
sive look.

When the house detective reached the lobby level, the headwaiter was still standing there, fingering his chin. The gumshoe asked, "Who's the fat little lug?" and the headwaiter told him.

Up till that point, there could be no mistake as to the man above being Dahl.

Concerned with tempting Dahl in to witness—and possibly blurb in his column—the new floor show, the miffed head-waiter watched thoughtfully. He saw Dahl reach the top mezzanine. He watched him bob his way around two sides, part of a third, finally come to rest at a point directly opposite and, of course, high above, where the headwaiter was standing. A queer trick of refraction—a blinding beam of light evidently trapped by one of the chandelier's crystals—made a blazing yellow spot against the gold scrollwork of the railing behind which Dahl was a dim, motionless head and shoulders.

A FLURRY of activity—a few parties arriving, a few departing—occupied the headwaiter for maybe ten minutes, but when he looked again, Dahl was still there, though in a different position. He was leaning over the railing now, as though striving to see something far below.

The headwaiter got his first intimation that something was wrong when Dahl's hat fell off and the columnist seemed utterly oblivious of his loss.

Peering in sudden concern, the headwaiter caught his breath. Dahl slumped a little—just enough to bring his face into the blazing yellow spot of light—and it became apparent that his eyes were not open.

Then everything happened in seconds yet, seemingly, with stunning, heart-squeezing deliberation.

Dahl's head and shoulders seemed to be worming, slowly, further and further over the rail. Bald, he looked for all the world like a fat, pink slug. Then suddenly he was far enough over to slump, jackknifing at the waist—and his eyes popped open. It was as though he had been touched by an electric wire. His head came up, whipped queerly from side to side—and his scream knifed through the lobby. He tried frantically to lash around, clutching at air, frenziedly grabbing for the rail. Then his legs suddenly flew up behind him—flew higher than his head—and he was like a huge, screaming frog.

He screeched—again and again—as he pitched over. He was a clawing, flailing madman, pink hands grabbing crazily at the scrollwork. One hand caught and for a heart-beat it looked as though it might hold him. Instead it somersaulted him and his whirling body, jerked too hard, whipped his hand away.

There was a macabre instant when it seemed that he was suspended, clawing, shrieking, in mid-air—then he plunged, straight down, a hundred and fifty feet, a writhing, clawing, plummet. The frantic watchers below got one ghastly flash of his terror-distorted face, mouth wide open, screaming, eyes mad—then he flung his arms over his head and struck.

It was an explosion. His head seemed to go right into the cracking tile. His head, arms and neck were utterly destroyed. And as if that were not enough to complete the horror, his fat little legs, protruding from the mess, shook and shook and kept on shaking, as though animate of themselves.

A veteran police inspector, off-duty, raced out of the Men's Bar, collided with the green-faced house detective as both fought through the panic-stricken mob to reach the thing.

The inspector gasped, "My God, do you—who is it?" and the house detective told him. Then, presently, they checked back to make sure and eliminated all doubt that it was Daniels Dahl. This was the only way they could get positive identification for there was nothing in the sopping pile of wet cloth and flesh that could help.

IT WAS ominous sensation, of course—that Dahl was dead, regardless of how it had happened. Nearly everyone knew him for a vicious little blackmailer—even I, and my work keeps me mostly outside of New York. And blackmailers, dying, sometimes leave behind them more than footprints on the sands of time.

When it was first revealed that he had not fallen accidentally, the sensation stepped up. That came with the discovery of Dahl's stick and glasses on the balcony. Beside the stick was Dahl's wallet, empty, rifled, and a short piece of lead pipe.

Under the stick was a note. It was printed crudely, in green ink, on hotel stationery.

> I am either going to get my papers back, or silence every mouth that can harm me. If you want a taste of this, just refuse me—as he did.
>
> Green

There was no mystery about the way the killer had accomplished his crime. Lieutenant Drinkwater, pink-eyed dapper ace of the Homicide Squad, gave the official version in a bulletin, fifteen minutes after his arrival at the scene.

"The killer—this Green—hid in one of those darkened phone booths back of where Dahl was standing. The house detective had no reason to inspect those booths—and the killer knew that—also knew that Dahl was coming here. He stepped out and slugged Dahl unconscious. While Dahl lay on the floor, he went through his wallet, evidently failed to get what he was seeking, coolly and deliberately penned that note, then—loaded Dahl over.

"I hold no brief for Dahl, but any killer vicious enough to carry out this murder should not be at large, etc....

"To the person or persons who understand the import of the note—who fear the threat of death made by this Green—please get in touch with us immediately, for your own protection."

I was just taking a short one in the bar of the Club Ostend, on upper Broadway, when all this came in, via the radio loudspeaker, hushing the packed night club to intent, interested—and for all I knew, frightened—silence.

Then the sea of clamor closed in again and I sampled my drink. I was mildly curious about who had murdered the columnist but only mildly. My object at the moment was a little well earned relaxation and I had no slightest intention of having anything to do with the muddle. I did not even know that Dahl was a policy-holder in the Acme.

That is, I didn't until after the phone call pulled me away from the bar.

CHAPTER TWO
I PROMISE A KILLER

FIFTEEN MINUTES after that—one hour exactly from the moment that Dahl was pitched to his death—I stood facing the gun in the hand of the trembling blond girl.

I stood in the hall of a cheap, furnished-apartment establishment in the West Seventies. The girl had the door open on a chain while her desperate, long-lashed blue eyes raced over me, the .25 automatic steady on the belt of my topcoat. She was lusciously rounded, her skin transparent pink, mouth a ripe cherry color and not stingy. She was all in black—black caracul bolero over black jersey and pleated skirt, black silk stockings and ties—but those curves would have showed through a coffin.

Her frightened, tense eyes examined me so long that I asked politely: "Am I saving my company a hundred thousand dollars by just standing here, miss? Or did you have something else in mind?"

She glanced up, caught her breath and closed the door. I heard her fumble with the chain then. After a moment, her choked, frightened voice told me to come in.

I did and was in a sleazy apartment. She had retreated behind a wicker table that bore the only light in the room—a table lamp. She was just a dim face beside it, her gun now lying on the table. She swallowed twice and urged me to close the door.

I did so. There was a moment when we stood looking at each other—then she tumbled words. "You—you've heard about Daniels Dahl, the columnist—his being killed?"

I said I had.

"About the—the note that the murderer left? About this Green—and his threatening to kill someone else?"

"Yeah," I admitted. "I heard about that."

"It's me—I. I'm the one he's going to kill."

I stared.

She gulped some of the huskiness out of her throat and repeated it.

I eyed her sharply, but she meant it. I let out breath and asked: "Who are you? Why would this Green…?"

"I'm Doris Zimmerman. I'm—I was— Daniels Dahl's secretary."

"Why would—wait a minute. You know Dahl's dealings with this Green? Know why he killed Dahl?"

She came out from the shadows, a step at a time, shivering with clenched hands. "No, no! I never even heard the name Green until tonight! But he thinks I do—thinks I have what he wants. He—he phoned me, forty minutes ago—five minutes after he'd killed Dahl. I didn't even know Dahl was dead—much less about the note. He—on the phone—he demanded that I have some papers at his hotel before dawn tomorrow—or I'd join Dahl. I didn't know what he was talking about. I thought he was a crank and hung up on him.

"Twenty minutes later I heard about Dahl's death—and the note—and I understood. I ran to this hole to hide— and I've been trying desperately to reach you ever since."

"Me? My God, lady, why me?"

"Because I know about you—know you're Acme's most dependable investigator. I know you can find this murderer—and I've got to see him—got to talk to him— before the police get him! I've got to!"

"Why?"

"I—" Her hollow eyes ran away from mine. Her body was so close now I could feel its warmth, feel her shiver. Her voice was husky, gulping. "Unless I see him—he may say something—may make it seem that I—" She suddenly put tiny hands over her cheeks and blurted desperately: "Oh, please—I can't tell you—you wouldn't want to know! Just—just do it for me—let me see him—talk to him—

before you take him to prison. Just for a minute! If you will, I'll do anything—anything—"

SHE HAD me half-hypnotized, even by then, but I tried to explain. "You've got this wrong, lady. I can't—"

"How? How have I got it wrong? I swear—"

"I mean about me. I couldn't do anything."

"Oh, what are you talking about? I know you've solved—"

"Nothing like this. I'm just a country boy. New York's tough enough at any time, for me. Now, it's too hot. Even without figuring, I don't have to be told that Dahl had a lot of victims. They'll be going crazy tonight—wondering where the dirt is that he held over them. Some of them may go crazy enough to do something about it. Then, every money-hungry cop on the force, half the private detectives in town, all the newspaper reporters, will be thinking what *they* could cash in for, if *they* had that stuff. They'll all be deadly, with that fortune at stake—and the best brains on the force aren't dumb. They'd freeze an insurance dick out—never let me near a lead—and if I got too numerous, I'd probably get a bullet in the head. With a potential fortune loose, and me without even an excuse to put my nose—"

"But you have? You have! Dahl was insured with—"

"The Acme doesn't send investigators to cover murders as thoroughly covered as this one. Dahl's dead and they'll have to pay anyhow. What can they gain by having the killer caught?"

"Oh, I told you! I told you! If you prove that the beneficiary of his policy killed him—if you get him convicted—you don't have to pay! Ruth Snyder—"

I blinked. "You didn't tell me that. Who is this beneficiary?"

"His nephew, Armand Saltis."

"You think he killed Dahl? That he's the one behind the name Green?"

"Yes, yes!"

"He killed for the insurance?"

"No, no! He doesn't even know about it. It's payable to the estate but Dahl has no will. Saltis gets it all because he's the only living relative."

"Then why—"

"I don't know! I don't know! But I know he did it. They were always doing things together—underhanded things. Saltis works in a bank—the Park Avenue branch of the Security National. He never came near the office—I heard Dahl warn him not to—but he used to phone often. He'd tell Dahl people's names and mention big sums of money.

"Then last night—about five—Dahl called him and told him to meet him on Long Island. Something about an 'eighty-thousand-dollar item.' Dahl told him that if everything worked for the next twenty-four hours, his— Saltis'—troubles would be over."

"You don't know where on Long Island?"

"Yes, yes, I'm coming to that. Talbotville. As soon as he had hung up on Saltis, Dahl called the Penn Station and asked about trains to Talbotville. There weren't any so he called his garage and told them to fill up his green convertible and send it down. Then—then he took a gun from his desk and went out... Wait! Let me finish!

"I didn't hear from him last evening—not till two in the morning. He called me at home to say he wouldn't be in today and to use one of the spare columns from the files. Then—today at three in the afternoon—Saltis called me!"

"What about?"

"To tell me to have Dahl call him—and call him right away if he didn't want trouble. He was wild. Don't you see? They went out together on some crooked deal last night. Dahl tricked him some way. Saltis was looking for Dahl all day—and finally found him at night. My God—isn't it obvious?"

I TOOK a long minute to think it over. "Not obvious— but interesting. Where would I get hold of Saltis?"

"I—I don't know. I've been trying his boarding-house the last hour—but he isn't there."

"Where else would he be?"

"I don't know."

There was a second of silence.

"This started all right," I said. "But what do I do? You suspect this bird. We don't know where to find him. We don't know his business with Dahl. Above all, if he knew nothing about the insurance, we haven't any motive whatever to connect him with killing Dahl."

"Oh, but you will have—if you look in Talbotville. It's not far out—thirty miles. It's a tiny place. Dahl and his car would have been conspicuous. You could trace what he was doing—and if Saltis was with him—get an inkling of their business together."

"It's all pretty thin!"

"No! No! Not for you. Track down what they did there last night, and you'll know why Dahl was killed tonight. Oh, can't you see? Nobody knows this but you. Everybody else will be running around, looking everywhere else—while you hurry out there and sift out the real truth. You—you'll save your company money, help your own standing—and you'll save me from nightmare! I—please believe me—bringing him to me first won't hurt anything.

Nobody need ever know it, and I—" She swallowed and her eyes drove with desperate torment into mine. "I—I'll make you glad you did—afterward. I promise it."

She put her clasped hands out. Damn it, she was almost praying to me.

I felt my ears burning. I avoided her eyes—and caught myself looking at the gorgeous rest of her—which was worse.

I growled: "I'd rather get my hands on that Saltis. You don't know anywhere else I might find him?"

She hesitated just a minute, racing thought lighting the shadow of her long-lashed eyes. "I—no."

"Don't stall—if you have any ideas—for God's sake!"

"I—Dahl had a little secret apartment in a tenement house on Second Avenue, just around the corner from the Sentinel Building."

"What would Saltis be doing there? Did he know about it?"

"I—I don't know. I don't know who knew about it. I followed Dahl there one day, but I didn't dare look inside."

"Anywhere else?"

"No. But you could look at that Second Avenue place. It's on the way to the bridge."

I said, "Maybe," and hesitated. I looked around the room. "If I do give this a whirl, I've got to know where you are, every minute. You won't be safe here."

"Oh, I will, I will! Nobody knows I came here. It's the one place I would be safe—even if he wanted to carry out that threat." She looked quickly over her shoulder, retreated hastily and picked up her little gun. "Please—oh, please don't worry."

I looked at the miniature automatic. "That thing won't help you." I took my own .38 Police Positive and put it on the table, held out my hand. "In case anybody should come, take that in both hands and blast. I doubt if you'll need it—but if you do, take no chances."

She cried out: "You—you will do it? You will bring him—"

"I'll see what I can do—if anything," I grumbled, and for a second I looked squarely into the deepness of her blue eyes. I won't deny I went wilty inside. She looked so damn young! I caught myself thinking, "The price is certainly right," and she must have guessed my thought for she went crimson and her eyes fell.

I SET my jaw, looked round for the phone, stepped over and scribbled down the number. I growled: "All right— I'll give Long Island a try. Give me that Second Avenue address—though I can't figure it as important. Whatever I have to do I'll have to do fast. Cops are digging at his apartment and his office and they'll catch up to all this before long. You'll—are you damned sure you're safe here?"

"Yes, yes. I'll be right here when you want me—" I don't think that was what she meant to say, exactly. She suddenly wrung her hands, blurted: "Oh, go—please go! I'll be absolutely all right! Truly I will—you needn't worry!"

The thought crossed my mind that I was playing the sap for a girl—and I hesitated at the door, frowning. Yet it wasn't so. Damn it, if this Saltis had killed Dahl—it was pointedly my job to nail it down. Sparkling blue eyes, soft white skin and all the rest did not change that. And I could see no harm in letting the girl see the murderer before I turned him in—assuming that I ever did get to turn anyone in. It was a sweet chance to make a good score. If I could jump in, skirt the fringes of the ugly little mess and really find something out on Long Island, I might turn the trick like falling off a log. Anyway, I could see no way that I could get into trouble.

How wrong *that* was!

I said, "All right—but take care of yourself," and stepped around the door, closing it behind me.

I turned to go down the hall and—as simply as that—I was up to my neck in trouble.

A tall, thick-shouldered dark guy was talking to a bony, bleached blonde of indeterminate age in an apartment door two doors away. He was Shiverstein, first-grade headquarters dick, brother of a Bronx district leader, a smart, deadly cop who would have been a captain if he could have kept his hands off people. His head turned over his shoulder and his black eyes, under heavy black brows pierced me. His craggy, swart face took on a pleased look. He told the crone in the apartment door: "Never mind. Close your door."

I quickly reopened the door behind me and said into the crack, "Put the chain on this door quickly, Harry," and closed it again.

Shiverstein's dark eyes jumped as he strolled toward me. He hunched his shoulders to slide his big, broken hands into his pockets.

"*Mmmm-m-m-m,*" he said. "I traced her to one of these three buildings but I couldn't quite spot—" He stopped as the chain was shot home behind me.

I gave him a fishy stare and said, "Who?" dully, but my noggin was racing—mostly around in a circle, I must admit. Any other cop and it might have been different. This one—no. I'd even heard that his beating up folks had a touch of the psychopathic—and I went rock-hard in my decision that he was not going to get his hands on the frightened little blond kid—particularly not in a secluded apartment. I got ready to go as far as necessary.

"Doris Zimmerman," he told me rapidly. "Secretary to Daniels Dahl—little blond piece you could eat with a spoon. She ran out before the boys could question her and she's a material—"

I pursed my lips deprecatingly and shook my head again. "You got a bum steer, friend. She isn't—"

I hadn't considered the full extent of his driving determination. His sleepy manner had taken me in. I should have been on guard. He was a dollar-hungry type if ever anyone was. A chance at a fortune's worth of shady information—Dahl's—would drive him nuts.

IT HAD. Fortunately, it had shaded his discretion just a little. His left fist suddenly whipped out of his pocket, whistled at my head in a vicious hook. But he was a bruiser, not a fighter. He wasn't close enough for that tactic. Unprepared as I was, I still had time to poke him a good straight right in the mouth that snapped his head back.

Then I *was* sunk. Damning the frantic luck that had forced this on me, I had to go through with it—or let him get a hand to his gun. He did make a stretch for it as he staggered back. I jumped after him, feinted at his ear and he jerked his arm up to guard it, trying hastily to back away from me, his face turgid, his dirty teeth showing. I went after him, my heart in my mouth, pounding lefts and rights around his head to keep his hands up.

He let loose a vicious left suddenly, out of his crouch, that caught me on the breast-bone and damned near cut off my breathing, but I dared not give ground. I pounded in and in, till he had his arms fairly up over his face. Then I gambled everything on dropping down and pumping two straight ones with all I had, into his mid-section. I jumped back as he doubled over gasping, let him have my knee on the jaw-point so hard that my leg ached. I knocked him backwards in a semi-circle and he crashed on his back on the floor, woozy, his knees doubled up. I dived for him, lit with my knees on his chest and yanked the gun from his hip.

It had taken just about two seconds—the whole rumpus. I heard doors clicking down the hall and roared, "Get back inside or I'll shoot your ears off," and no doors came open.

I jumped up and swung back to the girl's door. Her frightened face peeped at me through a crack. I snapped "Open up—quickly!"

I dragged the groaning, half-conscious copper in by the heels, dropped him on the floor as she closed the door hastily behind us. I had to run back for his hat and mine, but no one saw me.

"Oh, my God!" she gasped. "What—who is it?"

"Get your stuff—every scrap of it," I told her, "and beat it down to my coupé—a maroon Buick—in front of the building."

She tried to argue but I roared "Get out—or I'll throw you in jail!"

When she was gone, I squatted down beside the groaning copper, trying desperately to think of some way to make my peace with him.

There wasn't any way. I was cooked—unless I murdered him, which, I assure you, is out of my line. I racked my brain, trying to put together some sort of proposition—but I had nothing to sell. I had to fabricate something.

Some of the agony went out of his face, though he was still holding his belly, doubled up. His black eyes shone into mine with pure, distilled hate.

I said carelessly, "My boss isn't going to like your taking a poke at me for no reason. Think your pull is as strong as the Acme Life?" and cursed the feebleness of the bluff even as I said it.

He might not have heard it. He told me in a hoarse, pain-wracked whisper, very distinctly: "You pulled this the one time it counts, gumshoe. I'm after captain's bars on this job. If you've made me miss out—I'm going to kill you, by hand."

"Yeah?" I tried to pretend I wasn't scared. "When? Now?"

He said nothing, but his labored breathing was like steam. I had visions of myself in a precinct-house back room, in a cellar.

I DIDN'T know what to do, except that I had to rescue myself somehow, here and now—or face disaster. I got up, mopping my skinned knuckles, my brain churning. I grasped desperately at one straw that I thought of. "Socking folks got you into plenty of trouble up to now. I mind a couple of newspaper reporters you put the slug on once. I guess I'll give them a break."

I suddenly dropped on him again, swarmed all over him, ripping, tearing, dodging his flying feet, his feebly clutching hands. Cloth ripped—and I got up, with his ripped-off trousers in one hand and his badge in the other. His shorts—mauve—were a gorgeous thing around his thick, hairy legs.

"Pants, gun and badge," I said. "That ought to give the boys at the *Sentinel* a thrill when they get them by special messenger in about an hour. *Maybe* it won't get you laughed out of that captaincy." I hesitated. "Or do you want to try to talk me out of it?"

He simply eyed me with that shining, vicious fury—and I realized desperately that this was not enough. I almost realized that nothing was going to be enough—that I was done for, no matter what, the minute I walked out of this room.

He was whispering again, through clenched teeth: "Have all the fun you can, gumshoe—before we catch up to you." There was almost gloating in his eyes. "I've got you dead to rights. If you didn't kill Dahl, you're an accomplice. If you're not an accomplice, you've still interfered with me—probably ruined my case."

I half-laughed. "Think you can prove it?"

He didn't even answer. His dirty teeth showed. I knew what he meant—that he didn't have to prove it. All he needed was an excuse to set the humming police machine on me—an excuse to get me picked up. And he certainly had it. I wondered hollowly just how long I would last, after I was once picked up—and I came as close to panic as I'll ever come.

I tried as long as I could to hold back the words that crowded up to my tongue. I knew—as well as you—how thin my chances of making out on them were—yet it was the only thing left—the only possible bluff that might hold him off. I walked over to the telephone, ripped it out by the roots.

I rolled his gun and badge up in his trousers and stuck them under my arm, stood over him, said carelessly: "You'll never get me in charge on this case, brother. I know who killed Dahl. I'm on my way to get him. Send out all the alarms you want. I'll still have him in tow before any of your cops can get to me—along with the whole story, which will make a monkey out of any frame you try to rig." I walked to the door.

Then I stopped, as if I had just thought of it. I walked back and looked down at him with thin eyes. "Does the pinch really mean bars to you? Wait a minute." I frowned, simulating a long minute of deep thought. "Yeah. Yeah, you could make a little trouble for me at that. I'll make you a proposition. I don't want any trouble with you guys right now—for certain reasons—you haven't the faintest idea what they are, so don't bother trying to figure it. I'll tell you what I'll do.

"I'll forget the sock you took at me, and I'll give you back your stuff—and I'll let you have the pinch. That's assuming you don't go around shooting off your mouth about this rumpus, or putting out any alarms for me. I'll call your office when I'm ready to hand the killer over to you and you can play the big shot."

My heart was sinking dizzily. It sounded sickly weak to me. I couldn't tell how it sounded to him. His black eyes did not change. Yet—whether it was getting over or not—I was all out. There was nothing more I could offer him. I tried to keep up my pose of nonchalance as I sauntered to the door. "And if you don't like that—you can go to hell."

I reached for the knob. His voice came back, hollow and grim from the floor. "I'll give you three hours, gumshoe—since you already know the killer."

I nodded casually. It was the only thing to do.

CHAPTER THREE
A GIRL NAMED GEORGIA

OUTSIDE, **I** raced down the stairs silently. If ever a man talked himself onto a hot spot, I had done it, and I was crawling inwardly—yet what else could I have done? I knew, as well as anyone, how pitifully thin my chances were of catching Dahl's murderer in the next three hours—but at least I'd chiseled myself three hours. And there would not have been three minutes of safety for me, had I not run the bluff—had I not held out to Shiverstein the chance of the pinch. Not that I was sure, even now, that he would lay off me for three hours. He might—or I might be grabbed by the first copper that saw me. But there was no use worrying about that.

I had gambled the works on being able to produce the killer within three hours. If I did—I was safe and my own company would back me against any frame. If I didn't—I was on my own. There was absolutely nothing to do but bend every effort to make good my bluff.

The girl was shivering, white-faced, in one corner of my car, as I piled in. I sent us shooting away, heading uptown, before she found her voice.

"Who—who was it?" she choked. "Was it—Green?"

"No, just a cop. Don't worry—he may think you were in that room but he doesn't know it. You were out before he could see much."

She almost sobbed in fear. "How—oh, what did you do to him? What are you going to do with me?"

"You are going to a nice hotel and register under a phony name—and sit there till you hear from me."

"The policeman. What did you do?"

"We struck a bargain," I told her. "Forget him."

I dropped her at a Broadway hotel where I knew the night manager, and put what safeguards I could around her.

I TOOK a minute to think, sitting in front of the hotel with my motor purring, my hand on the gearshift. There wasn't much thinking to do. Talbotville—and nothing else—seemed my one hope. I winced as I realized the time it would eat to go there but I had no alternative. I let the car roll, gunned it crosstown, headed for the bridge.

The Second Avenue hide-away of Dahl's I dismissed in my mind as unimportant. It sounded all right, but, somehow, I could not imagine the slippery little gossip-monger hiding anything of importance—I meant his collection of dirt of course, there. Nor could I imagine his killer sitting in that hide-away, waiting for the police to come and find him. Then, too, the police had probably located the place by now. Even if I could count on Shiverstein's holding his hand, the cops were poison for me. I wanted no part of them.

I decided to stop and phone Preeker, my boss. Running around in the night, trying to nudge cops out of a rich haul, was dangerous enough at any time. Doing it without any official assignment was asking for trouble.

I knew about what he would say and I was not wrong. His soft, purring voice was made for what he handed me. "It was a lucky day for Acme when we secured your services, my boy. A hundred-thousand-dollar saving is a nice sum. I will certainly point out to the board of directors—"

"Save it," I told him. "I don't even know that this Saltis killed him. But I want a man to sit right there on this phone and be ready to do chores for me, understand?"

"Yes, yes, of course. But remember—it *must* have been the nephew who did it—"

"If it's someone else, what do I do? Frame him?"

I didn't wait for his answer to that one. I climbed back in my car, angled swiftly toward the broad crosstown street that held the Sentinel Building—Daniels Dahl's newspaper. The plant was between Third and Second. Even if it had not been for the winking red searchlights on the police cars in front, I wouldn't have parked near there. I slid up Third, went up a block and crossed over—not far—maybe a quarter of the block. This street was black with parked cars—some doings in a nearby Masonic Temple—and I had to take the first parking spot I came to. I eased in, cut my ignition and lights and took my spare gun from the glove compartment.

IT WAS black as the inside of a cat. Impatient as I was, I didn't get careless. I hurried up the block, close to the building fronts, and without noise. The address the girl had given me, I estimated, would be just a few numbers down from the corner I was heading for, and on my side of Second Avenue. I was quite confident that I would find cops already in possession, and that I was wasting my precious time, but I played it safe.

I eased up to the corner, with painful care. An oblique corner-store niche beckoned me in the blackness and I slid into it.

The darkness here was oppressive. The moon was completely blanketed by black clouds and the shadow of the structure did its bit. I turtled my head out of the niche, squinting against the dark, looking along the shop fronts. I couldn't see a soul.

I had a foot in the air when I heard a subdued voice from the bulk of a roadster, parked in the blackness at the curb—less than fifteen yards from me. It was a girl's petulant, exasperated undertone. "I'm going up, anyway."

I set my foot down again.

A man's voice in the roadster was a husked groan. "You simply can't, Georgia. As your lawyer, I forbid it! If you were found there—"

"I won't be found there."

"But the risk! If you've told me the truth, you've nothing to fear legally. At worst, some publicity—"

"At worst! You fool—if that sanctimonious heel of a trustee of mine got hold of this, he'd go into a spasm, clamp down on my money. And you know I've got to touch him this week. This thing has broke me!"

"But what can you find here? Even if he did get that—thing—last night, it wouldn't be in a place like this—"

"Writing might be—to show where it was—or if he really did get it! Maybe he was bluffing. I still think—"

"He wouldn't leave anything important in a tenement rat-hole like this. Georgia—be rational. It's a marvel that we got you in the clear at all. Now you endanger everything by this rash—"

The girl swore wildly. "Say rash to me again, and I'll hit you with something. Why in the name of God did your uncle have to die and leave me in your hands? He'd know how to handle this! Isn't there a cigar lighter in this car?"

The man's husk was bitter. "If my beloved uncle had known how to 'handle' the funds of Blackstock and Blackstock a little better, maybe I'd have a car good enough to have a lighter. Here!"

There was a scratch, a match flared, hastily cupped between palms to be held to a cigarette, but I had a quick flash of their faces.

The girl was beautiful, in an intense, blazing way. Her features were regular, smooth, her hair a long, red-black bob. Her eyes were long, greenish, with a strained, driving look—and this was not just of the moment. Her skin was flawless. Only her mouth showed a cruel, puffy twist. She wore a green polo coat, green gloves, no hat. The man was a distressed, moon-faced, youngish owl with a mop of blond hair and tortoise-shell glasses.

She took two deep, crackling pulls of the cigarette, held it out. She cut off the hapless blond youth's beginning speech with, "Nuts! Hold this!" and was a quick shadow out on the sidewalk, the car door swinging closed behind her.

The youth groaned. Then she was a flitting shadow across the walk—at the door, undoubtedly to Dahl's hide-out building. She threw a quick look up and down, a hinge whined, a square of black appeared as a momentary silhouette, vanished again, and she was gone.

I just stood stupidly. I was caught unprepared, unoriented. Obviously I had stumbled on one of Dahl's black-mail victims—but I couldn't figure just what that added up to. There would be plenty of them prowling tonight. That the girl was patently one of the rat's contributors, certainly didn't make her connected with his death necessarily.

But that mention of "last night" kept me anchored. If tonight's killer stemmed out of last night's happenings—and if the girl knew something about those happenings....

It took me about two minutes, nevertheless, to get on top of the thing—make up my mind to walk in on her. I knew this spot was likely to become a storm-center any minute, but the chance of surprising her actually in Dahl's establishment would entitle me to all she knew, at any rate.

I fingered my tie, glanced at the spot in the darkness where the owl-eyed youth kept vigil. I eased silently out of my cubicle—and the girl suddenly reappeared from the tenement.

There was a soft whine from the door that had swallowed her and it opened, a little jerkily, slowly. Then it swung shut and I could see her black outline, standing clear, her hands to her head. She gasped: "Arthur!"

The blond youth flung himself out of the car. I took an unconscious step after him. The girl was swaying, stumbling—and then suddenly she crumpled. She fell to her knees, still nursing her head.

The blond youth scampered to her moaning, "Georgia! Georgia!" and almost sobbed as he grabbed her up.

Her gasp was a desperate whisper. "Get me in the car— get me home—someone hiding there—hit me."

I took a quick stride toward them and a sudden sharp noise jerked my head round. It was the sound of a man's flat soles whacking down on the sidewalk, a few yards down the pitch-black side street behind me—someone jumping from a high place to the sidewalk.

I swung back, my head buzzing. The girl's assailant? Escaping?

I whipped back, swung round the corner, whisking the gun from my pocket. I saw a dark shadow, thirty yards away, darting up from the sidewalk.

I called, "Hold it! Don't move—" and the shadow shot like a streak between two parked cars.

I damned the thick murk and the fact that I dared not shoot, and hopped between two cars myself, out into the road, trying to spot my man. I didn't realize that I'd been outsmarted till I heard the fugitive's footsteps pattering away in the blackness—still on the sidewalk. I swore, tried to hop back between two cars further down—and stuck my toe in a tin can.

It didn't hurt me but it threw me—and jammed my knee between two car-bumpers, just long enough to lose me the chase. When I jerked the can loose and hopped onto the sidewalk, the dark, racing figure, far down ahead of me, instantly side-leaped again—and I lost a second in indecision before I was able to follow that move.

By the time I finally reached the corner below, there was neither sight nor sound of my man in any direction.

OF COURSE, when I finally dashed back to the corner above, the girl, too, was gone. There was just an empty hole at the curb where the roadster had stood.

After I'd got through cursing and swung grimly back toward Dahl's hideout, I took exactly two steps—then froze. I backed swiftly, furtively, back into my store-corner niche. A party of noisy men had suddenly appeared around the next corner, heading my way. One or two uniforms were visible. Torch-beams started playing on the fronts of the stores, picking out numbers. Loud talk and profanity distilled the information that the Law was taking over Dahl's tenement hide-away.

I ground my teeth, sat once more in my car. Lost now, the opportunity suddenly seemed far more important than when it had been presented to me, my hesitancy far more stupid. I began to wonder if, had I taken a chance and cut loose with my gun, I could have cracked the whole puzzle right there and then.

I did not dwell on that too long. One thing was certain. If I had shot the fugitive down, I would never have been able to snake him clear of the horde of police—never been able to parade him before the blond girl for whatever mysterious purpose she wanted him—nor lay him in Shiverstein's lap. Not that that had occurred to me at the time. My restraint had been motivated, rather by a funny habit I have of wanting to know just who I'm shooting at before I go making targets of folks.

Yet, even if I did not feel especially steamed up over what might be in Dahl's secret flat, I wished the police had not discovered it. By not too great a stretch of imagination, I could picture some stony-eyed copper stumbling on Dahl's little store of discreditable secrets—and I winced for the folks involved. Furthermore—and I suddenly goosed my car alive in concern—there might be some reference to Talbotville. If they decided to chase it down—and why wouldn't they?—there was an end to my exclusive lead.

I backed silently out to Third, sent the car shooting uptown, toward the bridge. Almost there, I decided to consolidate what scraps I had picked out of the little flurry. I stopped long enough to telephone in. Preeker had left Harry Granite, a sharp lad, on the phone.

I told him: "I may want to know who a certain girl is. Here's what I know about her. Her name is Georgia something. She's evidently rich—how rich I want to know. She has a trustee, so she'll be an orphan. She was one of Daniels Dahl's subscribers. Her legal affairs are in the hands of a firm named Blackstock and Blackstock, I think. One of the firm died recently and the girl's affairs are being handled by the dead man's nephew. His name is Arthur and she moves too fast for him. Can you locate her from that?"

"Give me her physical."

I described the girl as best I could, and the owl-eyed lawyer.

Harry thought he could do something with it.

I said: "All right. Here's something else. The cops have discovered a hideaway of Dahl's at —— Second Avenue. It's right around the corner from the Sentinel Building. Get a reporter you know over there right away and keep tabs on what they find. Also, keep a line on what they discover in his other apartment, and his office. I'm on my way out to the Island. I'll call you back in a few minutes."

CHAPTER FOUR
A PAIR OF TIRE-TRACKS

LATE up the Middle Island Road. If I were racing the police, I was sure I was keeping ahead of them. There was no traffic. My speedometer hovered near the eighty mark. In less than twenty minutes after I quit the bridge, I swung to a long, grinding stop beside a roadside lunch wagon. I gave Granite, at the Acme office, another call.

He reported crisply: "Nothing in Dahl's hide-out—except that he evidently spent a lot of time there in the past twenty-four hours and developed some pictures."

"Anything at the other places?"

"Nothing of any consequence."

Going out of the lunch wagon I got a break.

I saw a red one-ton delivery truck, with lettering on its sides—*Heming J. Flattery—Fine Meats—Talbotville, L.I.*—parked by the diner.

I went back into the lunchroom, spotted a weathered-faced party with a turkey neck and white walrus moustache. Under his coat he wore a spotted white apron. He amiably gave me information.

" 'Bout three miles farther along the highway you'll see a sign says Talbotville. Turn right—toward the middle of the island—go over a couple rises, keeping the woods to your left. The road runs into a dead-end at the foot of Evergreen Mountain and *bang!* That's Talbotville."

"Mountain? On Long Island?"

"Well, maybe 'tain't a mountain. We call it that. It's a whopping big ridge."

"How big is Talbotville?"

"Oh, maybe three hundred folks."

"Were you at your store last night?"

"Till about nine I was."

I described Dahl and asked if he'd seen him, but he said he hadn't.

THERE WERE woods all right. From the time I turned off the highway, I was conscious of little else. On the left of the tarvia road they were thickly packed, tangled behind wire fence. On the other side of the road were farms, partly cleared ground, but on the left only the woods.

I went over two rises, down into two valleys, passed two roads that curved away into the woods at the left, dipped up over a third ridge and coasted down—into Talbotville. The moon overhead was only thinly veiled now and I could see the ridge. It towered above the town—a modest rise, with a huge cleft in the center.

I ran into difficulty here. The burg was only one street of stores and not more than half a dozen of them were open at night, but it took me about as long to canvass them as it had to get there from New York. I was plenty discouraged before I chatted my way through to the last store in the street.

A hardware-and-dry-goods merchant informed me, finally: "Yep. I see him. He come in here for fillums. I keep fillums. He wanted extra-sensitive, for one of them little candid cameras. I figured he was going to take pictures of the Signal Shack at moonlight—that is, I did at first, before all the goings-on."

"Goings-on?"

"Yeah. First he comes here asking his way to the Signal Shack. I told him—"

"What'd you tell him?"

"Well, this here Signal Shack's a historical spot, see? Right up the side of the mountain there—in that cleft. You can't get to it except from the other side. That is"—he gave me an athletic wink—"unless you don't mind a little trespassin'."

"How do you mean?"

"Well, all them woods across the road is part o' the old Talbot Estate. Ain't no one lived there for ten year and they don't keep no caretaker. The whole estate is kind of like an arch, laid on the mountain. Right at the narrerest part, it ain't more than a mile through to the Signal Shack. Which is what I told him."

"And?"

"He climbed in his car and went spang back to the first road, like I told him and, I guess, went on to the Shack. Then he came back, maybe twenty minutes—half-hour—later, askin' for a horse-van."

"A horse-van!"

"Yep. I send him to Charlie Riggs over to Syosset. He gives me a five-dollar note for my help, and for not tellin' the other one that he was here."

"What other one?"

"A young feller—city feller, too. Kind of dark, with big brown eyes like a woman's. He was plenty worried. He come up maybe hour—hour and a half—after the fancy little fatty had left the second time."

I took the hint and laid a five-dollar note in his horny hand. "You say I go back to the first road and turn?"

"Yup. Drive maybe two-three miles, till the road bends way in and way out. Then you'll be right opposite the Signal Shack." He took me to the door and pointed up at the mountain's cleft. "It sets right in that V, on a little level spot."

I drove as he directed, with my noggin buzzing. A horse-van and a dark-eyed, youngish gent trying to catch up to Dahl! What the hell!

I WAS still wrestling the idea of the horse-van when, twenty minutes later, I stood in darkness, my car safely hidden a hundred yards away, peering over a weather-rotted, overgrown fence.

Dense woods were on the other side, the moonlight only vaguely sifting through here and there, but there was a clearly defined trail ahead. I swung over the fence and was on a thick carpet of pine needles. I did not need my flash. It was impossible to get off the trail. Woods formed a barrier on each side.

Yet I had to progress slowly, over the mile to the foot of the rise that slanted steeply up to the Signal Shack. Then I had to scramble up a steep slope about sixty yards—clawing and hoisting—till I was eventually on a little circular plateau.

The Shack itself was just a stone hut with a hearth in the middle and a chimney pointing skywards. There was nothing—not even a footprint—on the premises, nor on the little plateau surrounding it. I took plenty of time to search and finally the moon came out full, to help me. It didn't help me. There was nothing there.

There was nothing to conclude, finally, except that I was in a blind alley. The trail had petered out here, as far as I could see, and I was left with my hand on my neck.

It was no easy thing to swallow—to believe that I had made the whole dizzy trip for nothing—had let nearly two hours whisk away. But eventually I had to realize just that. I tramped grimly back through the woods. What did I do now?

I was halfway back along the thick, tangled, woods trail when I saw the light.

It was a sharp sliver. It shone suddenly through the trees at my right—and was instantly gone.

I stood stock-still.

The beam did not come again, but there was a sort of diffused blue glow somewhere in behind the overgrowth. It took me a startled groping moment to comprehend its queer quality. Then I got it—there was a clearing near me, somewhere down below my own level, and something was reflecting moonlight in that clearing.

But the first sharp beam had not been moonlight. That had been a sparkle of white light. I hefted the gun in my hand, made swift estimate of the trees before me, then swung quickly and wriggled into them. Crawling, squeezing, painfully careful, I wriggled through the thicket—and checked myself behind a thin screening of saplings, almost at the clearing's edge.

I thinned my eyes.

I was above, and almost at the lip of a round pit cut out of the solid woods—evidently a clay pit. Water rippled shallowly in its flat bottom.

Directly across the pit, at a level twenty feet lower than my own, a flashlight was shining down. It shone at the point where a day road disappeared into the water. A dark figure stood behind the flashlight, evidently inspecting the water's edge.

Even before I caught sight of the individual behind the flashlight, I was desperately cursing the woods, looking around for some way to get out of my virtual trap—to get across the pond.

Then the light moved. Its owner was running it back along the road, and its dazzle left my eyes. In the process, the figure became a dim silhouette under the overhanging trees that lined the twisting road—and I pursed my lips.

The figure was a girl and she wore a polo coat, no hat. I could not swear that the polo coat was green, nor that her long bob was red-black—but I knew instinctively that it was so—knew that I was seeing the girl Georgia, whom I had seen slightly more than an hour ago on Second Avenue.

FOR THE first time it dawned on me that the name 'Green' might quite as well hide a woman as a man—and this one's sullen, spoiled face sprang suddenly back into my mind. There was nothing in her face—if my experience told me anything—that said she could not kill—nor that she would even have conscience pangs afterwards.

I whipped my head round, trying vainly to see a route through the trees. They crowded the pit's edge, were all but impenetrable, yet it was my only chance. I tried to slither through them, worm my way round the rim.

It would have taken an Indian to do it noiselessly and I am no woodsman. I snapped a twig on my second step.

It was like a pistol-shot in the silence—and the flashlight whipped up at me instantly.

Then before I could even shout at the girl, the light was gone—and she was off like a startled rabbit. I dived swearing, into a solid mass of brambles.

Long before I had cursed my way through the thick brush and stumbled down into the road, the sound of her flying footsteps had died. And even as I took my first step in pursuit, the churning of a distant automobile exhaust sounded—the quick roar as a distant car shot away.

I wiped sweat from my forehead. I was beginning to feel harassed, futile, a little desperate.

I sprayed my light down where the girl had been looking. A single set of automobile tires were engraved on the clay, as though a car had been driven into the water, but a glance out over the pool showed its extreme depth to be only a few inches. There was no car there now. It must have been driven away again.

It was minutes before the significance of that percolated—and my mouth went open.

I jumped back toward the clay road. I turned the flashbeam down, trotted along the bumpy, narrow, twisting road, following the sharp marks of the tires—a hundred yards—two hundred.

Then suddenly the road widened and I almost stumbled over myself stopping.

The sharply carved tire-tracks suddenly vanished. But others took their place—huge ones, flat-treaded, that had cut deep into the clay—the tires of a truck.

I half turned back, then realized that the road ahead of me must be another entrance to the estate and might bring me out as close to my hidden car as retracing my own route would.

I wasn't wrong. I piled into my own jalopy not two hundred yards from the mouth of the driveway.

I had places to go and Syosset was one of them. When I drew up in the silent little town, a patrolman trying doors pointed out a large sign above a white stone garage—*Chas. Riggs—Sales and Service.* I found a dim light burning behind the windows of the garage office, and a vague shadow moving about within.

When I pounded, the shadow opened the door—a yellow-haired youth with a long nose.

"You have horse-vans for hire?" I tossed at him, and his expression was answer enough. I pressed: "You hired one to a little fat man—a city man—late last night?"

"No. We didn't do nothing like—"

"He's been murdered," I told him flatly. "I'm from the D.A.'s office. You'd better not lie—no matter how much he paid you to."

The youth's Adam's apple bobbed. He gulped. "Wait! I—I better wake Pa. He—he may know—"

"Hurry up. I'll use your phone."

In a minute I had the Acme office again.

"No, no," Harry Granite assured me. "Nobody's found Dahl's cache of blackmail stuff anywhere. No. I haven't been able to tag that girl yet but I'm working on it."

"Well, get the lead out," I told him. "I need whatever you can dig up badly now."

The yellow-haired youth came back with a yellow-haired man—a broader edition of the youth. He was stuffing a nightshirt into trousers and his light blue eyes were startled, frightened.

I made my voice a snarl. "Come clean or I'll toss you in jail."

He burst into anxious explanation, winding up with, "He showed me how he worked for a newspaper so I guessed nothing was wrong. We picked up a car—a gray Packard— there last night. Been standing there, in the water, maybe a week, I'd say. We took it to this garage in New York." He handed over a scribbled receipt and I gazed tenderly at the address.

CHAPTER FIVE

FORMALDEHYDE

FOR A FINGER

I MADE a half-hearted attempt to juggle my scraps together as I raced back toward the city. Saltis, bank employee, calling Dahl and reporting names and large sums of money. Saltis missing Dahl at an appointment back on the Talbot estate, and being furious about it. Saltis seeking Dahl all day. And a gray Packard, parked for a week in a clay pit on the estate—a Packard belonging to a sullen, willful heiress who feared no legal difficulties, but only publicity. Dahl, apparently, moving this car away, appropriating it.

And New York going crazy trying to find the answer that might lie in the garage toward which I was racing.

It was not till I was almost there that it suddenly occurred to me that the garage was in the vicinity of Daniels Dahl's own apartment. It must be the columnist's own garage to which he had ordered the gray Packard taken.

And that suddenly turned on a new light in my mind. If it were the columnist's own garage, it would, probably, contain his own car—the green convertible. Could it be...? Why not? What a monstrous joke on the police who were searching Dahl's apartment, and his office—apparently vainly—if the slimy little blackmailer had chosen his car for his hiding-place!

It was in the district around East End Avenue—that new exclusive section of Manhattan that was rising from ancient dumps. The trim, yellow-brick garage had not risen very far. The dumps still slanted down from its back door—a vast mound of refuse.

As I braked to a stop, forty minutes later, there was a dim night-light burning outside the front door, over a sign that said: *Ring for the night man.*

Why I didn't do just that—ring—I wouldn't know. Everything was still, silent. I had a finger on the bell, yet I hesitated. Maybe it was sight of the little door-within-a-door—the pedestrian's entrance. It was not open, but it was ajar—just a little.

I looked quickly toward the dim-lit office window. Three silent strides put me in front of it, let me peek into the office. There was a safe, a bright-yellow maple desk, a table littered with metal junk, a hat-rack, a swivel chair, an arm chair, and—from behind the desk, on the floor, a foot protruded, toe upwards.

I blew out breath. I felt a brass pipe—a hose connection—against my leg. I hopped up on it and I could see over the desk.

The prone, unconscious man was the blond, moon-faced young lawyer, Arthur, who had been with the sullen red-haired girl, Georgia.

For a second, I could not figure it. Had the girl, somehow, guessed that Dahl had brought her car here? Had she sent the hapless blond youth to do something about it—and had he been surprised by someone else also here on sinister business? What business? Or had the killer, this 'Green,' also figured out that Dahl's car might hold the blackmail material?

Maybe they'd both come on account of the possible contents of Dahl's car.

I jumped down, hefted my gun. This sort of guessing was foolish—or worse—while the killer I sought might still be inside.

I crouched in front of the door, listening, and heard nothing. I touched the little pedestrian's door gently with my fingers, gave it a slight push.

Hell broke loose inside.

I jumped a foot, my face screwing up, as iron rang and clattered on the cement inside—a crowbar, propped against the inside of the door, which my push had dislodged.

Cursing, I dived through the door, gun ready, swung quick looks around. There was no one on this floor, but there was a car elevator at the rear, beside the elevator a whitewashed set of stone steps. Light shone up the steps.

I sprinted on my toes, reached the steps and dived down, burst into a basement workroom lit by one blazing incandescent on a cord from the ceiling.

CARS STOOD round the walls, one under the droplight half dismantled. A man in mechanic's overalls lay sprawled, eyes closed, on the cement floor, a gash over his right eyebrow.

I felt cold air and swung toward the back, ran for the open door that led out onto the dumps in the rear. I ran outside, listened, thought I caught a sound from around one side of the garage and raced after it. I was pretty sure, however, that I had no chance of catching anybody. The crowbar had been a clever alarm signal—and whoever had used the back door had had ample time to light out.

I wasted a minute or two running around before I gave up and hurried back into the basement.

I took a quick look at the prone man, found he was breathing regularly. There was a monkey-wrench on the floor near him, and a small jimmy and creeper—one of those little cradles used for sliding under cars.

Cars ranked the walls on three sides. I ran along them, looking for either a gray Packard or a green convertible.

I found the gray Packard.

It was in a corner of the basement—a brand-new coupé. Its left front mudguard was crumpled and torn, almost turned under onto the left wheel. The left front amber light was smashed, tilted at a crazy angle.

I let out breath. The car was in a corner and I had to make myself small to get in to the driver's door. I swung it open and glanced at the instrument panel, got confirmation of the fact that it was a new car. The speedometer registered exactly two thousand miles. An oiling tag from a New York garage showed its oil had been changed exactly one hundred and twenty-five miles ago.

I shut the door, stepped out again and around the half-dismantled car in the center of the room, peering for the green convertible. I did not see it at first.

Then I did.

The proximity of the slugged mechanic had fooled me. The green convertible was the car in the center of the room. It stood almost under the droplight, its cushions tumbled out on the ground, its rumble seat open, all its doors open. It had been so plainly under my eye that I had momentarily missed it.

It was not being dismantled. It was—or had been in the process of being searched.

I did not realize how thoroughly until I looked inside with my flashlight.

Every cushion, including the back-rest, had been taken out. The radio had been ripped apart. The glove compartment's lining had been torn out. The rubber floor-mat was up, the floor-boards in disarray. About the only thing intact was the heater under the dash and even it had fresh, bright scratches on it.

I stepped back, almost stumbling over the creeper and the jimmy as I peeked into the rumble seat. The rumble was in the same condition. Somebody had taken this car apart, inch by inch.

I bowed to the unknown's thoroughness as I saw the hood wings propped up, the air filter knocked from its pedestal.

Maybe it was the very thoroughness with which everything else had been gone over that jerked my attention back to the scratched heater. It stood out like a sore thumb—a spot the intruder had attempted to work on and then abandoned. I felt a sudden thrill. Could he have been in the very act of dismantling that when I frightened him away? In that case, maybe he had not succeeded in discovering....

I caught my breath, scooped up the jimmy quickly, tucked my gun under one arm and kneeled on the running board. I did not try to pry the whole heater out—that was not necessary. I got a skimpy purchase on the face of the dingus, applied pressure.

THERE WAS a snap and the whole grid-face of the heater clattered out on the floor-board. I felt a giddy awe. If the searcher had had one more minute....

There was no heater behind the grid-face—merely two neat little metal shelves. On the lower shelf lay two bottles—one, about the size of a bottle of aspirin, had *CONINE* on the label. The other, a squat brown pint flask with a wide neck, bore a label with the name *Talbot* scribbled on it.

I snatched it out, eyes flashing, unscrewed the wide cap and held it to the light. Then quickly I turned its mouth down. I shook—and liquid splattered on the running board. The sharp stink of formaldehyde rose—and then something solid plopped out.

My stomach knotted.

It was flesh—human flesh! A flap of skin clinging to the obliquely sliced finger of a man. The whole was dull gray, the knuckle-bone protruding through trailers of shredded skin.

There were dark splotches of black sludge and grease all over the gruesome little exhibit.

This was the break. My scrambling around had dropped me finally into the heart of the little puzzle—with the key not far ahead.

I whipped out my watch—and a little chill touched me. My three hours were exactly up.

I spotted a wall phone with a greasy directory hanging beside it, half started toward it—then swung back to look at the contents of the lower shelf in the heater. I licked my lips. A plain cardboard box was filled with envelopes of conventional size. As I clawed the box out, I saw a name scribbled across the face of each envelope.

I held them under the light, my heart speeding up, flipped through them. There was no 'Saltis', no 'Zimmerman', no 'Talbot'—which puzzled me for a minute.

But I had no time to be puzzled now. I crammed the envelopes into my pocket, jumped to the wall phone. I presumed it was an extension, but it worked. I got Harry

Granite at the Acme offices and told him in no uncertain terms: "I've got to know about that girl, Harry! I—"

"Keep your pants on! I've got the whole dope. Listen! Talbot—Georgia Talbot—"

"I know. I was just going to tell you that. Where does she live? Who is she?"

"She's filthy, dripping rich. She's most of the remaining business of that Arthur Blackstock. Her family left her a scad—the woolen people. She has a trustee who pays her fifty thousand dollars every quarter. That's only income, mind you."

"Where does she live?"

"A penthouse on Central Park West." Harry gave the address and I repeated it back carefully and urged him: "No—see if you can top that with finding where she was tonight—four hours ago—at the time of Dahl's death."

Harry gasped. "Gentle Tudas! She didn't do *that...?*"

"You tell me. Call me at her penthouse, any time after half an hour."

I hung up. I held the instrument, while I struggled swiftly with the mileage figures on the speedometer of the gray Packard. Then I called the State Police barracks on Long Island.

To the trooper who answered, I gave the name of Udall, a lad I knew in the D.A.'s office, and told him: "I want you to take down a message for your lieutenant. No, I haven't time to wait for you to put him on. Take it down—fast. Ask him if anybody lost a finger—that's right, a finger— somewhere within fifty miles of Talbotville, Long Island, within the past two weeks.... Yeah, I know, but that's the message and it's vitally important to get an answer in the next twenty minutes or so. Call me here—" I rattled off the phone number of Georgia Talbot's penthouse and hung up.

I LOOKED down at the prone mechanic. He showed no signs of life. I suddenly thought of the lawyer, Blackstock, upstairs. I ran up, hurried to the office, but the lawyer had tired of the game and gone away. The killer—yes, I was sure now that the killer, Green, had been in this garage just ahead of me—had evidently tapped Blackstock more gently than the lad downstairs. Though *he* was due to come out of it by now—unless his skull was fractured. I went back down—and he *was* out of it.

He was standing up, swaying, one hand clutched to his head, the monkey-wrench in his other hand, eyes groggy.

I put the gun on him and said: "Get them up, little stranger."

He made no move to obey, peered at me as though uncomprehending.

"Never mind the act," I told him. "Mechanics don't have manicured fingernails. Come on—fast!"

He gasped and raised his hands—and ran right out of mine.

I hadn't given him credit enough. Whether he was naturally smart or just spurred to brain-heat by panic, he was thinking brilliantly.

He raised his hands. He was standing right under the blazing single globe that lit the room—and he just had to tap it with the monkey-wrench. His big brown eyes were wide, innocent on mine—as the light exploded.

I sensed, rather than saw, the monkey-wrench whistling toward me. I jumped aside as the room went black—but he was even ahead of me there. He had kicked the creeper and it was skidding across the floor. I landed squarely on it when I jumped—and my feet went out from under me as though I had stepped in grease.

My gun went off and then I crashed down on my neck, my head whanging the stone floor like a ton of brick.

I wasn't knocked cold—but I was goofy, in a rocking, giddy haze. Pure instinct helped me out.

I knew there was a regular, ear-shattering banging going on somewhere. I knew it was near me. But it was a full minute before I realized that it was my own gun, in my own hand, and that I had been calmly firing it—at nothing—merely to keep the brown-eyed pseudo-mechanic from jumping me.

It was the banging of the back door that really brought my senses pouring back in a rush—and I staggered up in the blackness.

Then I was fumbling at the door myself, patting my pockets to make sure my treasures were safe, fingering out my pencil flash.

I burst out into the night air as racing footsteps went away from me—somewhere. I could not figure the direction I and I milled about in a quandary.

Then came a sound that shocked me fully back to my faculties—the shrill scream of a police siren in the near distance.

That ended my interest in the gent with the manicure. I estimated quickly, raced around the side of the garage, piled into my car—and got away just before the prowl car turned in to the block.

CHAPTER SIX
THE JUDAS TOUCH

FOR THE first ten blocks my thoughts were churning, but they didn't matter now. I had knocked the lid off the swarming little murder-pot—knocked it off just a bit too soon. I did not know yet who had killed Dahl. I did not even know—for sure—who the pseudo-mechanic was, nor who had sapped him. The ill-luck that had walked with me from the first was working full time now.

I found a dark street, squealed up to the curb a few steps from a dim stationery store, jerked out the box of envelopes. There were names on some of them that, another time, would have made me whistle. Dahl had had some rare prizes among his victims. I hurried in to the store.

I almost held my breath while I called the little blonde, Doris Zimmerman, at the hotel where I had hidden her. She was still there.

"I'll pick you up at the service entrance of the hotel in five minutes," I told her. She said: "Oh! Oh! You've got—"

"I've got nobody—but it's narrowed down. It'll blow off in the next few minutes—and there'll be no time for bringing folks to you. You'll have to be there when it pops, if you want to play with the killer."

She cried in sudden fright: "But—but he may—if he sees me—he may kill me."

"I'll be right beside you."

She hesitated so long that I thought she had gone away. Then she said: "All—all right."

I hung up and started out of the stationery store.

A loud crackle of static from the black street outside brought me to a quick halt. I stood where I was just long enough to hear a neat description of myself, and my car, coming from a radio prowl car parked at the curb outside.

I never did know if the cops from that car were just there by chance or whether they were, at that very moment, examining my jalopy and had left their loudspeaker turned up by accident. It didn't matter.

All that mattered was that I was out on a limb for fair now. Shiverstein had put the finger on me. Every cop in the city would be looking for me. There was dryness in my throat as I pictured again what would happen to me if they got me.

I cursed fretfully as I ran out the back door of the shop and found myself in a fenced-in back yard. The astonished proprietor of the shop was still staring goggle-eyed at me when I hopped his fence to the backyard of a tenement fronting on the street above and ran into the open basement door.

I plowed along a dark corridor, found the areaway entrance in front before anybody found me—and then I was up on the dark street, hurrying east as fast as my legs could carry me, my heart in my throat. If I could find a cab—if I could just stay free of the police net for a few minutes.

I caught a cruising hack over near Fifth Avenue. Once inside I had a moment's respite while the driver whirled me over to the Broadway section. I tucked myself in the dark corner of the cab till we drew up and I saw the white-faced, frightened girl huddling in the dark doorway.

Then we were turning around, racing back toward Central Park West.

"Where—where are we going?" she gasped. "Do you know—who...? Did Saltis...?"

"Maybe, sister, maybe. It could be anybody—anybody that ever contacted Dahl. Everybody he touched seems to have turned into a double-crossing heel—like Midas, the guy that everything he touched turned to gold. Call this the Judas touch. When Dahl got his hands on them they went bad—or it looks like that from here."

"Where—where are we going?"

I suddenly patted my pockets, found her tiny gun—and not my own spare one. Evidently I had left it in my car. I gave it back to her and said: "Give me mine. I'm going to need it here."

She snapped open her bag with trembling fingers, shoved it at me and repeated: "But where-where are we going?"

"Right here," I said, as the hack came to a squealing stop, just across the road from the towering apartment house that supported Georgia Talbot's penthouse. "Just follow me. Come on—I've dropped too many minutes already. Don't talk."

THERE WERE only a few apartments above us lighted at this hour. There was not a soul visible in the street. I took her elbow and steered her into a modernistic, glittering little lobby, dim now. There was someone moving behind the ground-glass screen behind the cork-and-chromium circular desk. Two chromium elevators were closed at the right rear of the lobby, but one opened just as we reached it.

A sleek youth in dinner clothes hurried out from behind the glass screen. "I—I beg your pardon, sir. You—you wished to be announced?"

"Not unless you want a rumpus," I snarled at him. "I'm from the district attorney's office." He couldn't think of an answer to that one, and I ushered the girl into the car and rapped at the operator: "Move this thing—fast!"

I held the girl's arm while we swooped up. "Roof!" I told the boy.

"I—the car only goes to twenty-five. You have to walk—"

Then we were in a luxurious hall of aquamarine and salmon that glowed with indirect lighting. The elevator dropped down again behind us.

I held her arm long enough to bite out: "Don't say a word till I tell you. Got that? Not one word."

I took a glance at my watch as I piloted her down the long hall toward the carpeted penthouse stairs. I took off my topcoat and hat, walking a little behind her so she did not notice it.

When she looked with her frightened blue eyes over her shoulder I shook my head, motioned her sternly up the carpeted stairs. I swung open an ornamental grilled-iron gate and we went up soundlessly. At the top a second gate already stood open. I checked her on the threshold of the roof. We were in a little tepee on the sodded roof. I looked past her at the penthouse.

It was a four-room bungalow, in the center of the roof—colorful, intimate, modernistic, cheerfully ablaze with lights. Most of the windows were wide open. On one windowsill there was a fresh highball sitting, crammed with fresh ice, full to the top.

I held the blond girl's arm while I looked it over. Then, in one long motion I swung my coat around her shoulders, coughing the while, clapped my hat on her head, kneed her out so she stumbled across the turf. I went into a crouch, swaying forward on my toes and dived, at just about the same instant as did the dark figure who had been huddled, waiting, in the shadow of the tepee.

He lunged at the girl's figure, blackjack upraised—and my shoulders caught him just about the waist, flung him staggering sideways. I saw the glint of a gun in his other hand, snatched and wrenched it away, flung it. The gasping man whacked wildly at me with the sap, but I got an arm up, took one blow on it, then had the gent's wrist. Simultaneously, I brought one up from the floor with my other fist, dotted him neatly on the chin-point, lifted him up and dropped him on the sod, out cold.

The girl was backing away, eyes frantic, hands to her mouth.

I calmed her. "Don't be excited. This is one of the candidates I tempted to come down here. Your friend, Mr. Saltis." I bent down, fanned him, scooped him up over my shoulder like a sack of meal and started toward the penthouse. "Better tell Miss Talbot—"

There was no need to tell Miss Talbot anything. The red-haired girl was already in the doorway. She hugged her bare arms in front of her as though chilly, but her small features were as smooth as wax, her oblique green eyes pools of shining shadow. She wore a dazzlingly white evening dress. She flung out: "How dare you people...?"

I put a little bite into my voice. "I've some urgent business with the person who killed Daniels Dahl. I'm going to transact it here. Udall, of the D.A.'s office."

Her green eyes jerked startledly to the limp man on my shoulder and she backed away slowly. "Who is he?"

I FOLLOWED in and dumped the little black-clad figure—the pseudo mechanic who had outthought me in the garage—on a cherry-and-chromium couch where he bounced on his face. I ran hands over his slight body.

"His name is Saltis," I told the bony red-head. "He's been minding your business."

"My business?"

"Yeah. He must live somewhere near your old family estate at Talbotville. At any rate he either stumbled on your abandoned car out there—or had it reported to him by someone in the neighborhood. He's the one who told

Daniels Dahl about it." I looked hard into her green eyes. "And put you to so much trouble."

Her thick lips curled contemptuously, opened—and just then the telephone rang sharply.

I stopped all motion by saying, "That's for me," and backed over, not concealing the gun that hung from my fingers and not losing sight of any of the three people.

Saltis' large brown eyes suddenly blinked, opened foggily. He hoisted himself up quickly, eyes going white-ringed as he saw me.

"Sit quiet," I warned him. Into the mouthpiece I said: "Yes?"

"Mr. Udall? This is State Police—Lieutenant Hathaway, Long Island. Hey—on that finger business. An old farmer was a hit-and-run victim near Huntington, a week ago—on one of the back roads. No trace of the car. It evidently went right over the old man and carried away his finger—we didn't find it. The old man's still in the hospital, dying. He didn't see what hit him and there were no witnesses. Hey—have you got anything?"

"I may have later."

I hung up, turned back and faced the red-head—and the white-faced, brown-eyed Saltis.

"All right. I've got the goods on both of you. Which one did it?" The phone rang again. I made the mistake of answering once more, thinking it was my office checking in with the report on the red-head's movements.

A gloomy, grim voice said in my ear: "Sorry to call so late but I got to speak to Miss Georgia Talbot."

I tried to make my voice sound like a butler's. "Who is calling, please?"

"This is Shiverstein, of headquarters. Hey—you sound like—"

He swore suddenly, and hung up the phone. It was like a stab in my stomach. I knew as well as I knew my own name that he had recognized my voice—and that I had now only a few desperate minutes left.

I swung, tight-jawed on the two again. "All right—which of you wants to confess to killing Daniels Dahl?"

The red-haired girl was at the open window, picking up her highball. She spoke contemptuously, her shoulders shrugging. "If you think you've any of these 'goods' on me, Mr. Policeman, you're in for a sad shock. Everything's all taken care of."

I couldn't make sense of that. "What?"

"You heard me."

"Just how do you 'take care' of murder?"

"Murder? What the hell are you talking about?"

"The murder of Daniels Dahl—the little pup you pushed over the balcony of the Montfalcon tonight."

She gasped. "Good God! Why should I murder *him?*"

"Why? Because he had you nailed to the cross. Dahl went out to Talbotville last night—on Mr. Saltis' tip. He spotted your car and snooped—"

"What car?"

"Drop it! I've only got minutes to deal with you. The car you drove out to Huntington—and killed a man with. The one you turned around and raced to your family estate in Talbotville and abandoned in the woods. And, unfortunately, for you, the one Mr. Saltis here guessed the truth about—and handed it on to Dahl. Including the finger of the man you ran over—which was in the crankcase."

IF I expected her to collapse, I was disappointed. Her voice was flat, contemptuous. "What of it?"

"Nothing of it—except that Dahl spent last night and today assembling the whole story—figuring where it occurred by your oiling slip and speedometer and so forth—and got the answer. He got in touch with you for a squeeze—a juicy plum it was, too—manslaughter at least. How much did he order you to bring to the Montfalcon?"

"Fifty thousand dollars," she drawled casually. "What's it to you?"

"A lot to me—but it couldn't be much to you. Why didn't you pay off?"

"Pay a blackmailer? I don't go in for it. Besides—it happens that I've had heavy expenditures. As well as my allowance, most of my bank accounts—"

"You mean you killed him because you were out of money?"

She put one hand to her head, ground her teeth. "Are you mad? I didn't have anything to do with killing him."

"He went to the Montfalcon to meet you."

"Maybe. When he first called, I wasn't sure what to do. When I found out, I just ignored him. What reason would I have for killing him?"

"I've just been telling you." I was beginning to think her wacky. "The dope he had on you—the dope you thought was on his person—the dope you've been chasing around to retrieve ever since."

"Nonsense. It's just that I can't stand gossip right now."

"You'll be standing more than gossip—"

The phone rang again.

As I stepped over to answer once more, I saw the flushed, green-eyed red-head suddenly look queerly down at the floor with a blank look. Then she made a hasty motion of her hand, spilling a little of her highball as she gulped half of it.

At last Harry Granite was saying in my ear: "Hey—about that girl. I got a line on her movements tonight."

"Go ahead."

"She didn't kill no columnist. She was in the Algonquin Hotel at eleven o'clock—there's a dozen people to prove it. She's got an iron-clad alibi."

I croaked, "Thanks," and hung up bewilderedly.

That was a sock—and I didn't like what was left. There was sweat on my neck and I was listening for the squeal of a police siren—or some other indication of police closing in on me. I swung on Saltis.

"So it was you, bank-clerk! You killed Dahl!"

His frantic eyes jumped crazily and he gasped: "I—no! Why should I—"

I raved: "Drop the bluff! Shut up! Don't waste breath. I know all about it. You worked for Dahl—worked in the bank—"

He cried desperately: "He made me! I swear! He had certain evidence—something I did once—"

"All right. He had something on you and forced you to notify him when any of your Park Avenue customers made a big cash withdrawal. Not a bad way to find an occasional blue-blood off base. He looked into whatever the gents—or ladies—that you reported on had been doing that made them require chunks of cash. He looked into Miss Talbot's doings—when she drew out eighty thousand. You looked too—because you knew her. Is that it?"

"No! No! He made me—he knew I passed her estate on my way home. I—I found the car and—and guessed what had happened."

"And made a deal with him—this valuable dope, in return for the evidence he held over you?"

"Yes! Yes! But he—"

"He crossed you up. He made a date to meet you at the estate—and promptly hurried out and got the car away ahead of you. You were wild. You started looking for him. You even called his office and made a threat. But you didn't catch up to him till eleven o'clock tonight—on the balcony of the Montfalcon Hotel!"

HE STARTED to speak but I roared: "Shut up! Even after you'd killed him—and found that you hadn't got the stuff he had over you, you still had to go on the prowl for it. You had it figured that it might be in his car. You went there and found Miss Talbot here had evidently had the same idea and sent her henchman. You knocked him cold and went to work to search. Unfortunately I interrupted the search and finally chased you off. But while you lay on the floor playing possum you'd heard me say I was coming here—so you came too, to retrieve the dope that you thought I'd gotten from Dahl's car."

He cried out desperately: "Yes! Yes! I told you he had something—something that I had to get back. I've been trying to—as you say. I was even willing to try and attack you—but I didn't kill Dahl! I wasn't even in the Montfalcon at eleven o'clock! I was at the *Sentinel* office at eleven o'clock, talking to Crum, the city editor. You can ask him. I was just starting out for Dahl's place on Sec—just starting out when Crum came out and caught me on the sidewalk to tell me Dahl was dead. Go on—call and ask him! I wasn't near the Montfalcon at eleven!"

For a second a touch of panic reached me. If they both had alibis—if neither of these two had done it—Shiverstein already on the way here—and I no nearer the answer to the puzzle than when I started.

Then, somehow, my eyes were on the luscious, peach-blond little Doris Zimmerman.

She had one hand in her bag, and her blue eyes were fixed on my face, white-rimmed. When she saw my questioning stare, she went terrified, rigid. Unreasonably her mouth went square and she screamed: "Don't you dare accuse me! Don't look at me like that!"

I looked at her hands. "What are you holding your gun for?"

"Why? Because I'm afraid of being murdered! Because if one of these people is Green—"

"Drop that gag. It ceased being good a long time back. I know there's no one named Green. I know that note left at Dahl's murder was completely phony—a piece of imagination created to confuse the issue! And I know that you were never threatened by anybody. You simply took advantage of the note to concoct a plausible story to make me work for you."

And then the fogginess went away from my mind and I saw the whole painfully simple answer. But I saw it too late, and the nightmare rushed up to its final peak of horror, utterly beyond my control.

I whirled back to the red-headed heiress. "How are you so sure there are no legal consequences to that accident in Hunt—" and that was as far as I got.

Georgia Talbot screamed.

It was a slaty scream, blood-chilling. It choked me off. The highball glass, half-empty in the girl's hand, suddenly exploded—crushed in her grip. She screamed again and again. Her feet did not move, but her whole body was suddenly jerked to the right. The right side only of her mouth flew open. Her eyes were those of a maniac.

Her right forearm suddenly clamped up against her breast as rigidly as iron—and foam suddenly spewed out between her gray lips, choking off the ugly screaming. Her teeth were clenched, her lips drawn back like an animal's— and her whole body jerked in wild writhing as she pitched forward onto her face, jaws grinding, feet lashing out crazily, thrumming on the floor.

MOMENTARILY, I was as horror-frozen as the rest of them. Then I shot at Saltis, beside the phone: "It's a convulsion! Get a doctor—fast!" As the strange, dank smell of mice bit my nostrils I suddenly remembered the bottle I had left in Dahl's car—the bottle marked *Conine*. I added quickly as the white-faced bank-clerk's shaking hands snatched at the phone: "Tell him to bring strychnine—for conine poisoning."

Even then there was a split-second when the monstrous sight of the threshing, mouthing girl on the floor was utterly beyond my ken—and then I got it. The highball glass in the open window—her queer attitude as she gulped it—

I spun on my heel and went out the open door onto the roof, fired instantly at the black figure who was jumping from darkness into the funnel of light that came from the stair-tepee.

My shot knocked the man sideways, against the open door. The door flung violently back, banging against the tepee, and the man stumbled, fell down. A long tongue of roaring flame licked out at me, but the lead went wild. I stood perfectly still and pumped three ripping shots into the crouching, writhing hulk of the murderer.

Then there was silence. Even the sounds from the house—the girl's unearthly convulsion-sounds—were suddenly stilled.

Somebody threw the switch and floodlights blazed up on the roof.

Arthur Blackstock, the blond owlish lawyer, lay perfectly still, bleeding from the head, his pistol a few inches away from his slowly stiffening hand.

I dived for him, dropped to one knee, my hands flying over the dying man's clothes. I felt the thick bulk in his inside pocket, yanked out a sheaf of papers. I riffled through them, saw a white envelope with *Doris Zimmerman* on it, and another with *Armand Saltis*. The envelopes matched the ones I had already found—Dahl's blackmail ammunition.

I jammed them in my pocket, ran and snatched up my hat and coat from the ground nearby.

I turned to find the little blond girl, eyes mad, face starch-white, pointing her little gun at me with shaking hands. She gasped: "Give me—"

"Later," I snapped. "Don't try shooting that pop-gun. I took the shells out of it long back, just in case."

Saltis burst out of the penthouse. He babbled: "Doctor on the next floor down—coming right up."

His eyes dropped to the huddled body. "Who—who—"

"Arthur Blackstock, the girl's lawyer," I told him and quickly jerked out the envelope with the kid's name on it, tossed it to him. For a second he could not move, as it fell on the ground. Then he recognized what it was, made a queer little cry and dived for it. He came up, babbling: "Oh, my God, you mean—"

"Get it out of sight. The cops—"

A bald-headed, pink-pajamaed portly man raced up the stairs with a bag in his hand. He paused indecisively, then started toward the dead Blockstock. I waved him away.

"Not this one—he's gone. In the penthouse—" and he trotted away. I started after him—and then more feet were pounding up the stairs.

I stopped, swung back, my gun up—just as Shiverstein burst out on the roof, three men behind him.

He stopped and his dirty teeth showed. "Ah, killer!" he said greedily.

I shook my head slowly. "Better talk to me privately, if you know what's good for you," I told him—and his effort to make up his mind would have been funny under any other circumstances. It took him five full seconds to stammer finally, "Well, all right," and to snap at his men: "Go on—see what's in there."

I FACED him over the dead man. "Here's your killer," I said. "Not only of Dahl—but, I think, of Georgia Talbot, in there. I think she's dead."

"All right, smart guy—but that still leaves you just where I want—"

"Oh, no," I said. "Unless I tell it, you'll never in ten million years find the story. And I'm not telling it, unless I get a proposition I like. And don't waste time on those two youngsters—they know nothing."

Again we had minutes of dispute, during which time the doctor came from the penthouse, shrugging. "Too late. She must have had a terrific dose."

The phone in the penthouse had started to ring steadily—reporters downstairs.

Finally I reached a compromise. We waited till three reporters were with us, and then I told them: "Mr. Shiverstein and I were working together." He confirmed that by a nod. His face was purple, but I had him. I went on: "Georgia Talbot did a hit-and-run on an old man in Huntington two weeks ago. She ditched her car, went to her lawyer, this Arthur Blackstock. He hasn't a penny—evidently his uncle tossed away his family's money.

"He ran out to Huntington to see what had happened and found that there wasn't any evidence at all against Miss Talbot. But he saw a chance to get his hands on a small fortune. He did not tell her the truth. He told her there were witnesses—but they could be bought off. I don't know exactly how much he got out of her, but it was over eighty thousand.

"Dahl found out something was going on, and found the car, discovered the story. He tried to shake down the girl. Naturally, she went again to her lawyer. He was stuck now. He had to make good—so he told her to forget the whole thing and he killed Dahl.

"But he couldn't be sure yet that he had gotten all the written dope that Dahl might have had. He prowled around, in Dahl's garage, among other places. He saw me prowling there also, overheard me make a date to come here—overheard it on an extension phone—and was uneasy. He sneaked up here to find how much I knew. He listened outside the window, heard me questioning the girl, and he knew I was getting warm. Naturally, if the girl once came out with the story about buying off the witnesses, she'd have to name Blackstock—and that would bring the whole house of cards tumbling down around his head, so he slipped some poison into her drink, got her over to the window and got her to drink it—probably urging her to cover up the fact that she was talking with him by acting natural and all that.

"Mr. Shiverstein gets the credit. We had a little idea earlier—a wrong one—which we were trying to work out. It had to appear that I was wanted by the police in order to work a certain angle on another suspect, but that person is utterly clear, so pay no attention. Right, Mr. Shiverstein?" He had to nod slowly.

"Mr. Shiverstein had the ideas—and Miss Zimmerman and I get a slight assist. Also, Mr. Saltis here." I caught the grateful look in the bank-clerk's face and knew he could be depended on to take care of himself—not to let slip anything about his doings for Dahl.

I took the blond girl's arm and moved toward the exit. "I'm taking Miss Zimmerman home. She's had a tough night, and she can't be any more use to you anyway. You can reach her through me—most any time."

SINGLE INDEMNITY

IT WAS THE WACKIEST SET-UP
THAT HARD-AS-NAILS INSURANCE
DICK HAD RUN INTO A LIFETIME
OF CLAMPING DOWN ON PHONY
CLAIMS. HERE WAS A CLIENT
WHOSE JEWELS HAD BEEN
STOLEN—THE ACME MAN HAD
SEEN THEM HIMSELF IN A PARCEL
OF RECOVERED LOOT BROUGHT
INTO A NEW YORK JAIL—YET THE
OLD DUCK WHO'D INSURED THEM
GAVE HIS LIFE TRYING TO PROVE
THEY WERE RIGHT IN HIS OWN
SAFE ALL THE TIME.

I **HAD** been in Ancaster City before. It was about ninety miles upstate, on the banks of the Trotteville River—a busy little city of ninety thousand. At any rate it looked busy at two thirty in the afternoon when I drove through the center of town. The local white-light district—Debussy Street—was a slightly tinnier, slightly more callow, edition of Broadway, but I could not see that it was any smaller. The roar of the falls two miles away, below the famous Bleecker Dam, could be heard in almost every part of town. Even in the early afternoon, it made background on Debussy Street for raucous music, pitchmen, barkers, hawkers, rubbernecking crowds and taxi-honking. I felt as much at home as I would have in New York.

Hoag, Acme Indemnity's local manager, was a harassed, sane little veteran with pink hair, pink scalp where hair used to be, a pink shirt, and snapping black eyes. He jumped up from behind his desk as I came into his office.

"Thank God it's you! I been chewing my nails ever since I told Preeker to send me a sleuth, for fear of what I'd draw. Come upstairs."

HOAG HAS a tough job. Acme maintains a private-watchman patrol service in Ancaster, with a payroll of forty-two men and five fast trouble cars carrying more artillery than a tank. As well as handling the insurance office, Hoag is straw boss of the patrol service. The upstairs office to which he led me was the office of the Protective. We passed through an anteroom full of blue-clad men playing poker.

"Now let's get the straight of this," he said, as he handed me my full glass in his private office.

"The straight of it is simple enough," I said. "The emerald bracelet belonging to Mr. Morton Cameroon—which Acme insures for twenty-five grand—is, at present, in the Mercer Street police station in New York City."

"He swears it isn't. He swears he's got it in his own safe right this minute."

The harbor police saw her being thrown
in the river, but the killer got away.

"I know he does," I said, "but he's a liar by the clock. I
happened to be in the Mercer Street station-house late last
night on another matter when they kicked O'Donnell—
he's a regular and well-known fence in New York—into
the station. The cops had a bag of jewelry they'd found in
his rooms. Naturally, I stuck around and took a look.

"Most of it was slum but there were three good pieces. I took descriptions of them and went up to Preeker's master-file. Maybe you don't know it but he keeps a complete cata-logue of every piece of jewelry Acme insures. Anyhow, the only piece that checked against the file was this emerald bracelet of Cameroon's.

"Now don't tell me it was a similar piece. There are no similar pieces. The bracelet—according to the policy—was designed especially by Grandmother Cameroon, forty years ago or something, and made to order by a New York jeweler. There couldn't be a duplicate. The one in New York is your client's—and don't make any mistake about it."

"Then why does he swear it isn't?"

"That's what's got Preeker in a spasm," I said. "And it's what I'm here to find out. Do you know anything about this Cameroon?"

He almost choked on his drink. "I guess I know all you *can* know about him. I waged a two-year campaign to sell him the insurance in the first place. He's about the town's richest man."

"And?"

"He and his brother owned the Cameroon Textile Mills, down by the river. The brother died and then this one owned them. But they don't mean very much now. Just before the brother died he—or the brother, I don't which—invented some loom that did trick things in knit-ting textiles. They patented it and the royalties from the damn thing bring in more now than the mills themselves ever thought of producing."

"Then this Cameroon is rich enough to snap his fingers at twenty-five thousand?"

"I guess so. If anybody ever is."

"Is he the kind of guy that would?"

Hoag thought it over bewilderedly. "Well, he might. He's a quiet, sort of vague old duck. What's your theory?"

"Hell, I haven't any. Suppose some employee pinched the bracelet and Cameroon found him out. Would he be tenderhearted enough to cover up for him—or her?"

"Well—I guess—maybe. I really don't know. He's only got one employee—a witch-faced old housekeeper named Emma. He lives all by himself up at the north end of town and doesn't go near the office once a month. You want to see him, of course."

"Yeah…. No, don't do that." I stopped him reaching for the telephone. "Let's just go drop in on him. Where would he be?"

"At home, I guess."

WE DROVE into a pleasant residential section and finally stopped before a corner plot completely surrounded by a high box hedge. Many trees poked their heads up, inside the large square plot. The house was invisible till we were exactly in front of a gate that gave on a narrow cement walk.

Up the walk the ancient, old-fashioned little gray-brick house sat smugly, its one turret red-leaded and most of the windows in the house shaded. Hoag stepped off the walk to peer around the side of the house.

"His car's in the garage, though that doesn't mean much. He hates to drive it," he told me and ran up the two front steps to whang away at a brass knocker.

The door was opened by a stringy, tall, old maid, with a severe face and severer black-and-white uniform. When she recognized Hoag her sour expression suddenly shifted into the most rakish leer I have seen in many a day.

"Why, hello, Mr. Hoag," she bade us welcome, wiping her hands on her apron and flinging open the door.

Hoag stammered embarrassedly as he went in and, in his confusion, blurted out an introduction which I didn't think necessary, then asked: "Is Mr. Cameroon in?"

"Nope." She thumbed over her shoulder. "He walked up to the asylum to see Mr. Lawson. He said he might go downtown to the dentist afterward, but I doubt if he will. He's an awful coward when it comes to a dentist. He's had a tooth-ache, off and on, nigh onto a year but he funks going down and getting it fixed. Dopes it up himself, though I'm sure I don't know how he expects—"

"Thanks very much, Emma," Hoag managed to stem the torrent. "We'll come back later, maybe."

We sidestepped her invitation to a nice cup of tea or maybe some of the old man's—with a knowing wink— sherry, and got back to the car.

"I slipped her a piece of change when I sold the old man the policies," Hoag told me uncomfortably. "You know—a little information here and there. I dunno what other ideas the old fool got."

"The hell you don't," I said. "If you want to knock off for an hour or so, it's all right with me. I'll come back for you."

"Cut it out," he begged. "Do you want to pursue Cameroon to the asylum? It might not be a bad idea. He's kind of hard to see—no matter how important the business may be. I think he's afraid of people or something. Anyway, he hasn't got his car and we might just catch him and drive him downtown."

"We can give it a whirl, anyway," I decided and we drove out to the highway.

The broad driveway to the asylum—Lynchland State Hospital, by name—ran a half-mile through thick woods before we came out into the open. It is always a gruesome wonder to me how large these bughouses are and how many of them there are. The one in front of us was in a valley and there must have been quarters for a couple of thousand nuts. Red brick buildings were scattered all over the landscape and little groups of patients speckled the distant fields.

"Speaking of employees," Hoag told me as we wound round toward a certain building which he seemed to know, "this Lawson used to work for Cameroon. The old man visits him every week up here. Maybe you can make something out of that for your protecting-employee-who-snitched-bracelet theory. The old loon's been here fourteen years. Cameroon tried to take him out and put him in a private booby-hatch but not being a relative or able to find anybody who was, the state wouldn't give him a tumble."

We parked our car with others in a yard behind a red brick building. "If Cameroon's here, this is the spot where he visits Lawson," Hoag told me. "If he's been and gone, they can tell us inside."

The sun was low in the sky and it seemed to redden all the barred windows. I suddenly had the creeps, and would have preferred to remain in the car, but Hoag gave me no chance.

"Come on," he said. "But stick close to me or they'll never believe you're not a patient."

We went up steps and into an immense, highly polished, high-ceilinged hall.

Hoag checked me just inside the door. "There he is."

HE WAS a forlorn-looking little old man with white hair and mild, pale-blue eyes. He was sitting all alone on

a bench halfway down the long hall, following anxiously
with his eyes each of the long stream of nurses and interns
who were constantly passing up and down the hall. His
hat was beside him on the bench and he had a white pad
of some sort pressed against his cheek—something for his
toothache, I supposed.

"Well?" Hoag looked questioningly at me.

"What's he doing? Waiting to see this Lawson?" I asked.

"I guess so. I'll ask him."

"I'll wait here."

I watched him walk down the long hall, bend over and
speak to the old man. Cameroon jumped a foot, looked up
quickly and reached for his hat before he saw who it was.

There was pantomime—the old man gesturing, shaking his head anxiously, glancing down the long corridor
at me when Hoag nodded his head my way. Finally Hoag
straightened and said something. The old man shook his
head. Hoag's shoulders made a vague shrug.

The girl came by just then and he almost backed into her.

She was breath-taking. A number of the nurses in sight
were plenty decorative but this one was top. She was a
redhead, about medium height, and even the hideous gray-
and-black uniform she had on could not hide her curves.
She had long-lashed blue eyes and a generous cherry
mouth that even from this distance got a man to thinking.

I thought Hoag's sudden bow and gesture with his hat,
and his wide smile, were a little overdone for an apology. So
did the girl, evidently. She looked straight at, and through,
both Hoag and the little old man on the bench, shrugged
and looked bored, did not stop.

As she came past me I gave her a closer look and decided
that I hadn't given her any the best of it, at long distance.

She paid me no attention, disappeared around a corridor corner.

"The old boy has been kept waiting two hours," Hoag told me when he finally left Cameroon and came back. "He says they always keep him waiting nowadays, but he's going to wait on. He doesn't want to see you right now and he says it's too late to go to the dentist. So what?"

"Let's get out of here, anyway," I said and we went out.

When we got in his car, Hoag said: "You know—there's a funny one. Did you notice that red-haired girl I spoke to?"

"Yeah."

"Name's Brenda Hale. She was a registered nurse here in town for a couple of years and took care of old Cameroon when he had the jaundice—nearly a year. Yet she didn't even speak to him when she passed us. Or me, either."

"Probably forgot him."

"Hell, it's only three months ago since he got better."

"You do things funny around this town," I said. "What's the etiquette when you've chased a man to the nut-factory to call him a liar and then can't work around to doing it?"

Hoag looked vague. "Well, I thought you were in a big hurry to see him. Say—are you sure of your ground here? The more I think, the less I believe that old man is a liar."

"Well, he is. Maybe somebody made a paste duplicate and substituted it for the real one when they took it. All I know is, the real one is in New York."

"What are you going to ask him when you do catch up with him?"

"Damned if I know," I said.

"Listen," he said suddenly, after a minute. "It just occurred to me—whoever stole that bracelet might have fenced it around here and it went down the line to New York that way."

"Quite probably," I said.

"If we could find out the local fence who bought it, maybe we could trace back that way—make him cough up who sold it to him."

"Do you know the local fences—and how to break them down?"

"I don't but Burroughs should."

"Who's Burroughs?"

He started the car quickly. "He works for the Protective. He used to be a safe-and-loft detective. Say—suppose we go and see him now. You can catch Cameroon later."

"Why didn't you think of that before?" I growled.

WE RAN downtown and saw Burroughs. He was a hatchet-faced, gray-eyed grouch of a man with a toothpick in his mouth and his blue uniform fitting somewhat too late.

"The only two fences in this town that would be big enough to send a piece like that to New York," he told me gloomily, "are Feitlebaum, the pawnbroker on Allen Street, and Ditmars, the phony auctioneer-jeweler on Debussy. If any of the rest had it, they'd peddle it to them two to ship out."

I went down and found the dingy little pawnshop on Allen, its windows crammed with clothes, musical instruments, the cheapest kind of jewelry. Feitlebaum was an ancient with a rim of white beard that ran around under his chin and up into his scant white hair. His eyes were red-pouched, as lively as two black toads.

I leaned on his dirty counter and gave him my card, told him in a confidential tone: "I'm a square shooter. I do plenty of business with fellows in your line in New York. I work for an insurance company and not for the cops. I want you to bear me in mind if you happen to run across any item that you think I'd be interested in. We pay ten percent and sometimes higher—and no questions asked, or answered. Get it? And listen—we sometimes even pay for information. We forget where we got that, too. For instance, right now, I'm trying to get a line on an emerald bracelet—old-fashioned—gold rosettes—a high-class piece but kind of tough to get rid of. Maybe we could do a little business now—or maybe some other time. You can ask around about me in New York."

His voice was like a broken clock attempting to strike the hour without being able to hit anything. "I wouldn't known nothing about this," he told me slatily, but he put my card in the pocket of his greasy flannel shirt.

I went down to Debussy Street next, but I was too late to see Ditmars. It was dark now and the street was a blaze of incandescents, red, blue and green neon lights. The sidewalks were crowded. I stood outside Ditmar's pitch and watched him work. It was exactly the same game I had seen a hundred times in New York—a brightly lighted store, full of cheap but gaudy jewelry, a red banner announcing—*Auction Today*. The shirt-sleeved auctioneer, his fingers blazing with brilliants, high enough above the counter so his chant could be heard outside on the street. A mess of slum jewelry with weird price tags attached being "auctioned". I was even in time to hear his shill in the crowd urge him to throw in the diamond ring from his finger to the little collection in front of him, and hear his scornful laugh, but I wasn't paying attention to that.

I was interested in this Ditmars—I presumed he was the auctioneer—a big, heavy-framed man, with bulging muscles, a craggy, grim-jawed face and brown eyes hidden far back under black eyebrows that met thickly above the bridge of his nose. His square head was completely bald. He was, if I judged correctly, a tough baby, but somehow the kind of crook you can't hate. There was a dull, aggressive light in his eyes, as though he'd slug you for your roll with the best will in the world, as cold-bloodedly as a fish, but prepared to take the risks and the rap promptly if he slipped up. I don't know how else to put it. Most of the crooks you meet in my game are snivelers, once the heat is on them. He looked dangerous enough—but also as though he could take it—and would take it—as it came.

I decided to try and reach him after he closed for the night, and found a restaurant where I ate till it was time to go see Cameroon.

I PARKED my car a piece away from Cameroon's queer little house and, in walking around two sides of the high hedge, found that there was a back entrance—a driveway that ran behind the house and ended in a garage at one end, then went through a gap in the hedge to the street, at the other. The lights of the house were almost invisible in the blackness imposed by the trees. I went around and in the front way.

The long-faced, strange, old-maid housekeeper let me in and was prepared at a moment's notice to be chummy with me, but I managed to get shown into the old man's library, where he was fiddling behind a desk. His mild blue eyes looked at me apprehensively and he seemed to be about to duck under the desk. The room smelt of some aromatic medicine and one of his pink cheeks was more than a little swollen.

I said: "I've had toothache myself, Mr. Cameroon, and I know you don't feel much like talking, so I'll make it very short. The company sent me out to check on that bracelet of yours. It seems incredible that the one we saw in New York was not yours, but we can make it positive in about one minute. The policy, as you know, says that we may inspect the piece twice a year on demand. So suppose you let me have a look at it now and then everything will be cleared up."

His mild eyes looked wonderingly at me. "But—but I can't do that," he said in a quiet little voice. "It's in the vault at the factory."

"Authorize someone to open the vault and show it to me, then."

"No, no, I can't—"

"Otherwise," I finished, "I'm under instructions to cancel the insurance. The rules make us do that."

"But this is Friday," he wailed. "The vault is a time lock. I—or anybody else—can't open it till Monday morning."

I stuffed my hands in my pockets and cursed myself for not carrying through earlier. But I was sure now that no miracle of duplication had occurred—that his bracelet was in New York. I looked troubled and thoughtful.

"I'll have to phone my boss in New York," I said finally. "I haven't the authority to wait till Monday."

"All right," he said with alacrity and jumped up, waved at the phone. "Go ahead." He walked to a door at the end of the room and opened it. "I'll be in here when you're through."

I hadn't exactly meant it to go that way, but it wasn't a bad notion at that, so I called Preeker.

I no sooner had him on the wire than I knew I was being listened in on. There was the unmistakable click and the sort of breathless humming that can mean only one thing.

Naturally I thought of the old man and wondered why he would be wanting to hear what was said.

I told Preeker: "Mr. Cameroon wants me to wait till Monday morning before showing me the bracelet. I got in this afternoon on the Erie." Everybody (except Cameroon, I hoped) knows that "on the Erie" means to be careful—that someone is listening.

Preeker—curse his dollar-frantic, unscrupulous soul—tried to take advantage of me by saying: "No, I'm afraid we can't do that. The policy expressly states—"

"I really think we should," I cut in irritably. "Mr. Cameroon is an important client of the local office here. I think he is entitled to every courtesy."

Preeker finally said, "All right," in a puzzled tone, wondering, no doubt, why I had called him at all, inasmuch as Acme sleuths have authority that would more than cover this, when in the field.

I hung up and went over and opened the door the old man had gone through. It was a little dining-room and he was sitting on a window seat nursing his jaw. There was no sign of a telephone in the room, or wires or box—unless they were concealed in the sideboard.

"Who else is in the house?" I asked him.

"Why—why only my housekeeper," he said bewilderedly.

"Where is the extension phone?"

"There—there isn't any."

That, of course, set me thinking about a tap.

More and more, I was getting a hunch that the item of the bracelet itself was only a scratch on the surface of what went on here—though I hadn't yet a notion of the truth.

I mumbled something finally about it being all right till Monday and left.

I STOOD in the darkness beside the front steps for a few minutes till I was reasonably sure they thought I'd departed. Then I started looking around the house to see if by chance I could locate the tap.

I didn't get very far with it. I had covered maybe four yards when a brilliant flashbeam slapped me and a harsh, crisp voice snarled, "Turn out your flash—fast!" and there was enough menace in the voice to make me do it.

"Keep your hands away from your body. Drop the flash and turn around." I turned. There was enough piercing light from the flash to make the man behind it practically invisible. He said, "Start walking," and walked me over to a spot behind a thick clump of evergreens. Then he growled: "Who are you?"

I told him.

"Yeah? Let's see your papers."

I handed them to him and told him: "You smell copper to me, mister. If you are, buzz me. There's no use our working at cross-purposes."

"Isn't there?" He handed back the papers. "Do you know a Miss Brenda Hale?" he shot at me.

"Yeah," I said, after a minute. "She's a nurse at the asylum, isn't she? I don't know her to speak to, but I've seen her."

He didn't say anything. The light pierced my eyeballs, made my head ache. It didn't move. It didn't move for such a long time that I said, "Well, what do we do—stand here till somebody in the house spots us?" and when even that brought no response, I discovered the trick he'd played on me.

The flashlight was parked in the crotch of a small tree, but my man was gone.

I found my car and sat in it with my ears strained. The night was so silent out here that I could hear small sounds inside the house—the phone ringing, a door close inside the house, people walking around.

But I heard no automobile starter *whirr* into life.

Bewildered, I tried to guess why the copper—that's how I identified him anyway, by his manner and way of asking questions—had stopped me, and having stopped me, what I had said that sent him scooting away like that. The only thing I could possibly figure was that the news that Brenda Hale was at the asylum might have been fresh and important to him somehow.

Acting on this line of thought, I drove out to the highway and as near as I dared to the broad driveway that led into the asylum. I parked about a hundred yards away and walked the rest of the distance. If my man had no car I might head him off or, if he had beaten me in, I might catch him going out.

I SAT there for nearly an hour, my curiosity growing, not to mention my impatience, trying to put a logical construction on all this secretive, meaningless business, but I couldn't.

Cramped and chilled, I stubbed out my fourth cigarette and was just about to pass up the asylum when headlights danced in the trees far within the grounds. I leaned against the bole of a huge oak and waited, on the off chance that this might be my party.

The headlights came nearer and became a Vitacar Victoria coupé, practically new. The dashlight gave orange glow and in the glow I saw the man driving—a youngish, dark-eyed, hard-bitten face, under black hair *en brosse,* hatless. His face had a stiff look as he slowed to a stop before turning onto the highway.

He was not alone in the car. Beside him sat the luscious red-haired nurse, Brenda Hale, with her appealing face as stiff as his.

I had just that flash of them as they went by me.

They turned up the highway in the direction of my parked car and I could run after them with assurance that they were not getting too far away from me in the meantime. They were driving at a moderate pace.

They were still well in sight when I jumped in my car and got it started after them. I was traveling faster than they were—overhauling them steadily—till a clock somewhere started booming out the hour, ten o'clock. Then they spurted.

Startled, I tried to spurt with them but their car was new and mine was three years old and they fairly ran away from me. I crowded down on the gas, wondering what was the matter with the speed cops in this town and managed to keep their distinctive tail-lights barely in sight.

And then the tail-lights suddenly vanished.

I almost slammed into the slowly moving string of freight cars muddling across the grade crossing before I realized what had happened. The driver of the car—or the girl or somebody—was apparently a native and knew that this slow freight passed here just at ten o'clock. Hence the spurt to get by before they reached the grade crossing.

I sat there for ten full minutes, cursing, waiting for the endless, sluggish stream of cars to get out of my way. When they finally did, the coupé was, of course, gone. And I hadn't bothered to get the license number of the Vitacar coupé.

I sat there, burned up and finally turned around and drove back to Cameroon's house.

FROM THE front, the place looked exactly as it had when I had left it two hours earlier. I prowled round, inside the hedge. No sound or movement came from the lighted house. I approached the back door, keeping out of the square of light that came through it.

I don't know how long I stood there before I noticed the condition of the grass in the patch of light. It was trampled, and heels had dug up loam, as though some sort of frantic milling had been taking place there. There was a small black smudge in the grass.

I dropped down and rubbed my hand over the smudge. There was dew on the grass so that when I turned my flash beam close to my hand it appeared as thin pink rather than red, but one smell of it and I knew what it was—blood!

I jumped for the kitchen door. It opened under my hand and I ran in on tiptoe. There was not a sound in the house.

Two minutes later I faced the surprising truth that there was not a soul in the whole place.

I went to the telephone, hastily called Hoag at the Protective offices downtown. Instead of Hoag, I got the snarling voice of the ex-safe-and-loft detective, Burroughs.

He rattled at me urgently: "Hoag just called in a minute ago. He says for you to rush like hell to Mercy Hospital." He quickly gave me the route I needed to get there, and assured me that he didn't know what it was all about.

Hoag was waiting for me just inside the door of the modern, trim hospital when I slammed on my brakes and piled out.

"It's Emma," he told me breathlessly. "She's been horribly attacked and is almost dead. The harbor police saw her being thrown in the river a few minutes ago with her skull fractured, and she's dying. The killer got away. She's raving something about somebody not being crazy, not crazy....

I ran toward a door at the end of the hall that had a sign—*Emergency Receiving Room*—on it, pushed in and had one confused impression of a room full of men in white, men in brass and blue, and the bewildered, frightened face of old Cameroon in the background. They were clustered around a small operating-table. Even as I came in, they drew back as though by common consent and somebody said flatly: "No soap. She's dead."

Then I was beside the table and looking down at the blackened, half-naked body of the old-maid housekeeper, Emma. A piece of her scalp hung down over her eye. There were ugly black bruises on her throat. Her hair was still wet from the river and little rivulets dripped down on the surgery floor.

Maybe it was the angle at which I was standing that permitted me, exclusively, I guess, to see the little blob of red in the corner of her eye. I almost reached for it, but some intimation of its importance must have stopped me. It was tiny, no larger than the head of a pin, but it was so intensely red that I knew it could not be blood. I was suddenly intensely curious about it.

Cops were barking questions at me, but Hoag rallied round and protected me. Finally, I got up courage to put my finger in the dead woman's eye and snake away the red stuff, saying, "Can't you at least close her eyes," and then retreating at the blasts of official wrath that blistered me. I kept on retreating till I was outside in the hall with Hoag.

I couldn't make anything of the bit of wax I had acquired except that it was just that—red wax. Hoag stammered questions that I didn't hear. I stopped him with: "Exactly what was the old witch mumbling that you heard?"

He repeated anxiously: "Just—just what I told you. That someone wasn't crazy. Probably the one who choked her and slugged her, eh?"

"Maybe. Listen—how many Vitacar dealers are there in town?" and when he said two, I sent him to the phone. "Find out who owns late-model, last-year's Victoria coupés—Vitacars. Where's a good chemist?"

He stammered an address and I told him "Meet me there when you've found out what I want—or phone me, if you'd rather." I hurried out of the hospital.

I DROVE the few blocks to the chemist's, went in and tendered him my envelope with the little blob of red wax. "What's that made of?" I asked him. "Is it identifiable?"

"I should say so," he told me after five minutes. "There's oil of cloves, chloroform, eucalyptus, creosote and carnuba."

I said, "Gentle Annie," and ran out of the shop.

It suddenly occurred to me to wonder what had happened to the bewildered old Cameroon in the rush, and then I remembered that he had been at the hospital when I was there, but that I had been too busy to pay him any attention.

I hurried back to the hospital but he had gone, after making what arrangements he could for burial for the old housekeeper, when the authorities should be finished with the body.

I went back to the chemist's shop, having missed Hoag en route, and found him waiting. I told him: "Better get some of those special cops on guard around old Cameroon. I don't think he's any too safe. Did you get that list?"

"Yes," he gasped. "What—what do you think...."

I don't know the rest of what he said. My eye, traveling down the list of Vitacar owners had stopped at the ninth name—*R. Ditmars,* and the address, the phony little auction shop on Debussy Street.

Suddenly, I got the whole picture, filled in by a couple of guesses. I ran out, almost knocking Hoag over, got into my car and sent it shooting down Debussy Street. A block from the auction-room, I piled out.

The place was closed, the windows tightly shaded. I had a sinking feeling as I stood out front and then, through a flaw in one of the blinds, I caught a chink of light. Apparently someone was inside.

I hurried down the street to a cross-avenue, trotted up it and found, as I had expected, that there was an alley which ran behind the shop. I could see glow at the far end of the pitch-black little slot. I ran noiselessly along the uneven cobbles, fishing out my gun. I had every reason to believe that I was right on top of the climax of the whole queer, desperate little puzzle.

Then I was at the back door of the building which was the auction shop in front. It was a solid door and I could not see through any nearby window. I had my case of picklocks half from my pocket as I turned the knob but I didn't need the picklocks. The door opened to my touch.

I eased it open, by inches.

The building was divided into three narrow rooms, all in a row. The front room was the public auction-room, containing the glittering glass cases of jewelry and so forth. The middle one was a little office with all the behind-the-scenes paraphernalia of the racket. The third—the one in which I was standing—was a storeroom full of bales and boxes.

The door at the front of this storeroom stood open and, through it, I saw three people. Ditmars, the hulking racketeer, stood beside an auction block, holding by the collar the youth I had seen at the wheel of the coupé, the youth I had taken for a copper. The youth's rocky, hard-jawed face was bruised and swollen, his eyes a little glazed. His coat had been ripped off and his tie was awry. He wore an empty shoulder holster.

He was handcuffed, with an ancient pair of iron manacles, to the lovely red-headed nurse, Brenda Hale. The girl was gagged and her eyes above the gag were terrified.

I was in, the door closed silently behind me, in one swift motion. Ditmars, speaking to someone in the room with him, someone I could not see, said cheerfully: "No, pal, I don't know who the young hothead is, either. All I know is that you phoned me in a panic tonight, when you heard some insurance dick was in town, and wanted the girl picked up. Fair enough. I told you two grand was the price—but you can do your own killing. The only way I could pick her up was when she left the asylum and met up with this guy. So I had to bring them both along and it's just too bad if you didn't want him. You'll take them both, or neither—and the price is two grand, on the line."

I stepped into the doorway, saw I had the narrow room—including the muffled figure sitting on a chair with his back half to me—fully covered, and put in my bid. "I'll pay three grand," I said.

EVERYONE IN the room—except the slug-nutty stiff-haired youngster with the girl—jumped a foot. I saw the gleam of metal in Ditmars' big hand.

"Drop the gun," I warned him, and he let it bounce to the floor.

He swallowed once and then his face was sardonic, grim, even cheerful. "Why not?" he said. "So I've got another bidder for this pair? All right. Let's do it properly." He suddenly picked up a sign with a lot number scribbled on it and in one motion hung it around the girl's neck, simultaneously picking up a gavel from the auction block and tapping it gently. "All right, gentlemen," I could see his sharp, wary eyes trying vainly to pierce the darkness where I stood, even while he put on his cool, stalling, act. I watched him closely as he rattled on: "Three thousand I'm bid, three thousand I'm bid. Who'll make it four...."

I was watching him too closely. I did not see the slug-nutty youth come out of his fog. Nor had I noticed any too carefully where Ditmar's gun had fallen.

Both matters were brought to my attention at the same moment. There was a sudden, wild flash of movement as the youth dived for the dropped gun. I say he was out of his fog. He wasn't really, or he would never have made such a hopeless play. I could have shot him through the head before he touched the gun but I didn't want to. I yelled, "Don't be a sap—drop it!" but he paid me no attention. Then, as he whipped the fallen pistol up at me, I had to fire.

Our shots were one-two. I heard glass explode behind me. I saw—believe it or not—my slug hit the top of his gun, run up his sleeve and slam a furrow in his cheek. He was smashed sideways, against the girl and they went down in a crashing heap. I roared at Ditmars, "Stand still!" and he stood perfectly motionless, with his hands high in the air—a wise gent.

It was the third gent who was unwise. He threw something.

Somehow, I was so occupied watching the others—and, I may as well admit, so contemptuous of the little bundled figure that I didn't expect anything from him—that I didn't see the flashing silver coffeepot till it was in mid-air. I didn't know what it was and I fired, as I ducked hastily, slamming the little man fairly off his feet, pitching him into the corner and dropping him to the floor, squealing, his hat rolling across almost to my feet.

"Fancy meeting you here, Mr. Cameroon," I said grimly as I stepped over and drove a fist into his frantic little starch-white face. He lay down, sobbing.

I said: "Open your mouth—and if you bite me, I'll beat your brains out."

At that I had to force his slobbering jaws open. The mild blue eyes were almost black with fear and panic, rage and fury, now. I inserted a finger and dug around till I pried a soft mass out of his upper molar—the wad of red tooth-ache gum with which he was attempting to alleviate his toothache.

"What did you do? Cough when you were strangling your housekeeper?" I asked him. Then, with pardonable mendacity, I bluffed, "This finishes you—puts you squarely in the electric chair," and put the wad of wax in a fresh envelope in my pocket. "It's all over. It'll match up with the bit you coughed in her eye."

His frantic hysteria suddenly seemed to evaporate and he was a deflated, shivering little madman.

"What in the world did you have to kill her for?" I asked.

His dry lips moved. He had to lick them to croak out dully: "She listened in on the extension phone in the kitchen hall. She heard—her"—he nodded at the now-kneeling, frantic Brenda Hale—"tell me that Lawson wasn't crazy any more. I knew if—if anything happened to Lawson and Miss Hale—that Emma would know I had done it."

"A nice guy. You were going to knock off both Lawson and Miss Hale. Why? Lawson was the real inventor of the loom? He went bugs just about the time he perfected it and you and your brother stole it? That it?"

He said nothing.

"But why—"

The frantic girl behind me had succeeded in tearing off her gag. She burst out wildly: "An ambulance—get an ambulance! Max is shot in the face—we have to get him to a hospital."

"Behave, Miss Hale," I snapped at her. "The cops will be here in a few minutes and I've got to know the truth of this thing. Your boy-friend isn't hurt much, as you ought to know. I've a hunch you two are going to need help and I've only got seconds to learn how to help you. Why were you spying on Lawson and reporting to Cameroon?"

SHE HESITATED just a minute, then looked down at her hands. "He—Mr. Lawson had letters from Mr. Cameroon's dead brother—letters about the loom, proving that Mr. Lawson was the real inventor. The letters had never been found since Mr. Lawson was—was declared insane. Mr. Cameroon feared they would come to light and he wanted me to try and find out where Lawson might have hidden them."

"Was Lawson really sane? Railroaded by these—"

"No, no. He really was insane—until last month. I—I think he's better now and just shamming. He must realize that the Cameroon fortune is all rightly his and he's afraid of what might happen to him if Mr. Cameroon found it out."

"Smart guy," I said grimly. "He's not so crazy. So Cameroon was paying you to spy on Lawson, to try and get out of his goofy mind where he had put those letters?"

"Ye—yes. But he wasn't paying me. I—oh, he's coming to."

The man on the floor groaned, struggled to sit up.

"Go on, hurry up," I raved at the girl as the sound of sirens came on the night air. "Finish it up. If he wasn't paying you—what were you doing it for?"

"We—about three months ago—Max came down from upstate to see me. We—we hadn't seen each other in a long time. We went out to Taplin's Roadhouse on the Turnpike. We drank too much and—and stayed till almost dawn and—"

"I get it. You left there drunk. Go on."

"I was working for Mr. Cameroon then. I had to get back quickly, and we—we were speeding in Max's car. It was one he had borrowed from the barracks upstate."

"Barracks? Is he a state trooper?"

"Yes. We—we were speeding when we ran down a switchman on the railroad tracks. He was drunk and stepped in front of us but his brother was there with him and saw it happen. He wasn't killed, but he was badly hurt. The brother said he'd forget he saw us if we raised five thousand dollars for the injured man's family. It wasn't blackmail or anything—he really was sincere. He gave us twenty-four hours to raise it. We were desperate. If it came out, I'd be blacklisted and—and Max'd probably go to jail.

"I knew of an emerald bracelet Mr. Cameroon had around. I stole it. I had once nursed Mr. Ditmars in the hospital and I—I knew I could sell it to him. We paid off the brother that way.

"Then Mr. Cameroon told me he had seen me take the bracelet—made me believe that he had traced it all the way and that he was going to prefer charges against me. I was frantic. Max had gone back upstate. I begged Mr. Cameroon not to prosecute me, promised him I'd work and pay it back. Then he said he wouldn't put me in jail, and that he'd let me keep the money—if I'd do this thing for him."

"You mean find where Lawson had hidden the letters?"

"Yes. He made me sign a full confession but he promised to give it back to me the minute he found the letters."

"Then Lawson got better and Cameroon's whole house of cards started falling around his ears. Right?"

"Yes."

"Where is this confession you signed?"

"I don't know."

"Where is it?" I whirled on the crazy-looking little Cameroon. He was a weak sister now and he cringed, put his hand in his inside pocket and found a wallet.

Doors started to burst in as I ripped the confession to shreds and threw them in a waste basket.

To Ditmars, I said: "You keep your big mouth shut and I'll do what I can for you. You've got a rap coming. Start talking and I'll see it's attempted murder. Otherwise, probably receiving."

"Fair enough," he said promptly.

To the old man, I said ferociously: "You'll be in jail a long time awaiting trial. If you bring up anything about these young folks stealing things or running over people, I'll see that my friends in the jail beat you up every day. Furthermore, I'll guarantee you'll get no medicine for your toothache."

He hadn't a chance to say anything before the store was full of brass buttons, hoarse shouts, glittering pistols and flashlights. The party was led by a hatchet-faced prosecutor named Enslow, and somehow Hoag had attached himself to the prosecutor's shoulder.

I told the story, leaving out the jewelry, making it appear that the girl had been paid merely to furnish information about Lawson and was perfectly innocent. I finished up by telling the prosecutor: "You'd better find some way to detain me in town, so I can't leave the jurisdiction before trial time."

He swallowed twice and assured me I'd get a subpoena within an hour.

"What was that for, for God's sake?" Hoag asked when we got outside.

"Hell, we insure old Cameroon's life for fifty thousand dollars. I don't want to be within Preeker's reach when he finds out I've put the old pirate practically in the electric chair."

Cameroon helped me out, at that. He hanged himself in his cell the next morning with his belt. His policy had a three-year suicide clause in it, and we just got under the wire on that, so it all wound up costing Acme nothing.

Made in the USA
Middletown, DE
20 December 2020